SUMMER OF SECRETS

SUMMER OF SECRETS

Grace Thompson

This first world edition published in Great Britain 1994 by
SEVERN HOUSE PUBLISHERS LTD of
9–15 High Street, Sutton, Surrey SM1 1DF.
First published in the USA 1994 by
SEVERN HOUSE PUBLISHERS INC., of
425 Park Avenue, New York, NY 10022.

British Library Cataloguing in Publication Data
Thompson, Grace
  Summer of Secrets
  I. Title
  823.914 [F]

  ISBN 0-7278-4694-9

Typeset by Hewer Text Composition Services, Edinburgh.
Printed and bound in Great Britain by
Hartnolls Ltd, Bodmin, Cornwall.

CHAPTER ONE

Bettrys stood at the window of her London flat and stared along the street as far as she could see, stretching her slim elegant body across the armchair, unconsciously hoping that by doing so she would catch sight of Brett more quickly. The road was empty of people. The evening light was fading, guilding the row of houses opposite with the beauty of the dying sun and casting shadows deeper and deeper as she watched. She spared a second to glance at her watch. She whispered his name, "Brett," willing him to appear. He wasn't coming. But she still stood waiting, hope fading but, like the sun, not quite gone.

At the distant corner, the road joined a busy thorough-fare along which traffic was heading out on the Friday-night nose-to-tail exodus. The pavements on the main road at the end of her row were filled with people hurrying towards the District Line station a couple of hundred yards to the left of the corner. Somewhere among that mass of humanity was Brett. But was he walking towards her? Was he bringing her hope of a return to the exciting and loving relationship they had enjoyed for the past months? Or was he hurrying away, putting as much distance as he could between them? Off to search for someone new, someone who wouldn't put a sister with a drinks problem before him and what he offered.

Her slow, gentle manner and her kind heart had, in the past made Bettrys Hopkyns many friends. But since the death of her parents and the arrival in her contented life of her sister Eirlys, she had gradually drifted into a life

1

almost devoid of social contacts. That was why Brett was so special.

He had blown into her life one day when he came in answer to her advertisement for a buyer for her car. He stayed to talk and brought with him a breathless excitement, a zest for life which she had almost forgotten.

Bettrys was tall, three inches under six feet, but he was taller, and as dark as she was fair. What she lacked in confidence he more than compensated for and together they laughed their way through the whole of that Spring and Summer. He had never once called for her at her flat. And he had refused her repeated invitations to come for a meal and meet her sister, Eirlys.

"Let's eat out instead," he would say, patting his wallet pocket. "Live, laugh and love while we can, eh?" As she prepared to protest, he would add, "Plenty of time for staying in and meeting family and all that stuff when we're bored with each other. You aren't bored with me yet, are you, Bettrys?"

The fear that he might think so quickly settled any further attempts at persuasion. He was often away on business, about which he was very secretive. All she knew was that he was a Property Developer called Brett Cavendish. He had borrowed money on three occasions, and so far had not returned it. Not that she minded. He had spent so much on her with his extravagant treats she had no regrets at helping to pay for them.

When he was in London they met often, and ate and danced and went to the races and learnt to ice skate, and he taught her to manage at least the easy slopes on the dry ski runs. Something new every moment. She had never known what to expect when he phoned her and arranged for them to meet.

He took her to Paris for a weekend of sight-seeing, to York for breakfast, to Scotland to sail around the Western Isles, where he amused her by developing a fine Scottish accent. They once went to the summit of Snowdon, in

North Wales, where he developed an accent that varied from North Wales to that of the South, depending on whom they were with.

His fascination was endless and when she thought he could spring no further surprises, he told her he had tickets for Greece and promised her six weeks of utter bliss. In a haze of happiness she bought new clothes, ordered her travellers cheques and made all the necessary arrangements.

Then Eirlys started drinking again and she had to tell him she couldn't go with him.

Her sister's recurring problem began in the usual way with a lack of interest in anything, a refusal to go out even to work at the local school, where they were both teachers. Then the aggression grew, and questioning, pleading and reasoning developed into desperation and frustration, then anger.

Every time she entered the flat, Bettrys searched it for hidden bottles. As hiding places were exposed, more were found by Eirlys, who was terrified at the prospect of not having a drink available at any hour of the day and night. She had to know it was there and her agitation if her last bottle was discovered and poured away was pitiful, but the look on her sister's face did not prevent Bettrys from doing what she knew was right. But, for Eirlys, the need to know she had a bottle secreted away was a constant anxiety which led to her hating her sister with an intensity that was frightening for them both.

Bettrys found brandy behind the fire, under the imitation coals, and in Eirlys's bed, at the bottom of the wardrobe, in shoes, in pockets and behind pictures. There was a time when she thought there was not an inch of space she didn't know about and then found two bottles on the meter cupboard high up where she needed a ladder to reach.

The binge would slowly end and then would come the remorse and the promises and things would settle back

3

to normal. Eirlys seemed to really believe she was strong enough never to touch alcohol again and each time, Bettrys began to hope that this time it was true. Then it would begin all over again. The lethargy, the lack of interest, the refusal to go to work, the money missing from Bettrys's purse, the search for hidden bottles and the lies. Her beautiful sister changed in days into a vicious stranger.

Now she was standing at the window, waiting for a man who would never return, while her sister slept an ugly, noisy sleep, sprawled on a stale, foul-smelling bed. Self-pity threatened and she moved away from the window and stood staring at her own reflection and wondering how it would all end. Was her whole life to be spent dealing with Eirlys's disgusting bouts or waiting for the next?

Now she was alone again, she knew that Brett had tired of her loyalty to her sister and was on his way to the airport, heading for a dream of a holiday she had been looking forward to so much. Surely her parents hadn't really meant to burden her with all this? To expect her to give up everything she wanted to look after a sister who was determined to destroy herself?

Downstairs, a door slammed shut and she watched as a young girl left the building carrying a rucksack and headed for the underground station. At the corner, the girl stopped and waved at a group of people who were obviously waiting for her. Just as Brett would have been waiting for her if Eirlys hadn't ruined everything.

Leaving the window, she went to the bedroom where her sister lay sleeping. Taking a deep breath, she looked inside. The room was over-warm and smelled unpleasantly of vomit, even though the bed had been changed that morning. A fact most people didn't consider when thinking about caring for heavy drinkers – sickness and other symptoms of too much alcohol and not enough food. The excessive smell of the body's varied functions was not something Bettrys had been prepared for.

4

She called her sister's name, then frowned. The hump in the bed where her sister lay sleeping looked odd, illshapen. She had been snoring, flat out on her back when she had left for school that morning and, apart from rolling her onto her side, Bettrys hadn't disturbed her, knowing from bitter experience that if she woke her she would have a difficult few hours before settling her again. After a bout of drinking she was better left to sleep it off. But now, something about the shape on the bed puzzled her. She investigated and found the bed empty. She sighed. Once again Eirlys had given her the slip.

Hardly caring, thinking only of Brett and the holiday, both lost to her, she went back to the window. Brett might still come. He must come. She wanted to hear him say he would be back, and everything would be as wonderful as before. Even though, in her heart, she knew that by choosing to support her sister instead of going away with him, she had effectively told him goodbye. The words, the formal words, were all that was left.

She pushed her long, honey-coloured hair back from her face and stared at the corner from where he would appear, but there was nothing to see but her own reflection. Her eyes glazed, gave up trying to see beyond the glass and she remembered instead the expression on his darkly handsome face when she had told him she wouldn't be going with him. Disbelief, a half smile as if expecting to be told it was a joke. Then resentment, then a cool, hard tightening of his mouth and the instantaneous disappearance of the loving look that had been a part of his expression every time their eyes met. The love she was used to seeing was gone as if a door had slammed, shutting off a light from within.

The flat was in a quiet corner in London, in a street filled with busy commuters during the week but emptying quickly on a Friday evening and remaining comatose for the two days of the weekend. The house had been divided

5

into three flats and two bedsitters which were let mainly to students from the nearby college.

Below her she could hear the sounds of people busily preparing to go out for the evening, or entertain friends. The students had already gone, off on holiday, or to visit mum and dad probably with a bag of washing and an appetite, each of enormous proportions. The sounds increased Bettrys's loneliness.

She pulled the heavy curtain across the window, turned on the imitation fire and filled the kettle for a cup of coffee. With Eirlys off on a bender it was going to be another long night. The knock, when it came, startled her. She hastily switched off the kettle and ran to the door, a smile of welcome, a forgiveness for his lateness already on her lips. If only he would talk to her, perhaps, after all, there might be a happy outcome. If only she could make him understand.

The sight of a young policeman standing there startled her and at once she felt fear rising. Her thought was not for Brett Cavendish, but her sister.

"What's happened?" she gasped breathlessly. "Is it my sister, Eirlys? Is she ill?" Eirlys tried to keep her drinking private but occasionally drank to excess outside the flat. She had twice fallen in the street and been taken to hospital.

"I'm sorry, but you didn't give me a chance to speak. No, there's nothing wrong. I'm very sorry I startled you. You must be Bettrys." He held out a hand. "I'm a friend of your sister, Eirlys. We had an arrangement to meet after I finished my shift and she didn't turn up. I just wondered if you knew where she might be?"

"I'm sorry. I thought – a policeman knocking – silly of me. Please come in." She stood back and gestured to an armchair. "I'm just making coffee, will you have one? Eirlys will be back soon." She hoped that was not true. Eirlys wouldn't want a friend to see her in the state she was in!

He followed her into the kitchen, watched her put coffee in the cafetiere and stood with her while the kettle began to make encouraging noises. He was an inch or two above her own height, strongly built, his hair was almost black, matching the thick brows and the dark outline of a beard showed strongly, suggesting he had a problem keeping himself neatly shaved.

Bettrys searched her mind, trying to remember if her sister had mentioned this young policeman. There were times, she thought with a stab of guilt, when she did not listen too closely to her sister's chatter.

"Eirlys has told you about me?" the young man said rhetorically. Then he frowned at the lack of response in Bettrys's blue eyes. "I'm Jonathan Crawley." Still no sign of recognition. "We've been going out together for more than two months," he said, slightly dismayed at the lack of interest. "In fact, we were going to meet my parents, staying the weekend. She must have told you?" he added doubtfully, as the frown on Bettrys's brow deepened. "I'm Jonathan," he added stupidly, unwilling to accept that Eirlys had not talked to her sister about their growing romance.

"Eirlys sometimes chatters non-stop. At other times she says very little. You must know that," she smiled. "If you've known her for more than a week you'll have seen all her moods!" Except perhaps the one she's presently enjoying, she thought with a feeling of guilt. There was no point in warning anyone about Eirlys. She only had to laughingly deny it and at once a suspicion of jealousy was attributed to Bettrys.

"I found her very lively, funny, joyful and very much a chatterbox. I can't believe she didn't tell you about us. But where can she be? I tried the school, but she left after her final lesson. The caretaker said she was carrying a suitcase and had ordered a taxi, so where can she have gone?"

"She was at school today?" Bettrys frowned. "I left her in bed this morning. She was – she was ill."

7

"She arrived late apparently, but in spite of a severe migraine she took her afternoon classes.' He glanced at the phone and Bettrys nodded.

"Please, ring anyone who might know where she is. I want to know too." She thought of the holiday and the love she had turned aside, while her sister went calmly off somewhere without a word.

After several calls Jonathan shrugged. "No one has seen her since she left school. She told none of the other teachers where she was going."

"This really is a day for disappearances," Bettrys said. "A – a friend of mine said he'd call before going abroad for the summer." She didn't think it wise to explain to this pleasant young man that the reason she hadn't gone with Brett, was because her sister might need her, that she was drinking again and needed constant watching. Or that, because of her sister, she had lost the man she loved. Or that she was aching inside because he hadn't even bothered to say goodbye.

Jonathan left after finishing his coffee, leaving his address and that of his parents. "I would appreciate your letting me know when she does turn up," he said.

A day later, when Bettrys was sufficiently concerned by her sister's absence to consider reporting it to the police, Eirlys telephoned.

"I'm all right," she laughed. "Honestly I am. Stop fussing and allow me my privacy and freedom. I'm a grown woman. I'll be home soon. Bye." She hung up, having given Bettrys no clue as to where she was or whom she was with.

It was almost two weeks before Eirlys returned; laughing, glowing with happiness and unrepentant at letting Jonathan down.

"Oh, don't be cross with me and spoil a wonderful ten days," she said, hugging Bettrys and pushing a small gift into her hands. "I've been to Brighton, staying at a beautiful hotel, with a beautiful man and spending lots of beautiful money."

"Who have you been with?" Bettrys demanded. "A young man called for you, expecting to take you to meet his parents, and you've been away with someone else? He was puzzled, to say the least, when you vanished without an explanation."

"Explanations are best avoided, darling Sis. They only ruin everything with disapproval and guilt and they serve no useful purpose. What's happened can't be changed, so why go on about it? 'The moving finger writes, and having writ moves on' – you know how true that is."

"But Eirlys, who have you been with?"

"As for who I was with, well, just imagine the most wickedly worldly and wickedly wealthy man you've ever met and that will be him. And that's all I'm telling you!" She went into her bedroom and tipped out the contents of her suitcase and, leaving it as it fell, she went, singing cheerfully, stripping off her clothes and dropping them with the rest, to run a bath.

The sisters were not alike. Eirlys was small and extremely fair, her hair was almost white and her complexion flawless and milky. Her eyes, although the same blue as Bettrys's, were larger and set wide apart. They indisputably promised mischief. She was slightly over-weight, but her plumpness had always brought admiring glances, which she fielded with her own, leaving no doubt in the eyes of the receiver that she was a woman for whom fun was a priority. The ravages of excessive drinking and poor nourishment were not yet apparent.

Besides her sister, Bettrys felt plain and unattractive, but never resentful. Eirlys's attractions and her own poor copy of them were facts of life that could never be changed. Her sister's brightness and beauty lost her in their shadows and she never attempted to compete. Until the drinking began she was proud of Eirlys and wanted

9

nothing but to support her and bask in her reflected glory. It would only be until Eirlys married, then she would be free to develop her own life.

This latest adventure was different. She was treating people badly and it was no longer fun if others were hurt. She shivered at the prospect of a lifetime spent apologising for her beautiful sister and picking up the debris. That wasn't what her parents made her promise, was it?

Bettrys's dismay grew rapidly, until she was very angry, but she held back from shouting at her sister. She knew that only led to wilder and wilder laughter and, eventually, to guilt and the terrifying round of drink and remorse, followed by more drinking and yet further drinking until remorse was no longer important.

She bent to sort out the tangle of clothes and was relieved that she didn't come across a bottle hidden away in the carelessly packed luggage. A man was one way Eirlys kept sober – for as long as the intense passion and deep physical attraction lasted. She wondered how long this affair would continue and whether it would be long enough to justify her own loss, of Brett, her lover, and their Greek holiday. She suspected not.

The school holidays drifted by with mundane and cloying boredom. Bettrys spent several hours each day making jewellery, mostly earrings, with silver wire and beads, which she donated to the various fund-raising activities at the school. Her skills were growing and she bought some more expensive materials and devised larger, more imaginative pieces. These she put aside, toying with a vague idea of marketing them more professionally and earning extra money for herself. She tried not to foresee a future in which she was tied to the flat looking after her sister and unable to continue to teach.

Eirlys filled her time with shopping trips, overloading her credit cards with apparent disregard for how they would be paid. Several times she disappeared for a day or even two, always returning glowing with happiness, describing seaside resorts she had visited and the swish hotels in which she had stayed. She refused to say anything about the man who was her companion. Bettrys did not even know if it was the same person, or several. As there seemed no break in the whirl of activities, she presumed it was the same person throughout that summer holiday.

Her mystery boyfriend remained anonymous but as long as he was keeping Eirlys happy and away from the dreaded bottle, Bettrys did not care. She knew the weeks of euphoria wouldn't last, but just kept hoping for one more day, and another, trying not to think about Brett and her unnecessary sacrifice.

Thoughts of Brett, who hadn't even sent her a postcard, eased into a dull ache and succeeded in taking Bettrys's mind off wondering too hard who her sister was seeing. Her own life was empty and she hated herself for the moments of envy of her highly-strung and beautiful sister, who was never alone unless she wanted to be.

He knew it was time he moved on. Eirlys was a charming and fascinating companion but he had soaked more than he should from his most recent activities and knew that if he stayed any longer the chances of the police catching up with him were high.

Part of the fun of stealing and cheating was the buzz he got from the threat of imminent capture. Taking Eirlys away from her policeman had been satisfying. He even persuaded her to introduce him as an ex-neighbour from Wandsworth. He had bought the man a drink, with the money he had taken from an old man who had paid him to have his roof repaired! Hell, that was a laugh!

But deep inside he knew he could never cope with prison. The dancing with danger was a pretence. The truth was he had a growing fear of the police catching up with him. He knew he had outstayed his time here,

11

and all because of the vivacious and fascinating Eirlys Hopkyns. Now he would give her one final, love-filled weekend and depart.

To Bettrys it seemed that this latest infatuation of her sister's would go on for ever. Eirlys was completely wrapped up in her mystery man who took her out every night and every weekend. Although she tried on occasions to find out something about him, Eirlys seemed to enjoy keeping everything about him a secret. Once she let slip the name Gregory but this was never repeated and Eirlys denied that it was the name of her lover.

Bettrys thought with sorrow of her own love, Brett, and the holiday she had turned down out of family loyalty and tried not to resent her sister her happiness.

On Bank Holiday Monday at the end of August she returned from St James's Park to find her sister spread out on the bed, with the unmistakable smell of brandy filling the room. She turned Eirlys, prostrate and unconscious, onto her side, sent for the doctor and prepared for a spell of more battles against booze and lies and all that went with them.

"He's gone, Bettrys," Eirlys said, between bouts of sickness, later that evening. "He went without a word. I don't know where to find him."

"I know how you feel. It happened to me, remember?"

"To you? You've never felt a deep and passionate love for anyone else! When did you ever have a love strong enough to break your heart? You can't begin to imagine what it's like!"

Bettrys didn't attempt to argue. Her sister's own problems were paramount and what happened to Bettrys was only half heard and immediately forgotten. Bettrys knew it was pointless to refresh her memory about Brett. Eirlys, she had learned long ago, wasn't interested in anyone but herself. Her thoughts were sad but without bitterness.

The drink was the reason her sister felt no sympathy for others. Her depression made her centre all her thoughts on herself.

The young policeman, Jonathan Crawley, called several times but Bettrys reported to him that her sister didn't want to see him. Bettrys wondered briefly if Eirlys felt ashamed of the way she had treated him, now she had been abandoned in the same way, but decided not. She had behaved insensitively and without a care, yet demanded sympathy and loving attention when she was at the receiving end. Bettrys sighed. What a burden her parents had given her when they had made her promise to watch over her.

It wasn't until half term that the worst happened.

"Your sister is pregnant, Miss Hopkyns," the doctor said, "and I fear very much for the state of her health. Her mental state, you understand."

Bettrys understood all too well. Alcohol and the danger of suicide. And only herself to take care of her.

"For the present I have given her sick leave but I hope that once she has accepted the situation she will be well enough to return. Perhaps before the end of term. It would be better for her than wallowing in – her unhappiness."

"We can only hope so." Bettrys smiled hollowly. She knew that far from returning to work, Eirlys was going to make it difficult, if not downright impossible, for her to keep her own job! To stay in her teaching post she would have to employ someone to stay with her sister during the hours she was away from the flat. For the sake of the baby, Eirlys must not be allowed to drink for the duration of her pregnancy. They would both have to become virtual prisoners until Easter.

The world was filled with stupid people, he decided. And wasn't he glad of it! He fingered a fifty pound note. He had receive it from a woman who expected him to make a start on transforming her disgusting jungle into a beautiful garden the following week. In two days he would be far away.

He chose the next and final house with care. The garden was half-heartedly managed, with overgrown shrubs and abandoned flower-beds, weeds rampant everywhere. Well, he wouldn't mind doing a bit of weeding to help persuade them to part with some cash, but only if strictly necessary! He had watched the place for a couple of days and, as far as he could learn, it was owned by a young couple who both went out to work. The wife returned first, about four. He guessed she was a teacher like Eirlys.

It was so easy he was laughing as he walked away. Some impressive note-paper with few false directors listed was all he had. An imaginary business consisting of that note-paper and the natural charm he had been born with, which he had cultivated into an art. And here it was, a hundred pounds, simply for drawing a sketch of a garden with a barbeque, an exotic looking pond complete with lights, and a crazy-paving patio and path, leading to the dear old pergola. As long as he mentioned these "essentials" he could be certain of extracting some cash from the purses of his victims.

"Do forgive my wearing gloves, but my hands are so awful I have to hide them." He always used the same excuse. "I have eczema, and being such an enthusiast, I have to have 'hands on' experience of every job I do, so it doesn't heal. I simply cannot stand by and watch while my staff do all the work. I have to be involved." At this point he would laugh his charming laugh and add: "Instead of wearing gloves to work in the soil and the cement and for lifting all those rough stones, I wear them on occasions when I stay clean!" Like the others, she shared his laughter and offered her sympathy and her admiration for his dedication.

A hundred pounds cash! The silly woman had been intending to go to Portobello Market on the following day to look for second-hand china. Sheer luck he had chosen today. He hastened his steps. He didn't want the husband coming after him, although, as he had persuaded her to keep it as a wonderful surprise, that was unlikely. Yes, he thought with a contented smile, the world was full of idiots. God bless 'em!

By employing an elderly but very capable ex-nurse to watch over Eirlys while she was at school, Bettrys managed to survive the following term. When the woman was unable to come, Jonathan Crawley helped, sometimes staying overnight, when things were particularly difficult. Once, Eirlys stayed awake all night and Bettrys and Jonathan took turns in watching her for two hours at a time. During one of these long, exhausting occasions, she spoke about the man who had loved her, and then left her carrying his child.

Between them Bettrys and Jonathan learnt very little, only that his name might be Gregory, and that his home was a place in South Wales with a name something like "er trow".

"Not much help if she wants to find him, is it?" Jonathan said grimly.

"I hope she doesn't try. What would be the point? He would only deny he was the father, and seeing him again would put her back to the mess she was in when he first left her." She peeped in and saw that Eirlys had succumbed to the sleeping tablets and was quiet. There were times like this when everything seemed so peaceful it was hard to imagine the bad times. But even when Eirlys was sleeping like an innocent child, there were never more than a few minutes when Bettrys felt able to relax. There was an underlying tension that exhausted her. She lived with the knowledge that, at any moment, Eirlys might wake and start screaming and demanding to go out. Or worse, she might find her sister quietly crying. Tears flowing down Eirly's lovely face distressed her more than the tantrums ever could. If he was with her, Jonathan would hold her while she fought tears of her own.

At Christmas, Eirlys attempted suicide twice, and spent a little while in hospital, a time which to Bettrys was like a holiday, even with the daily visits. There was no Christmas tree, no turkey, not even a gaily wrapped gift. Just a much-needed break in the routine of exhausting days and sleepless nights.

Slowly, they limped through the weeks and kept Eirlys safe through the long, dark winter months. The baby was born at the end of April. It was a girl and Eirlys named her Cheryl. For a while the depression seemed to have lifted. Although she needed a lot of help in caring for her baby, Eirlys seemed to accept the constant attention that was needed. Yet, Bettrys sensed a lack of love between her sister and her little niece. What Eirlys did was automatic. She never nursed the baby or handled her unless it was necessary. There was a coldness about her that made Bettrys give an involuntary shiver at times.

When Cheryl was two weeks old, Bettrys apprehensively agreed to Eirlys's taking the little girl, strapped to her in a baby carrier, to register the birth. Bettrys phoned Jonathan and he agreed to follow her and make sure she didn't harm herself or the baby.

"We don't want her to know we don't trust her, yet we can't risk letting her go alone," Jonathan agreed. He saw Eirlys walk to the register office then come out and get into a taxi. When he called at the flat a while later, Eirlys was sitting drinking a cup of coffee and the baby was safe in her cot.

"I've been out to register the birth," she told him. He feigned surprise and asked if she had given Cheryl any other names.

"No, just Cheryl Hopkyns. I thought of calling her Bettrys but that would have been silly, mother and daughter with the same name."

16

"Mother and daughter?" he laughed. "Your name is Eirlys!"

"Oh yes, so it is."

Jonathan's spirits sank. She had been drinking again. He picked up her coffee cup and a sniff confirmed it. The coffee was laced with brandy.

CHAPTER TWO

With the baby to look after as well as trying to stop
Eirlys drinking, the prospect of any life of her own was
nothing more than fantasy for Bettrys. She had to get a
bank overdraft to pay for the woman to come and help
while she determinedly stayed on at school. After a while
even that seemed hopeless and she knew that if Eirlys
didn't come out of her depression soon she would have
to give up her job. To think ahead was so painful she
tried to concentrate on one day at a time but that only
made the hours a blur and the organisation of the basic
routines increasingly laborious. The weeks dragged by in
a haze of muddled survival, tiredness and a growing sense
of futility.

Jonathan called one day and found Bettrys asleep on a
chair with the baby crying in her cot and Eirlys drunkenly
trying to make up a feed. He put Eirlys to bed, picked
up the baby and after he had calmed her with a drink,
gently woke Bettrys. "You must get some help," he urged.
"Social services must be able to do something."

"No. I don't want them to know. I love little Cheryl and
there's a strong chance that, if they knew about Eirlys,
they'd take her into care. I couldn't bear that. That would
make me feel a complete failure."

They were both silent while Jonathan fed the baby, then
Bettrys changed her napkin and put her in the cot beside
her mother's bed, where Eirlys now lay snoring noisily.

"Then let me help," Jonathan pleaded. "I work shifts
so I can be here some of the time when you have to be at

school. You can't go on like this and – I want to help her. Don't ask me why, but she gets to me. I feel protective towards her even though she doesn't care for me at all." He looked at Bettrys, who was trembling with the shock of coming too soon out of much needed sleep. Jonathan touched her arm and, emphasising the words, said, "I'm not offering to marry her, for God's sake. Only let me support her, and you, for a few weeks, just until she gets through this post-natal depression. The doctor believes she'll come through this and, with the baby to care for, return to the bright, happy person she once was."

"He doesn't know all the facts. He doesn't know, because we've never told anyone. My parents kept her away from psychiatrists and the rest and I've tried to do the same." She looked up at him through eyes that were ringed with tiredness. "Every family has its secrets. Eirlys is ours. She's always been fragile, you see."

"Let me help."

"Helping Eirlys is grabbing a tiger by the tail, you can't ever let go," Bettrys warned. "Best you walk away before you're dragged under, like I was."

"Tell me about it," Jonathan encouraged.

For the first time, Bettrys spoke aloud her despair of ever being free to live her own life. "I know it sounds like some silly fairy-tale, but I did promise our parents that if anything should happen to them I would look after her. I was sixteen and I never thought anything would take them away from us. Then there was a car accident while they were out walking the dog and they both died. They were only out of the house ten minutes and those ten minutes ruined everything for me, although I didn't think so. Not then. Until recently I was happy looking after her. When she's well she's so lively and amusing. Even her awful drinking was periodic and between those times she was fun to be with.

"I suppose I was living vicariously, through her. But I loved it. She showed me glimpses of a life so different from my own." Her voice was distorted by a sob. "I love her you see, and I still feel tied by that promise to our parents, even though it's ruining my health, and my hope of any existence other than as her slave, nursemaid and keeper."

"You've been wonderful," Jonathan leaned forward and kissed her wet cheek. "But even you must have some prospect of eventual freedom. This is a life sentence, isn't it? No one deserves that."

"I'd love to be able to count the days until it all ends happily," she said in a low voice. "But I can't see anything changing, ever."

A fleeting shadow disturbed momentarily the sunshine playing on the wall of the kitchen, where Bettrys and Jonathan sat deep in melancholy thought. The figure of Eirlys slipped out of the front door and went down the stairs to the pavement.

"What was that?" Bettrys asked. "I felt a draught. Did you see anything?"

"I thought a shadow passed over the sun."

In sudden alarm, Bettrys ran to her sister's bedroom and saw that the bed and the cot were empty.

"She's gone! She's taken the baby! Oh, Jonathan, she must have heard us!" With a wail of anguish she ran to the door, followed by Jonathan.

They saw her in the distance, running, clutching the baby. Moving in slow motion, dream-like through the throng. Knowing without being told that she was heading for the underground station. Losing sight of her. Crying in frustration and fear. Finding her again. Seeing her glance back, white-faced, glassy-eyed and desperate. Drawn to her by the baby's screams. Real? Or imaginary? The image of the helpless infant forcing them to greater and greater effort. Disregarding those they pushed aside in their race for a life, or maybe two. Pushing through the station entrance. Knocking into a man buying flowers and sending him staggering. Unaware of his shouts. Fighting past slow-moving passengers. Why wouldn't they under-stand and let them pass? Causing furore, forcing their way into a queue of patient people buying tickets. Jonathan shouting "Police!" and her echoing it in a scream that didn't sound like her own voice. Searching the platform. Frustration making them cry out as if in pain. Seeing her then, on the edge, a train approaching fast, so fast there wasn't time. There wasn't time! Running on leaden feet, wading through glue, movements impossibly slow. Jonathan shouting, pleading, reaching her, grabbing her clothes, then reaching slowly, oh, so slowly for the terrified child. Then, seeing the distraught mother vanish under the relentless, gigantic machine of death, amid crazy screams and panicking people.

Jonathan was a great comfort to Bettrys in the following weeks. He stayed as much as his work allowed, occasion-ally sleeping on the couch and answering the demands of the baby, whom Bettrys had accepted as her own.

Sadly, she realised that by dying, her sister had freed her from her promise to her parents, but by leaving little Cheryl, her freedom had been irretrievably taken from her. She was now committed to the care of this helpless baby, unless she could find the child's father. And, would she be willing to part with the little girl if she succeeded? Could she hand this beautiful infant over to strangers? Yet she had to try and find him and give Cheryl the opportunity of being cared for by her own family.

"Where would you start? What do you know about him?" Jonathan asked one evening as they sat in the flat eating pizza and drinking red wine. "You say you don't even know where he lived when he and Eirlys were together. Not that that would be much help anyway. This is bedsitter land and the population probably moves faster here than anywhere else in the country. Even people who share a house or flat know little about each other. It seems impertinent to ask."

21

"I don't even know his name."

"Then you'd better forget it. You'll only waste time and effort. You should concentrate on making plans for the future. Feasible plans, so you can have some sort of life for yourself, and the baby, if you're determined to keep her."

"Cheryl. That's her name."

"Nice name," Jonathan said vaguely. "Terrible start to her life, but, a nice name."

"That's not all she'll have that's nice. I'll do my best for her."

"You always do your best, don't you, Bettrys? That's the sort of person you are."

"How dull that sounds." Then as he was about to disemble, she added, "But I *am* dull, compared to Eirlys." This time he didn't even pretend to disagree.

"I wonder if she gave her a second name," Bettrys said. "I've never looked at the birth certificate."

"She said not when I asked her. But you'd better check. She was drunk at the time. I remember she said she wanted to call her Bettrys but the daughter couldn't have the same name as the mother!"

Bettrys searched in the box where death and birth certificates gave the outline of their recent family history. She gasped. "Jonathan! She registered the baby in *my* name!"

Bettrys tried in vain to discover something that would lead her to Cheryl's father. All she discovered, by talking to Eirlys's friends and colleagues, was that the man was from a small coastal village in south Wales. Like Bettrys, they thought it sounded something like Er Trow. Then she had two encouraging pieces of luck. A parent of one of her pupils, called Rae, who occasionally went out with Eirlys, gave Bettrys a little more information.

"He sold encyclopaedias, and there was some doubt as

22

to his entitlement to sell them," Rae chuckled. "Quite a boy he was, by all accounts."

"You don't think he worked for the company legitimately?" Bettrys asked, hopeful that such employment might have led her to him.

"Don't tell none of this to your policeman friend," Rae joked, "but no, he never worked for anyone but himself from what I gathered. A real crook he was. Not that I ever met him. She kept him to herself."

"You didn't find out where he lived?"

"Different place every week if you ask me. But I think his family's home was in Wales. And he did tell her once that his father was as big a crook as he was!" This was another excuse for laughter and Bettrys left her wondering what it was about men who cheated people that made women think they were marvellous.

The second clue was found in a box of memorabilia hidden in Eirlys's wardrobe. Her sister has obviously kept souvenirs of the times she had been out with her lover. Theatre tickets, cinema tickets, a few pressed flowers and some chocolate wrappers. It was on one of these, scribbled untidily in pencil, that she found a telephone number.

With great excitement and a thudding heart she dialled and a voice with a strong Welsh accent answered.

"I'm sorry to bother you, but I'm trying to find a friend of my sister. She is away and I need to get in touch to give him a message," she invented.

"What d'you want to know, then?" the woman replied.

"What part of south Wales do you live. Near Er Trow?"

"Not far away. I take summer visitors so perhaps your friend stayed here?"

"If I could have your address Mrs – ?"

"Mrs Draco," the woman supplied.

"Mrs Draco. If you'd give me your address, I will write, tell you what I know and perhaps you'll be able to help find him."

23

"What's his name then? That'll be a start."

"That's the problem. I've mislaid her address book and now I'm not sure whether it was Williams, or Jones or Davies or some other Welsh name." Bettrys chuckled. "It's so embarrassing."

"You write to me, love, I'll help you sort it out. Been living here all my life and I'm sure to know him if he lives at Yr Tro."

Bettrys didn't write but kept Mrs Draco's name and address with the intention of one day visiting the area. She made a list of all she had learnt. It wasn't very much. Once or twice she had managed to persuade her sister to talk about her lover but she had never been told his name, or where he lived. She knew only that the small village was called something that sounded like Er Trow. The only other thing she remembered was that the beach further along the coast was something to do with Ffynon. Ffynon, she discovered, meant a spring.

The man who had loved Eirlys, then left her, was in Nottingham. It was his fifth address since leaving London and although the towns were different, his procedure was the same. Finding his way unerringly to the poorest area of the town, he rented a bedsitter, and three lockup garages.

A walk around the town satisfied him that his plan would work successfully. A garage selling Ford cars was situated just far enough away from his lodgings, there was a phone box that seemed to survive attempts to vandalise it, on a corner about ten minutes away from where he lived and there were enough people with money to round it all off satisfactorily.

To celebrate his newly prepared scheme, he picked up a prostitute and spent a pleasant hour being flattered and admired. That he believed her extravagant praise was due to his vanity not his stupidity. The woman had no idea just how clever, even brilliant, her eight-thirty pickup really

24

was. Such a pity there was no one to whom he could boast his brilliance.

The cars were stolen at night. Two were taken from driveways and one, purely for the daring thrill of it, from a locked garage. He drove them to his lockups and slept contentedly.

A few days later he wrote down three registration numbers of cars on the garage forecourt and wrote to Swansea for papers, stating that he had just bought the vehicles. Each time he gave a different address and, when the forms were returned with the cars in his, false, name, he advertised in the local paper, offering the cars, individually for sale – going cheap, the advertisement stated, owing to redundancy. It also added that he would accept cash only.

Once the money was safely in is wallet he disappeared, taking minimal luggage in a small expandable briefcase, and travelling first class on the train.

It was vanity that was nearly his undoing. He was walking through the town of Shrewsbury, looking for a suitable place to lodge and begin what would be his final series of car thefts for a while, when, in a second-hand bookshop, he saw one single copy of a new American Encyclopaedia of Knowledge. It tickled him to think that for the price of a couple of drinks he had the means to make a few hundred pounds. He could always move elsewhere to do the final deal with the cars.

He bought it from the ageing assistant, who hardly looked at him as she took his five pound note and placed the one pound coin back in his hand. At one of the motorway services stations he had printed four sets of business cards, purporting him to be: Richard Forbes, a second-hand books dealer; Reginald Porter-Black, a double-glazing salesman: Percival Tremain, a garden designer and finally, Grant Rochester, an American, selling encyclopaedias. Taking one of the latter, he knocked on several doors.

At the first house he had no luck but accepted a cup of coffee and helped himself to a silver frame and a small candlestick – Georgian if he wasn't mistaken.

At the second and third he received a deposit of fifty pounds and on the fourth he made his excuses and swiftly hurried away, having seen the unmistakable uniform of a policeman on the hall stand!

In three days he made £560 and was once more on the train, wearing a new overcoat and a satisfied smile.

"Mr Rochester?" a voice asked, as he settled to enjoy a new Dick Francis novel. He looked up and then froze. The man standing beside him was unfamiliar but had the hard expression that meant trouble. Behind him was the woman from whom he had tried to take a fifty pound deposit on some encyclopaedias. She was from the house from which he had hurriedly made his departure, having seen the police uniform.

"Rochester?" he asked in a Welsh accent. Quickly gathering his wits, he took out a business card. "Mistaken you are, sir, Madam. I am – " he quickly re-checked the name on the card he had produced. "Mr Richard Forbes." Dammit, why had it been the other one referring to books! "Barchester did you say? Never heard of anyone with that name. Sorry."

"I think you'd better come with me, Grant Rochester, or is it Percival Tremain?"

"Percival? Duw, what a name to be saddled with, eh?" Outwardly calm, his mind was racing in an attempt to escape from his predicament. He knew that flight was the only way. The man went on in his quiet voice:

"We have descriptions of you from Nottingham and London and a few other places besides. Car thefts, that's a new departure for you, isn't it? The name Francis Fellows ring any bells? Or Gregory Hillman? That was London I believe."

Gregory Hillman? That was the name he had used when he was with Eirlys. They had done their homework!

The train was slowing down. The station was a small one but he thought it better to risk a small place where everyone noticed a stranger, than the certainty of Nottingham, with this quietly dogged policeman, accompanied by his granite-faced wife.

The moment the train had spilled its impatient passengers and accepted the equally fraught newcomers, he pushed against the man with a suddenness that knocked him to the floor and darted out of the door as the platform was dizzily receding.

He fell heavily but, ignoring the pain in his ankle, he made his way towards the exit as the train squealed once more to a halt. Somehow, by sheer good fortune, no one saw him as he squeezed in between a loaded trolley and the wall. By lifting up his elegantly shod feet so they weren't visible beneath it, he miraculously evaded the first rush of a search.

The waiting room was quickly scanned and when it was vacated with the approach of another train to an adjoining platform, he went inside and listened to the voices outside telling him, as clearly as if he could see, what was happening on the platform and on the station approach.

Voices close by revealed that he was believed to have re-entered the train, which had not yet departed. Relaxing slightly, he visited the toilets and dug out a few items from his small case. He didn't move for half an hour, then returned to the waiting room, his face fatter and with a straggly moustache, and a wig of long untidy hair over his own neat style. A couple of elderly women entered and sat opposite him. They were meeting someone and when the train came in, he walked out beside them, a battered hat on his head, carrying his overcoat in a plastic bag, a scruffy jumper over his smart, silk shirt. His shoulders slouched and he was wearing a rather vacant expression on his face. He stood close to them as they greeted their friend.

With the station slumbering in the heat of the afternoon,

he walked with them through the unattended entrance and back into the town. Tomorrow he would "borrow" a car and get away from this unlucky place as fast as he could. Staying within the speed limits of course. No point in being doubly stupid. Once was enough. It was time to give things a rest. Time to pause and re-assess. Time to make plans for the future.

He abandoned the Sierra at the edge of the town and walked to the railway station. A shiver of apprehension chilled him as he prepared to step onto the train. If he were recognised he would be on a moving prison. Shaking off the dread of seeing the policeman and his wife staring down at him, he bought his ticket and a newspaper and settled himself in a first-class carriage. He wasn't concentrating on the paper in front of him, he was still edgy, watching people passing, afraid of seeing the uniform representing the law. Then as the train began to move, his eyes caught the headline reporting Eirlys's suicide and he smiled.

The baby was news to him and he sat thinking about the girl who had been such a delightful companion. What luck he had left when he did, she'd have ruined his memories of their time together. She'd have expected him to be sympathetic and even supportive; and everyone knew that these days it was up to the woman to deal with that side of things.

He thought of her face and wondered how it had looked in death. There had always been a fascination for him in death. The light fading from the face, the strength and determination vanishing as if an artist had painted something then wiped it out and replaced it with nothingness. It had been like that when he had witnessed a car accident when he was twelve.

The image of Eirlys became distorted as he tapped his hand with the rolled newspaper. She had intended to use him. All that charm had been nothing more than a devious plan to make him marry her. She had been like all the rest.

Memories of the beautiful Eirlys faded and slowly a hatred of her grew instead.

The bitch. She had been trying to trap him. Anger flared and he screwed the paper into a tight wand, hitting it against his hand and wishing it were her beautiful, scheming face.

Throughout the journey he stared into space, the image of Eirlys falling to her death becoming more and more real. He wished he had seen it, wished he had been there, perhaps even – his eyes widened with painful yet wondrous shock – perhaps even to push her. His hand felt warm as he imagined touching her, making that fatal movement, just a slight push, almost a caress, that was all it would have needed, but he would have been a part of it.

He stopped the dream abruptly, like snapping off a switch when it came to the part where police were hunting him with the intention of locking him up. He paused a moment for the panic to ease then began again, with the best bit, the warmth of her back and the gentle push.

He was living the dream over and over again as he alighted from the train. His mood alternated from anger with Eirlys from depriving him of a share in her death and pleasure at the prospect of the brief holiday he had promised himself.

Being responsible for baby Cheryl had changed Bettry's life in many ways, and had altered her attitude to other aspects of life too. She began to feel critical of their surroundings. A small flat that seemed trouble-free and convenient for two working sisters had now become poky, too close to the unpleasant traffic fumes and too far from a park. It was time to move on. The decision to move away from London altogether was just an extension of that idea.

"What will you do? Where will you go?" Jonathan asked on one of their regular evenings sharing a meal at the flat.

"Perhaps I'll go to Wales. Our parents came from there you know. It's hopeless, I know that, but I'll make an attempt to find Cheryl's father. It's as good a reason for settling on an area as any other," she smiled.

"After all this time? What would you hope to gain?"

"I don't want to give her up!" she said hastily. "I want to give her the chance of knowing where she came from. Learning about her background will be valuable later on, help her understand who she is. Perhaps there'll be half sisters or brothers; or cousins, aunts and uncles. There might be a grandmother, can you imagine what a joy that would be? She might be a part of a huge, loving family instead of having no one apart from me."

"It's dangerous. If you manage to find them you might not like what you find."

"Then we'll move away again. But really, Jonathan, the chance of disliking them is slight, surely? I'm hardly likely to find a gang of criminals, murderers or worse. Or a family of semi-literate idiots!"

"Keep in touch, will you? I'd like to know how you are, how you're getting on with your . . . quest."

"You make me sound like an ancient heroine searching for a dragon!" she laughed.

"Well, it's to the Land of the Dragon you're heading!" He laughed with her and then a mood of melancholy settled on them as they became aware that the close friendship was going to end.

"There's something I learned a couple of days ago that might help you," Jonathan said. "I spoke to a Welsh colleague and told him about the place you hope to find. He said it might be Yr Tro, which means The Bend. There are several places with that as a local name."

Bettrys wrote the information down in her notebook. It wasn't much, but it was a start.

"Let's sum up what we know," Jonathan suggested. "We think he was Welsh, and his family live on the south coast of Wales." He held up a second finger and added,

"We have to face the fact that he might be a criminal. He deliberately covers his tracks and gives nothing away. And because of that, we can't even be certain of the little we do know." A third finger was raised. "This Mrs Draco, who knows the area called The Bend, is obviously a good place to start as the phone number hastily copied must have meant something to Eirlys. Perhaps she too was trying to discover more about her man in the hope of holding on to him."

"He sells encyclopaedias," Bettrys added and a fourth finger went up.

"Bettrys, I don't want to alarm you, but please be careful. If he has hidden his identity so successfully, there has to be a reason. Promise me you won't ask any direct questions about him, or try to find him until you are certain he wants to be found. Don't give away the reason for staying at Yr Tro. Go there and pretend to be looking for a place to settle, pretend Cheryl is your daughter. You mustn't mention anything about Eirlys in case the man thinks you are intent on disclosing his identity to the police. We don't know him and he might be dangerous."

Bettrys laughed but Jonathan frowned and repeated urgently. "Promise me you'll be careful. Promise that you'll tell no one why you are there. Not until you are certain you've found the man and even then, think carefully before you reveal your reason for searching him out. If he is a confidence trickster you could be a threat and there's no knowing what he's capable of doing."

"All right, Jonathan, I promise I'll be a casual visitor looking for somewhere pleasant to spend the summer. Will that do?"

"Just be careful," Jonathan said gruffly. "I only wish I could come with you."

It was at Easter, when Cheryl was almost one year old, when Bettrys resigned from her teaching post. As a

31

preview to her search for Cheryl's father she went to south Wales and spent a weekend with Mrs Draco. She was given a delightful room facing the sea and Mrs Draco did everything she could to make them comfortable. At breakfast on the first morning, Bettrys asked her about the place called Yr Tro.

"There's a beach not far away called The Bend, but there might be others. Many of the names used by the locals are descriptive see, but it's so close it must be worth a try." She reached for a map from her crowded bookshelf and, as an afterthought, took down a bus timetable. "You'll have to get there by bus. It'll take for ever, mind, but it's a pretty run through the villages."

Bettrys noted the information in her book but, on such a brief visit, decided that Cheryl had done enough travelling. The exploration of Yr Tro would have to wait until next time.

Returning to London on the train, Bettrys's mind was filled once again with the hope of finding Cheryl's father. Didn't she owe it to the little girl to at least try? She decided to spend the summer searching for the man whose name she didn't know, then, if she had no success, she would rescue her career and forget him.

She wouldn't stay longer than the summer. There was a definite need to return to London after a few months away. Always in the deep recesses of her mind was the thought, the painful hope, that Brett would return and look for her. She had to leave a trail he could follow. She had to return to where he could find her.

She loved Cheryl and it would be no hardship to concentrate on making her happy. She wondered vaguely if Jonathan would be a part of their future and hoped he might remain her friend. Nothing more than that. She would herself be free of love and entanglement for when she and Brett met again. It was a foolish dream and in moments of honesty, she knew it was nothing more than a fantasy, but it was a dream which kept the edge off despair.

CHAPTER THREE

Bettrys stepped off the country bus and with Cheryl in her arms and all her worldly possessions on her back, stood on the roadside and stared out over the sea. It was so still and silent she could hardly imagine it in storm. The pebbles and crushed shells that made the shallow beach, seemed undisturbed by the sea's comings and goings. More like a pond than the sea, she thought. She put Cheryl down and knelt to encourage the little one year old to examine the stones and gravel, then she turned and looked inland.

The coast at this point was almost flat, only rising slightly beyond the road to a low, green hill, on which there were several scattered buildings, a row of farm cottages and the large stone farmhouse itself, half surrounded by pine trees. Sheep grazed peacefully and occasionally she heard the anxious bleat of a lamb briefly separated from its mother. Apart from the sheep there seemed to be no other living thing.

This must be the place Mrs Draco told me about, she decided, turning from the view of the hill to look down at the narrow strip of land below the road and slightly above the beach. Among low shrubs and trees that had been distorted into fantastic sculptures by wind and storm, other habitations, some with smoke slipping out of their chimneys and floating up to join the grey cloud above, were visible amid the greenery.

There was a roughly cemented path leading down through the trees from where the bus had dropped her, and she followed it, heading by a tortuous route around the trees and thick bushes to the beach. At the end of the path the shoreline was edged with rocks and a variety of wild flowers. She helped Cheryl to build a small stack of pebbles and laughed as the child pushed them over with an air of achievement.

Bettrys was tall, slender and had about her an air of superiority, developed to hide her natural shyness. Her elegance made the casual clothes she wore both suitable and attractive. Her black, grey and white skirt was long, full and flowing, and made of flimsy cotton that had been fringed at the hem. As rays of the sun pierced the cloud, silver threads showed. Her blouse hung outside the skirt and that too was flimsy cotton, this time in dark red.

When she had sold the London flat, she had kept only a few items of clothing, choosing those easiest to wear and care for, and which would tolerate being bundled into a rucksack. Similar clothes for Cheryl, plus a few toys, meant they were not encumbered with possessions and the problems of transporting them. Until she was sure she had found the right place, they might be doing a lot of travelling.

Her hair was tied in a bun on the top of her head but strands fell in burnished tracery round her face. She stood for a while, the hesitant sun touching her with a periphery of gold, and allowed the little girl to play. As she looked out over the sea, her eyes were the same colour, giving a hint of melancholy to her serious face. The houses slumbered silently, there was no sight nor sound of any inhabitants. Several places looked as if they were holiday chalets and had been locked up all winter. The door of one, called Colin's Place, stood open but there was no one to be seen.

Lifting the child into her arms she left her bundle against a rock and walked along the beach past the secretive huddle of houses nestling in the trees.

Beyond the houses, the beach began to curl around and the land changed. Instead of the low plateau, and the green hills beyond the road, cliffs rose high with hedges and fence guarding its edge. The beach was more sandy here and several boats were drawn up above the high-tide level. On the sea itself she could see floats marking moorings where, she guessed, the summer months would bring more sailors to enjoy the quiet harbour.

They stopped and played as the tide came closer, its progress imperceptible, the small invading waves hardly making a sound. Cheryl slept for a while, then woke and played some more. Bettrys dug into her pocket and gave the little girl some tinned food, some biscuits and a bottle of fruit juice.

A couple walked along the highest part of the beach, the first people she had seen since leaving the bus. They were holding hands, laughing. She was pretending to slip on the uneven surface and he helped her, finally picking her up and carrying her amid increased laughter. It was a lovely sound and made Bettrys aware of her solitary state.

She had no family now Eirlys was dead, and no love in her life. Brett was lost to her, she had to face it, even though a tiny glimmer of hope remained in her heart. What they'd been together had been good. It couldn't have been so trivial to him that he had forgotten her. How could it have ended without explanation? There was little chance of seeing him again now she had moved away. She didn't even know where he was living. Perhaps, she thought with a stab of jealousy, he'd found someone new and had stayed in Greece. "Oh, Brett," she said aloud. "Where are you when I need you so much?"

She missed him and ached to feel his arms around her, his lips touching hers and telling her she was his only love. A practical side of her came to the fore then and she thought of the two hundred pounds he had borrowed and not returned. That would be handy now, her money wouldn't last very long without work to replenish it. Foolish hope surged as she thought it might have been posted, and was now, this minute, waiting for her at the flat. She decided to telephone to see if any mail had been delivered. At least that small optimistic glimmer of hope would keep her happy for a while.

A hint of self-pity crept over her and she forced herself to invent games to amuse Cheryl, counting pebbles, drawing faces in the sand. There was Jonathan of course. She smiled as she remembered his kindness. No love in her life, just two men around whom to wind her fanciful dreams.

Cheryl gave a little cry and held up her arms to be lifted and cuddled.

"Yes, my darling, you're tired and it's time we found somewhere to stay." Bettrys kissed the little girl and they began to walk along the edge of the beach to the nearest, and largest, of the houses. A scream rent the air and she turned back to see a woman near the bottom of the cliffs in the distance beyond where she had walked. She was screaming and looking up. Above her a man was teetering on the edge of the cliff. Behind him bushes trembled and Bettrys thought she saw someone hastily moving away. She caught a brief glimpse of darting shadows between the branches.

The man was swinging now, clinging to the trunk of a slender tree growing out of the side of the cliff, his feet flailing, searching for a foothold. The woman on the beach was screaming instructions, sobbing in fear and calling for help. Bettrys ran towards them then turned back, deciding instead to get help from the nearest house. Then another glance showed the man had used the pendulum motion of the tree and had managed to somehow swing himself back to safety and was crawling down from the edge on which he had been balancing.

The woman had covered her face with her hands and was wailing as the man slowly disappeared, to re-appear moments later on the beach below the cliffs. He walked towards the woman and appeared to be comforting her, although her cries could still be heard. Bettrys saw them both look up, the man pointing, but Bettrys could see no one else there. They must know she was there but they made no attempt to speak to her, or ask if she had seen anything or anyone. It must have been the man's own shadow she had seen. He had probably slipped, perhaps as he was trying to call down to the woman below him.

As Bettrys turned once more towards the houses, a young man came out of the large one nearest to her, a spaniel bouncing around him in great excitement. Bettrys paused and waited for him to reach her. She reminded herself to be careful in what she said. Every word had to be considered if she were not to reveal the reason for her presence. She must think before she spoke every single word.

"Hello," she said, her voice gentle and almost a whisper. "I wonder, could you help us?"

"Looking for someone?" the young man asked with a smile.

Bettrys smiled back, a slow, languid smile that made him want to help her more than anything else in the world. She did want to find someone but now was not the time to discuss it. Her thoughts and caution delayed her reply and the young man began to wonder if she had not heard him.

"I'm looking for somewhere to stay, a day or so, perhaps longer," she said at last.

"I think Mrs Cooper might help." He held out a hand to take the rucksack she had retrieved. "Come on, I'll take you. It isn't far." He groaned in mock dismay as he took the weight of the rucksack, to amuse them, and was rewarded with a slow, heart-stopping smile.

The dog had run off, nose down, following some trail that, by the look of his tail. was giving him great pleasure. "That's Potter," the young man said, as if she had commented on the animal. "He'll have to wait a bit longer for his walk."

He led her through the trees along a narrow path, to the

38

porch of what appeared at first to be little more than a hut. The door was open and he pushed it and called. A small untidy lady wearing thick glasses on her thin pointed nose appeared, smiled at him and gestured for them to enter.

"Who have you brought for to meet me today then, young Gordon?" she asked in a high voice. "Another new girlfriend, is it?"

"I'm sorry," Gordon glanced at Bettrys. "I didn't ask her name. Found her wandering on the beach. She's looking for accommodation. Can you help?"

"I'm Bettrys, this is Cheryl." Bettrys held out a hand. "I just want a room for a few days, while I sort out something more permanent. If you would be so kind."

"Sorry, love, I don't take visitors any more," Mrs Cooper shook her untidy head, her lips lost in a determined grimace. The girl was silent for a moment, deliberating over her words with caution. Again, Gordon had the impression that she hadn't heard. Then she said slowly, "Perhaps you'd break the rule just for one night? We'll be off early in the morning. Cheryl's very tired you see."

"Go on, Carys," Gordon urged. "Just the one night." He badly wanted this fascinating woman to stay.

When he had seen her standing on the beach, the wind gently playing with her long skirt and teasing the tendrils of gold-tinted hair, he had collected the dog's lead and set off to see who she was. She had stood still for so long. Then, as he stepped onto the beach she had been walking towards him. His first thought was relief that he hadn't delayed a moment longer and missed her.

Where she had come from he had no idea. The bus had passed hours ago. And the walk from the village was more than five miles. One moment the beach was empty, the next she was standing there looking out to sea. In his foolish imagination she had evolved from the rushes and cotton grass of the moorland. Or had been magically brought there by the wind and the tide, entering his life and bringing spice and wonderment.

He looked at her shyly, afraid she might have read his foolish thoughts. "How did you get here?" he asked. "There hasn't been a bus for ages."

"Nevertheless it was the bus that brought us," she smiled. Their eyes met and held.

"All right then, you can stay. But only for the one night, mind," Carys Cooper said firmly. "Just the one night. It doesn't suit me to have visitors at the moment."

Carys Cooper was a small woman; quick movement gave the impression of irritability. Her hair was carelessly cut and hung about her shoulders in a wild frizz; grey at the roots, an unbelievable black everywhere else. Her long nose seemed too narrow to support her thick glasses, which made her dark eyes seem enormous behind the magnifying lenses in the small, sharp-featured face. Her mouth was sunken, caused, Bettrys guessed, by a lack of teeth.

The room into which they were shown was obviously a work room. A treadle machine stood against a wall half hidden by spread paper patterns. A modern machine was on a table draped with the makings of a dress. Cottons and all the paraphernalia of a seamstress lay about the room in untidy abandoned piles. The floor was carpeted with fluff from garments made long ago and forgotten.

Stepping outside to collect her rucksack which Gordon had left against the door, she saw that the house was larger and more solid than she had first thought. Hidden by the tangled trees pressing in from all sides, it was built of stone, on a platform of rock, and it blended with the scenery as if it had grown there.

Inside, once past the workroom, everything was neatness. Furniture and brass and dishes and windows all shone with cleanliness. A dark-stained staircase jutted out into the living room and Bettrys was shown up into a front bedroom with a view of the beach and the calm grey sea. The windows were stained with salt, and, half apologetically, Mrs Cooper promised to "Get my husband to get the worst off later."

After one of her intriguing pauses, Bettrys said, "Please, don't bother on our account. It adds a touch of mystery."

So do you my lovely girl, so do you, Gordon thought. Aloud, he said, "Well, I'd better get after Potter or he'll wander off into the next bay."

"Would that be Ffynon Sands?" Bettrys asked.

"That's right, ffynon is Welsh for spring and there are several that pop out of the sand there. Lovely for picnics it is. Icy cold and as sweet as you could wish. There isn't a name for this part of the beach, we just call it 'The Bend', 'Yr Tro' some of the older ones call it. We're only a straggle of houses that, apart from this house, our grandfather's house and the Taylor's farm, were once holiday chalets. We aren't big enough to be called a village. There isn't even a pub!"

"Thanks for your help," Bettrys smiled, and Gordon had the feeling he had been dismissed.

"Mam and Grandfather live in the house they call Smuggler's Cottage," he said as he reached the door. "Daft name! I live in the chalet behind it. Call if you want anything, or if you'd like me and Potter to show you round the area."

Again that slight pause before she said, "Thank you, Gordon."

Leaving Carys Cooper to prepare afternoon tea, Bettrys went upstairs, washed Cheryl and gave her some toys to play with out of her rucksack. Then she took out her notebook and checked against what Mrs Draco in Swansea had told her. Carys Cooper is the local sewing lady, her husband must be Jake. And Gordon must be Gordon Howells. His mother was Gwen Howells and his grandfather was an ex-fisherman, Maldwyn Griffiths. "Yes, my love," she said as she knelt to cuddle Cheryl, "we seem to have found the right place."

Old Maldwyn Griffiths, Gordon's grandfather, had seen

the arrival of the young woman and the little girl. He had been sitting on the length of timber the tide had brought in after a storm twenty years before, and which was used as a bench by Maldwyn and his friends as a place for conversation, and for having tea, supplied by his daughter, Gwen.

The little girl was pretty, he mused. Dark curly hair, so unlike the woman, yet they must be mother and daughter, why else would they be travelling together? He wondered where the husband was. Perhaps he was coming later. Holiday-makers they were for sure. But they didn't carry much. No bucket and spade for the youngster. Perhaps the father would bring those. Idly, he wondered if the old tin ones his grandsons once used would still be in the shed, and serviceable.

He stood up, stretched and walked up the slight incline to the path and went to see if his daughter had the tea brewing. That bench needed a cushion if he was to sit there for long.

"Gwen?" he called. "That tea ready then? And what about a cushion for that damned bench!"

Maldwyn had been a powerfully built man in his youth but age had stripped the flesh from him and now it hung in folds around his jaw and his once brawny forearms. He wore trousers held up with a wide leather belt, and a Welsh flannel shirt with the sleeves rolled up to allow the sun to touch the pale skin that had once been the colour of mahogany. His hair was pure white and as thick as when he had been in his prime. Bushy eyebrows gave the gnarled old face an aggressive look, so he bristled like a dog sensing the prospect of a fight.

"You're back, Dad," Gwen said unnecessarily. "I was just bringing you tea out on a tray.

"That bloody bench is too bloody hard!" he said.

Chuckling, Gwen picked up a cushion, tucked it under her arm and, with the tray in her hands, coaxed him back outside.

"There'a a visitor come," he said as he sipped his tea. "Gordon went up and spoke, then brought her to Carys Cooper's. Young woman and a baby about a twelve-month. Pretty little thing. Must be holiday makers."

"It's a bit early, Dad."

"One of them daft walkers then. She had a rucksack and nothing else. Sign of the times it is, Gwen. If they did a proper day's work instead of using machines for every damned thing they'd get tired enough without wanting to walk for a holiday! Damned silly idea, walking and wearing yourself out and calling it a holiday!"

"Yes, Dad," Gwen chuckled. "Damned silly idea. Just as daft as you walking five miles to the post office in the village every week to collect your pension when there's no need, wouldn't you say?"

"That's different!" he snorted.

"Yes,'" she said with a wry grin. "I thought it would be, love."

"Pity help them staying with that nosy old bugger, mind," he said, handing Gwen his cup for a refill. "Carys Cooper will have the ins and outs of everything about that girl's life before bedtime. And what *she* doesn't find out that husband of hers Jake will!"

"Drink your tea and don't start on about Jake Cooper, Dad. Honestly, he's all you talk about."

"Jake Cooper is a cheat and a liar! What else d'you expect me to talk about. He cheated me out of my boat!"

"You don't know that. Not for sure you don't."

Maldwyn only grunted and added an extra spoonful of sugar to his cup. "It's stewed!" he complained.

"Yes, Dad," Gwen grinned. "I thought it would be. Tastes like old boots."

He caught her eye and turned away before she could see his echoing grin. He knew he was a misery. Who better? But the trick Jake Cooper had played rankled as fiercely now as when it had happened more than three years ago.

He was failing, he knew that too. Perhaps this would be his last summer. But he prayed to live long enough to discover Carys and Jake's secret, hear Jake admit his guilt. That's all he wanted now. That, and to see his grandson Gordon settled with a suitable wife.

In a monotonous chant that suggested she had said them many times before, Carys Cooper recited the house rules. They were reasonable in spite of the firmness of her tone, but she reiterated two with emphasis. "Please to use the door from the beach only, and please to remember that the kitchen is out of bounds. Strictly out of bounds. I won't have anyone going into my kitchen whatever the circumstances, not ever. It's my private abode and private it must stay."

"Of course," Bettrys said, surprised at the vehemence showing on the woman's face.

Cheryl nodded off to sleep almost as soon as she had eaten her tea and Bettrys put her to bed. She lay on her own bed, and thought what to do next. It was obvious Mrs Cooper did not want them to stay more than one night, but she had to stop in the area if she were to get to know the inhabitants of the small community. The village was five miles away, too far for her to become a friend of anyone here in – or was it on – The Bend. Apart from Gordon that is, she thought with a slow smile. Another man to dream about, but he wouldn't do. He wasn't Brett.

She looked down at the sleeping child and decided that when she woke they would go for a walk along the shingly beach as far as Smuggler's Cottage, and perhaps call and meet Gordon's mother and grandfather.

Gordon was sitting at his bedroom window staring along the stretch of beach he could see from his vantage point. His grandfather was sitting on the bench again, hoping, no doubt, that one of his cronies would join him for a chat. His mother was hanging out washing that moved surprisingly energetically in the almost imperceptible wind created by the sea. A sheet wrapped itself around her body and Gordon chuckled. Lucky she didn't have Grandfather's temper or the offending article would have ended up in the mud!

He had planned to sail along the coast and climb the cliffs to photograph the newly-arrived seabirds, busy on their nest sites. Gannets nested in an area that couldn't be easily reached by land and by using his boat and then climbing, he hoped to get some good shots of the young birds. Meeting the girl and the baby had changed his mind. He watched the area of the beach near the Cooper's house and hoped to "accidentally" bump into them again.

At four o'clock he saw her. Holding the little girl's hand she stepped onto the beach and began to walk in his direction, picking her way over the rough stones, carrying the little girl over the worst patches. He collected his camera and whistled for Potter and was leaning against the bench beside Grandfather when she reached it.

"Hello again," he called. "Come and meet Grandfather Griffiths, Mam's father, ex-fisherman extraordinaire and great thinker of the parish!"

"Hello," she said, offering her hand. "I'm Bettrys and this is Cheryl."

The old man took her hand and gripped it warmly, then smiled at Cheryl, but although he tried to coax her, the little girl didn't respond, just stared in the straight, disconcerting way of small children.

"She doesn't say much yet," Bettrys explained. "But she understands most of what she hears, don't you, darling?" The child looked up at Bettrys's face then, reassured, gave the old man a shy smile.

"Fancy going for a walk along the beach?" Gordon offered. "Or would you like a trip in my boat over there?" He pointed, and Cheryl began to pull Bettrys in

45

the direction of the sturdy clinker-built boat with obvious excitement. She knew about boats, having gone several times to the seaside with Jonathan and Bettrys.

Bettrys looked at the old man as if for confirmation that it was safe to accept, and he nodded. "You'll be all right with my grandson. Specially on a day like this. I don't expect he'll take you far, he'll stay in sight of The Bend, won't you, boy?"

Bettrys wasn't sure if it was a question of a command, but, further assured by the production or all the necessary safety equipment, she smilingly accepted the invitation.

The outboard was an intrusion and when they reached a point from which they could see all the houses on the stretch of coast, Gordon cut it, threw the anchor overboard and allowed the boat to wallow lazily in the warm afternoon sun.

"There's Grandfather on his bench," he said pointing. "And there's Mam standing beside him." He moved his arm, directing Bettrys's gaze towards the fields above the road and showed her the large farmhouse on the skyline belonging to the Taylors, Diana and Emrys.

"Diana Taylor is Emrys's second wife. She doesn't fit into the community very well, seems to resent not being treated like the old-style lady of the manor. Fat chance of people respecting her when – " he stopped and pointed to the houses lower down near the beach.

The Cooper's house was visible although half hidden. The one she remembered seeing with its door open, called 'Colin's Place', belonged to Colin Williams, he informed her. "He's here this weekend but not with his wife." Again, there was an air of something not said. This was certainly a place for secrets! Gordon pointed out several other properties, including one in which the farmer Emrys Taylor's parents now lived. "Quarrelled with Diana and moved out," Gordon explained. Then he brought her attention to a very smartly decorated chalet, brightly coloured even though evening was crowding in and mist was fuzzing everything at the edges and taking the colours out of the day.

"That's called 'Costa Plenty' would you believe," he chuckled. "Belongs to our local yuppies, if there are such things any more. Jeremy and Frances Baxter play at being quality-country-folk-among-the-peasants most weekends during the summer. They bring their friends so they can be admired for their 'back-to-nature' life-style, and cook meals on a barbeque – assisted by microwave ovens and any other mechanical aids they can discover. They commandeer the beach as if it's theirs and have bonfires and midnight bathing parties when the weather allows. Grandfather goes mad!" He laughed. "When they arrive for the first visit of the year they send cards to all the local houses announcing that Jeremy and Frances Baxter are 'At Home' to friends. They are unbelievable, but they do give great parties."

Behind Smuggler's Cottage, where Maldwyn and Gwen still sat watching, was a small wooden chalet. "That's where I live," Gordon told her. "We all lived there when I was small, but soon after Grandmother died, Dad died at sea and Mam and the others moved in to look after Grandfather. I stayed in the chalet. It isn't exactly independence, mind, with Mam bringing food and doing the odd bit of cleaning, but I like the imagined freedom."

"Free to bring your girlfriends home?" she teased.

"Fat chance! Eyes like a hawk Mam has, and I swear Grandfather has radar embedded in his skull! He can see through rock!"

He talked for a while about the wildlife on the seashore and cliffs, explaining to the silent Cheryl about the animals he saw at night. He started the engine again and they swung round gently and headed for the shore. They took off their life-jackets and Bettrys helped him pull the boat up onto the shingle above high-water mark, where he had a mooring ring embedded. Then Gordon carried Cheryl to where Maldwyn Griffiths sat waiting for them.

"Your mam says for you to wait and she'll bring some drinks," he told Gordon. Once more he tried to involve the little girl in conversation but she just stared with her dark eyes and didn't even smile. Then, after her solemn appraisal, she turned, put her arms up for him to lift her and when she was settled on his lap, pointed and said, "Boat."

Maldwyn looked inordinately pleased. She obviously approved of him.

When Gwen came out with a tray of tea and a blanket to put round Cheryl, she stopped and listened as the sound of a car stopped on the road above them. Two policemen came down the path and walked to where they were sitting.

"Been over at Ffynon Sands this afternoon?" One of them asked.

"I have," Bettrys said.

"Did you see anyone while you were there?"

"I saw a couple walking near the cliffs, then later a man seemed to be in danger of falling. I think he was trying to lean over and talk to the woman below. He crawled back safely though."

"You didn't see anyone else?" She thought of her vague impression that there had been a third person present, but she was far from certain. To mention it would be misleading. She shook her head. Then he asked, "Any idea who they were?"

"I only arrived this afternoon. Why? He couldn't have been hurt. I saw him a short while later, walking along with the woman."

"No, Miss, he wasn't hurt, but he said he was pushed, that someone tried to push him over the edge." The policeman turned to Gwen. "Colin Williams it was, but he refuses to say who the woman was."

48

"I could hazard a guess!" Maldwyn said in a rumble of disapproval, but he was hushed by Gwen.

"How could you know, Dad! You haven't left this bench all day!"

"Where was your sense woman!" Jake Cooper glared at Carys, who folded up the tea-towel she was using to dry the saucepans and glared back, her dark eyes huge behind the thick spectacles.

"Funny it would be for me to refuse. Best we take a chance than start talk about us behaving odd."

"What if she sees something!"

"She'll keep out of my kitchen and if that isn't enough, well then, I can't be expected to act as nursemaid!"

"She'd better be gone by morning!"

"I might offer for her to stay a couple of days, we could do with the cash."

"Out she'll be and first thing in the morning or – " Hands on hips, she glared at him, her eyes bright as a bird's, her attitude unrepentant. "Come on, Carys, you know as well as I do that we can't take no risks."

"I'll do my bit, but the girl stays until I say she must go. Tell him that from me!"

When Bettrys and Cheryl were sitting down to their evening meal, Carys Cooper leaned confidently towards Bettrys and whispered.

"Shouldn't have much to do with them Griffiths's if I were you, girl. Trouble they are the lot of 'em. The old man is the worst, mind. Accused my poor dear husband of telling lies when he claimed against him for an accident on his boat. Lost an arm he did, and there's that old fool Maldwyn insisting he was nowhere near the boat that day! Wicked beyond he is, that one."

"Gordon took us out in his boat," Bettrys said. "And his mother, Gwen, gave us tea and biscuits afterwards."

"Well, you weren't to know, were you? And you have to be polite, don't you? Even to the likes of them Griffiths!"

Satisfied with her own explanation, she went back into her kitchen, closing the door firmly against her guests, and put the finishing touches to the casserole of Welsh lamb she was preparing.

It was seven-thirty when they ate and Carys's husband joined them. He was small like his wife and dark-skinned like someone constantly out in wind and sunshine. One sleeve ended with a pinned pleat, the other arm muscled and capable of many tasks.

His expression was unfriendly, accusative, as if daring Bettrys to offer condolences or assistance. He ignored the little girl and only addressed the briefest of remarks to Bettrys. She watched fascinated, although with some guilt at her curiosity, as he used a fork and managed his food with neat efficiency. Cheryl, too, was interested and for once, Bettrys was thankful she was not yet talking. This was a moment when she would certainly say something embarrassing!

There was a tense atmosphere around the table and Bettrys knew it came from Jake. He made the air prickle and she had the uneasy feeling that this man had a temper that was quick to rise. Although she knew nothing about the disagreement between Maldwyn Griffiths and Jake Cooper, she knew she would side with Gordon's grandfather without a doubt.

As they ate, Carys Cooper questioned her with the casual ease of an expert. Bettrys found it exhausting deflating her with half-truths and inventions. But until she knew who they all were and how they fitted into her sketchy scenario, she had to be careful not to let slip the real reason for her being there.

"You a teacher then?" Carys asked. Bettrys cautiously agreed without stating where she had taught.

"I gave up a post in southern England hoping for work that will enable me to spend more time with Cheryl," she replied.

"Well, it must be difficult, girl, yes, indeed. A baby

and no man. But there you are, you knew what you were doing, didn't you? No good for to blame anyone else. You young people today, you can't plead ignorance for sure!" She laughed as if she had told an amusing joke and Bettrys politely joined in.

She didn't respond to the remarks that were intended to encourage an explanation. Carys smiled as if in sympathy and said, "But there you are, I don't suppose you regret having her. She's someone of your own, isn't she?"

Bettrys didn't disabuse her of the idea that Cheryl was her child. In fact, she thought, Cheryl *was* hers, or as near being her own daughter as was possible without having actually given birth. Unless she found the father, and he insisted on taking some of the responsibility for her, an unlikely event, Cheryl would remain her own.

"Yes," she said very belatedly, in reply to Carys's comment. "I'm very glad I've got her."

Cheryl went to sleep at eight-thirty and Bettrys was invited to come down and watch television. She declined and lay on the bed beside Cheryl, and waited for morning. She had to find somewhere to stay. If only she had thought of asking Gordon or Gwen. But the excitement of the boat trip, then the visit from the police with their enquiries about the man who almost fell from the cliff, had distracted her.

She decided to go to Smuggler's Cottage immediately after breakfast and see if Gwen or Maldwyn knew of a place to rent. Perhaps one of the chalets would be available. They couldn't all be in use so early in the season. It would have to be cheap. She was running out of money faster than she had anticipated and there was a long way to go yet, before she found what she was seeking.

At the Taylor's farm high above the Cooper's house, on the exposed hillside, Diana sat alone, reading the newspaper and half watching the television. Neither interested

51

her and she stood up with relief when there was a knock at the door. She glanced at the clock. Too early for Emrys to return from his darts match at The Ancient Mariner. She switched on the outside light and opened the door. There was no one there.

Irritated, she pushed the door shut and saw, sticking out of the letter box, a piece of paper. With a sigh she opened its folds. What are they asking for this week? she wondered idly. Money for something no doubt. Or jumble. Or the promise of gifts for the summer fête. There was always something to collect for. She was ignored by those on Yr Tro, unless they wanted something.

Walking into the room where there was a better light, she looked at the paper and frowned. It was an advertisement for a garage sale, amateurishly printed and out of date.

Diana Taylor looked, at first glance, like the uninformed person's image of a country woman, born to the role. She wore tweeds and jodhpurs and thick socks, her boots lay carelessly abandoned near the doorway. Her hair hung loose about her full-featured face in untidy curls, where she had freed it from the snood and hat she habitually wore. A closer look showed heavy makeup and the very long painted nails that belied the first impression. Discontent clouded her fierce blue eyes. Whatever role she was playing, it was not making her happy.

She flipped the television off and put the untidily folded paper on a stool. What an existence. She had run away from a frighteningly jealous man and, with a failed relationship still snapping at her heels, had married Emrys, thinking that an older man would give her love, security and peace. She had given up the freedom she badly wanted but greatly feared, for safety and sufficient money for comfort.

Now, at the age of thirty-three, she was caught in a trap that was squeezing away her youth. Dull husband, empty life, bleak future. Even a knock at the door brought nothing but useless and irritating information. Why would anyone think she'd want to go to a garage sale? Why would anyone think she would want to *look* at their pile of old rubbish, let alone buy it, even if it was in aid of some charity? What sort of person did they think she was? Worse, what sort of person were they trying to turn her into with their small ideas and closed minds?

She hated this place. She felt utterly isolated on this bleak hill with the quietly threatening sea all around her. She hated the life she was forced to live, and the people with whom she was expected to find interests and satisfaction. There had been love, of a sort, for a while, but now she hated Emrys, blaming him for everything that was wrong in her life. And, she thought, as she picked up the offending piece of paper to throw it in the fire, she hated worth-while causes!

Irritation grew, then she glanced again at the out of date advertisement. On the back was a pencilled message. There was a simple drawing of a clock face showing the hands both on twelve. Below it, in capitals were the words, "WELL, WELL, WELL!" The message was for her! The paper on which it was written chosen in case it was retrieved by Emrys. *He* was coming back to meet her at the well at midnight! He had returned at last.

Suddenly life was no longer boring. Life was exciting. Life was full of promise.

To Bettrys's relief, Jake Cooper did not appear at breakfast. His wife's questions continued though, as she bustled in and out of the kitchen, making sure to shut the door each time she passed through it. Bettrys became adroit at evading a full reply and thought it might have been simply unsatisfied curiosity that persuaded Carys to invite them to stay a while longer.

"If you'll be out most of the day I don't mind you staying a while longer," she said as Bettrys paid her for the night's accommodation. "I can't be doing with a child under my

53

feet, you see, and it isn't convenient at present, for to have the extra company. Not really."

"Thank you, Mrs Cooper, you've been very kind," Bettrys said. She didn't want to stay under the woman's roof, but a few more days would be helpful if she were to find a place locally. "Perhaps we could stay for two more nights?"

This was agreed and, leaving most of her belongings in the front bedroom overlooking the beach, Bettrys set off for the village, with Cheryl in a rather battered old push-chair borrowed from Gwen. First, she had to find an outlet for the jewellery she had made. The earrings, brooches and necklaces she had once made to swell school funds, would now hopefully help eke out her savings. Then she had to persuade someone at The Bend to rent her a room. Somehow, she had to stay near until she had done what she set out to achieve, either find Cheryl's father, or cross this area off her list and look for another place called Yr Tro.

Walking briskly along the coast road she smiled happily. With the Griffiths and Coopers at war, there would be no difficulty persuading them to talk about each other! Gossip might be wicked but it would certainly bring results!

She had no luck finding a place to sell her jewellery. Perhaps Gwen would have a few ideas. She might have to look further afield while staying in Yr Tro. There were enough secrets there to justify searching for one more. There was the odd incident with the man on the cliff, the kitchen to which she had been forbidden entry, the feud between Old Maldwyn and Jake Copper. She pictured the few inhabitants she had met and tried to fit them into the role of Cheryl's father. The one who fitted was Gordon. Somehow she hoped he wasn't the one who had left her sister and his unborn child.

Diana waited until Emrys was deeply asleep. Fortunately, having to rise early, and especially after a few pints with his

54

friends, he slept within a few minutes of settling his head on the pillow. She slipped off the peach satin night-dress and reached for her clothes. Skirt and jumper, better than jodhpurs on this occasion. There was no need for her to dress as if she were a satisfied farmer's wife when she was off to prove the opposite!

She walked without need of a torch to the dovecot, stopping in its shadow, her eyes trying to pierce the darkness, her ears expectantly attuned for the sound of his approach. She was so excited her breathing was irregular and unnaturally loud in the still night. Slowly, another shadow unfolded itself from the gnarled trunk of the oak tree and moved towards her.

"My darling!" His voice was choked with emotion. "My darling, darling girl. How I've missed you," he said as he reached her and held her in his arms. "You'll never know how much."

"Brynley, my love, it's been so long I thought I'd die."

CHAPTER FOUR

Walking along the beach to see Gwen and ask about a gift or jewellery shop, Bettrys and Cheryl were hailed by an elderly couple who seemed to be washing sheets in a bath balanced on a wooden stool.

"You must be Bettrys," the thin old lady said. "We're Emrys Taylor's parents. Him up at the farm. Live down here we do because she's up there," she pointed vaguely in the direction of the farm, "That Diana, she can't abide the sight of us."

"Hush now, Petal," the old man said. "You mustn't talk about her like that." He smiled at the little girl and said to Bettrys. "My wife misses the farm, see, and blames Diana for us getting too old to run it any more."

"She threw us out," Petal insisted. Then she half covered her mouth with a hand and her eyes twinkled like those of a mischievous child as she said, "I nagged her something dreadful mind! Hopeless she is, isn't she Gar, you have to admit it. That Diana, refuses to learn anything about the farm." She smiled at her husband. "I hates her I do and there's no pretending I don't." She looked at her husband, as if daring him to stop her saying it and added confidentially, "And there's that Colin Williams down here again without his wife. Falling off a cliff indeed. Pushed more like!"

"He *says* he was pushed, damn it all! And Petal, you mustn't repeat – "

Bettrys left them still arguing and struggling with a sheet they were rinsing in the tin bath. So they were Diana's in-laws. She smiled as she imagined some of the arguments that must have taken place before "Gar" and "Petal", as they called each other, moved out.

Having arranged to stay with the Coopers for three days, Bettrys was startled when, after two, she returned from a morning stroll on the beach to find her belongings had been searched, and a stiff-faced Carys Cooper was standing waiting for her and demanding that she left at once. There was no explanation and no apology. Bewildered and not a little angry, Bettrys gathered her things together and walked down to see Gordon and his family.

"There's lucky! I found a chalet for you now, this minute!" Gwen said when she began to explain. "I said you'd be moving in in a day or so but I'm sure you can take over today. Filthy it'll be mind, not being used since last summer. I'll have to come and help you clean it so it's fit for you to take Cheryl there."

"Why did they ask you to leave in such a hurry?" Maldwyn asked, his heavy white eyebrows frowning in disapproval even before he'd been told the answer.

Bettrys shrugged. "There was no explanation. I didn't sneak into her kitchen, or do any of the other forbidden things." She smiled ruefully. "Carys gave us a long list of rules but I didn't disobey!"

"Banned you from the kitchen, did she?" Gwen looked as disapproving as her father. "What's she got to hide in there, then?"

"Twpsin they are the pair of them!" Maldwyn snorted.

"Come on, let's get started. Will Cheryl stay with Dad, d'you think? While we get the worse of the work done?"

Cheryl refused to leave Bettrys so three of them, closely followed by Potter, Gordon's dog, walked past the Cooper's house to the small chalet next door. To Bettrys's eyes the place looked perfectly clean, but Gwen wasn't satisfied until the floors had been washed, the beds wiped with disinfectant and the mattresses "aired proper".

The chalet was almost hidden from anyone passing, by overgrown and neglected gardens, although a narrow path, possibly made by foraging animals, was visible through the undergrowth. On the beach in front of it the "bones" of an old boat were visible like the carcase of a strange, prehistoric animal.

Like its neighbours, the chalet was situated on the ground between the road and the beach but being small, only its chimneys could be seen from the road above.

It was built mostly of wood, with some corrugated iron sheets for a roof and had metal windows. An ugly place, but one in which Bettrys felt comfortably at ease after the barely perceptible tensions at the Cooper's. There was little furniture, only a couch, a hand-made mat and a terrifyingly large and odd-looking stove in the kitchen. The living room from which the single bedroom led off, was also sparsely furnished, with two Windsor chairs, an armchair and a small, rickety, cane table.

The bedroom contained a double bed plus a small couch-bed. The mattresses had been wrapped neatly in waxed paper. When they were unwrapped both mattresses and pillows looked new and clean. A wardrobe stood with its door open and a dressing table had been placed at one side of the surprisingly wide window.

"At least this looks as if it's been lived in!" Gwen laughed, as Bettrys carried the bucket of soapy water in to wash the linoleum covered floor. "I'd be happier if we could have given it a good airing, mind. Pity you couldn't have stayed at the Cooper's for another day or so. Funny they asked you to leave so sudden."

"They didn't want me to stay at all. They only took me in because Gordon asked them."

"Strange, really," Gwen said and she gave the dressing table a furious polish. "They've taken in summer visitors for years. Then suddenly they don't want to do it any more. They even cancelled some that had booked."

"This is certainly a place with secrets! A man being

pushed from a cliff and refusing to say who his companion was, the Coopers throwing us out without an explanation . . . "

"Every family has stories they don't want others to know, fach. Yr Tro isn't unusual in that. What did she say when she told you to go?"

"She said it wasn't convenient just now. Perhaps they're expecting other visitors. Or, perhaps she finds it a bit too much, she does a lot of dressmaking and odd sewing jobs, it must be hard to fit it all in," Bettrys defended.

"She's always done that too. No. there must be another reason but I can't think what it is and she'd never tell me. The enemy I am, with her husband and my father at odds with each other."

They worked for another hour before Gwen declared that "it'll have to do for now". Then they went to sit beside Maldwyn on the beach below the Howell's Cottage and drank several cups of tea.

"I'll go into town and buy some bedding and a few things," Bettrys said, after walking back for another cursory examination of the rooms. "It will soon look like a home."

"Come back to the house. What am I thinking of! I'll lend you some until you can get your shopping done."

"There's probably a few toys left in the loft, Gwen," the old man said when they explained their intentions. "I'm sure little Cheryl would like something to play with."

So the afternoon was spent sorting through Gwen's neat cupboards. "I'm not ashamed for anyone to see *my* kitchen!" she couldn't help remarking.

Gordon returned and was sent up into the loft for a few toys and a high-chair that had once been used for himself and his younger brother, Pete. The chosen items were carried across the sandy beach to Bettrys's new home. The beds had been aired with an old-fashioned bedwarmer filled with hot ashes and several hot water bottles, and by six o'clock, when they went to Smuggler's

Cottage for a meal, the place was finally declared fit for habitation.

There was no sign of Gordon when Bettrys set off the following morning with Cheryl in the pushchair to walk into the village. It was a five mile walk and she intended as before, to walk there and return on the bus with her shopping.

There was a tractor chugging across the field to her left, pulling a trailer full of straw bales. The driver raised an arm and waved and Bettrys stopped and pointed out the vehicle to Cheryl. "See the farmer waving to say hello?"

She could see the lane leading to the Taylor's farm, and several houses on or near it which, she presumed, belonged to those who worked for the Taylors. Smoke issued from the chimneys and dropped low, heading across the fields. Several windows were open and lace curtains blew like white flags in the impatient breeze coming in from the sea. "Look," Bettrys laughed. "The houses are waving to you as well as the farmer on his tractor."

Before she had lost sight of the last of the houses on The Bend, she was aware of being followed. Potter was sneaking after her, hoping not to be spotted before it was too late for her to turn back. Slipping in and out of the wayside flowers, he wagged his tail hopefully when he realised he had been spotted. Bettrys looked at him for a long moment.

"Now what do I do?" she sighed. "If I go back there won't be time to walk and do my shopping before the next bus." As Cheryl held out a hand for the dog to lick, Bettrys smiled, shrugged and said, "Oh, all right, you'd better come." She searched in her shoulder bag and found a large headscarf that she thought might be used as a lead in an emergency and whistled her permission for him to go with them. Wagging his short tail and dancing in delight, Potter ran ahead of them, appointing himself their protector, and settled to lead the way, sniffing the ground for signs of danger.

The early morning was hazy with the promise of sun and the sea had that mysterious colour and texture in which it blended with the sky without it being apparent where one ended and the other began. It was a little chilly and at first Bettrys set a fast pace to warm herself. She stopped occasionally to admire the scene or enjoy the sight of a group of waders feeding on the shore, or the slow flapping flight of a heron, or the seagulls, with their strident "kee-ough kee-ough", complaining cries filling the sky with their complaining.

An hour and three-quarters later she reached the village and began to explore its shops. The community was well served. Besides two small grocers there was a bakery, a hardware store, a chemist, a fish shop and a butchers. What she wanted first was a gift or craft shop, which she had failed to find on her previous visit. Surely there would be one in an area where summer brought coaches and car-loads of visitors? She found it tucked in a narrow lane alongside the church next to the post office. She struggled to get the pushchair into the small, overcrowded shop and searched in her pack for her samples.

"I make earrings," she began, when the proprietress stepped forward with a smile.

"Oh, well, I'm afraid I have all the jewellery I need right now," the welcoming smile faded and the woman shook her head. Unperturbed, Bettrys handed her a blue velvet covered tray on which she had fixed some of her best work.

"Perhaps you would be kind enough to look at them?" she asked politely. "They are hand-made and my own designs."

They were made of silverwire and mostly consisted of coloured beads. Some were simple, many ornate, but all were beautifully crafted. Bettrys knew from the woman's expression that she would make a sale.

They discussed terms and Bettrys promised not to sell to another outlet within a radius of ten miles. She intended to go into Swansea and find shops there but that was eleven miles distant so she agreed readily and promised to deliver the order the following week.

She telephoned to the London flat and left a message on the answer phone for her mail to be redirected now she had an address. She hoped for a letter from Brett, telling her where he was and assuring her of his love. "But", she sighed, hugging Cheryl, "it will probably be more bills." She sat on the bus with Potter under the seat, all her shopping around her, Cheryl dosing on her lap, and smiled contentedly. It seemed that everything was starting well, apart from having unwittingly upset the Coopers that is. Everyone was so friendly; she felt warmed by the welcoming smiles she met everywhere she went, and the willingness of strangers to help. It would be easy to settle here, she thought, in the land of her fathers that she was seeing for the first time. She had to remind herself of what she came here to find: Cheryl's father.

"I thought that was where he got to, bad dog!" Gordon was waiting for her when she stepped off the bus on the road above her new home. "Several people saw you walking to the village and I guessed what had happened." He took the sleepy Cheryl in his arms and took hold of the heaviest carrier. Pretending to scold the dog, he smiled to include the solemn little girl and said: "I know what you did, bad boy. Skulked in the bushes until you were too far away to be brought back." He smiled again at Cheryl. "He does that every week when grandfather goes to collect his pension."

He dropped the shopping carrier at the door and turned to Bettrys, waiting for her to invite him inside.

"It isn't locked," she said.

"Now, Cheryl, what have you been doing? Where have you been? Did that Potter behave himself then?" The little girl went to where her newly acquired toys were waiting and busied herself putting a teddy bear in a rather battered pram. "Doesn't she speak?" he asked. "I can't get a word out of her."

"She manages a few words but she's only a year old," Bettrys laughed.

When Gordon had gone and Cheryl was sleeping, Bettrys explored the garden. Overgrown and very untidy, it nevertheless had some flowers. The remnants of daffodils and primroses drooped sadly but bluebells were plentiful, filling the air with their wonderful scent and showing a rich greenness under the trees. Straggling branches of forsythia made arches of cheerful yellow. Their vibrant colours were startling in the subdued tones of late spring. By sitting quietly and watching, she saw a pair of robins darting to and fro, obviously feeding their young in the macrocarpa hedge. Careful exploration revealed the presence of lizards, a slow worm and, in a crevice in the wall, a toad whom she at once named Ichabod – "glory departed". Surely he must once have been a prince?

The crevice in the wall which Ichabod called his own was below the single tap from which she could draw water. She had been warned that in high summer the source failed, but the spring which supplied the disused well on the Taylor's farm never dried up. It trickled through the ground and into a small stream between her chalet and the Cooper's house, before reaching the beach below, and would, she was assured, keep her and the rest of the houses reliably supplied.

She pushed her way through the overgrown bushes and examined the stream. A few oddments of litter were decorating its edge and she bent to pick up a cigarette packet, her heart lurching with revived memories. It was his brand. The gold packet seemed to burn her hand with sharp, painful recall. The sight of him reflected on her inner eye: the scent of his clothes, his aftershave and the smell of his cigarettes were vividly renewed, and flooded back to torment her.

She had tried to believe that thoughts of Brett had begun to fade, but seeing this carelessly-thrown litter reminded her of what had been casually cast aside. She carried the packet towards the chalet and placed it sadly in her rubbish bin. An empty packet, symbolising her empty life.

If only she hadn't refused to go with him that last time. Perhaps everything would have been different, perhaps she wouldn't be here, pretending that new acquaintances were sufficient, that the loss of Brett was no longer an ache.

Walking further through the thick tangle, she saw that the thin stream of clear water fell from a passageway in the rock wall and drifted on over the stones. She followed it with her eye as it meandered between the bushes on its way to the sea. A small trickle on which the people of The Bend might depend.

She wondered if she and Cheryl would still be there in high summer, or whether they would have achieved their objective and departed. The thought of finding Cheryl's father was a happy one but, with no Brett to return to, leaving this place where she already had so many friends, was disturbingly sad.

News of the newcomer spread rapidly among the inhabitants of Yr Tro, so that by the time she and Cheryl had spent their first night in their new home everyone shared what little was known about them. Among the first people Bettrys met was Diana Taylor, daughter-in-law of Petal and Gar, and the wife of the Emrys Taylor, whose farmhouse dominated the stretch of coastline, high above the road, around it; its cluster of buildings included a dove-cot and an ancient well.

Diana knocked on her door at eight o'clock one evening, bringing a quart of fresh milk and a dozen eggs.

"Diana's the name. Diana Taylor." She spoke loudly and briskly. Like a sergeant major, Bettrys thought with a half smile.

"Pleased to meet you. I am – "

"Bettrys. I know," Diana said, interrupting almost irritably. She wasn't one to waste time on repeated information. "Emrys and I live at the farm," she said, pushing the gifts into Bettrys's arms. "We thought you might like these."

"Thank you! That's very kind," Bettrys smiled. "Come in, won't you? I'm working, so the place is a mess, but – " she was almost pushed aside as Diana hurried into the room.

"Emrys and I hope you'll enjoy your stay here, and hope you'll call and see us soon," Diana said, looking around the poorly furnished room with some distaste. Then her eyes lit on a half-made earring and she picked it up. "You make these?"

"Until I settle and find myself a job, it's a small addition to my income," Bettrys said.

"I'll buy these when they're finished."

Bettrys began to explain that the order was for a local shop but changed her mind and nodded agreement. She sensed that this woman was not one to argue with. Diana Taylor would hear only what she wanted to hear. Another pair would have to be quickly made.

Diana Taylor, who Bettrys guessed was in her early thirties, was not a tall woman but held herself straight and tilted her head back so she looked down her nose, giving the impression of height. Her fair hair was long, and held back in a snood. Her greeny eyes sparkled as they looked at the half-made jewellery on the table and the pile of toys in the corner. Bettrys had the impression that the sharply-spoken woman could have made an accurate inventory of the contents of the room after one sweeping glance.

The wife of the local farmer looked as if she did not involve herself even slightly with her husband's business. Her country-style clothes were a deception. She was more Bettrys's idea of a lady-of-the-manor in a theatrical comedy. Her hands were pale and slender with long, bright red nails, that were obviously unused to any sort of work.

She was wearing jodhpurs and a perfectly-fitting check jacket over a green cashmere jumper. Her riding boots were well polished and of excellent quality. Everything about her, Bettrys decided, suggested wealth. And perhaps idleness.

"Thank you for the eggs. I don't think I've ever had eggs straight from a farm before." Careful, she thought. Don't say too much, specially to this perspicacious young woman.

"Here on your own, are you? You and the child? No husband?" Her outspokenness made Bettrys hesitate longer than usual before replying. She would have to be careful of this one. Impatient of waiting for a reply, Diana said, "All right, if you don't want to talk about it. I was wondering, that's all."

"I'm not married," Bettrys said softly, hoping Diana wouldn't ask about Cheryl. She did so hate lying.

"Stuck on your own with a child? Poor you!" The words were sharp but to Bettrys who intercepted a softer glance, they seemed more an expression of regret or jealousy. "Well, I'd better be off. Just thought I'd introduce myself. Come and see us some time. Evenings preferred, when Emrys has shed his working clothes and looks more human."

Bettrys was left with the impression of a forceful and rather unhappy woman.

"You'd better go," Gwen Howells chuckled when she called the following morning to see Bettrys. "An invitation from Diana is a royal command!"

"I would like to see the farm house," Bettrys admitted.

"Gordon or I will go with you if you like," Gwen offered. "She's rather exhausting to be honest."

"So I gathered!"

Gwen stayed to admire the work Bettrys was doing and chattered openly about the area's history and the people among whom she lived. Before she left she offered to look after Cheryl while Bettrys visited the farm later that day. "Go with Gordon," she suggested. "Diana would prefer to see my son than me, I'm sure." Gwen gave her new friend a saucy wink.

Gwen took the little girl to her own house to look after her on Saturday afternoon and Bettrys and Gordon walked up onto the road then turned briefly left, away from the village, to where the track with its heavy gate led to the large farmhouse overlooking the sea. The houses situated on the rough road leading to the main farmhouse and its surrounding buildings provided excellent views of whoever came and went. "I have the eerie feeling of being watched by several pairs of eyes," she admitted as they passed the final one and approached the farmhouse.

A door opened and a voice called. Bettrys looked up as a man approached them, dressed in jeans and heavy boots and wearing a thick cowboy-style shirt.

"Meet Ray Newbank, Emrys's right-hand man." Gordon introduced them and then Ray's wife, Jessie, opened a window and stared blatantly until Gordon walked over to the house and introduced her too. "Jessie works in the farmhouse and Ray on the farm itself," he explained as they walked on. "Nosy buggers the pair of them. Don't tell them anything you don't want spread faster than ice melts in hell!" Bettrys learnt that the Newbanks had a son, Leyton, a few years older than herself. "Leyton works on the farm on occasions, and does other odd jobs when he needs money," Gordon explained. "He objects to regular work and spends a lot of time fishing. He sometimes borrows my boat and pays for the loan by leaving a fish or two for Mam."

Windows in the farmhouse provided a clear view of their approach. As they walked towards it, the door opened. Diana shouted at the dog who came out of the barn and it slunk away, ignoring the presence of Potter, who had followed the couple.

"Come in, come in," Diana said in her brisk way and they hurried forward, afraid she would shut the door before they were through it. "I'll make tea; Emrys will be here in a few moments for his mid-afternoon snack."

"I used to come here almost every day when I was a kid," Gordon said. "I knew these buildings as well as Mr Taylor does."

"Did you?" Diana asked quizically. "Of course, that was before my time. With the first Mrs Taylor of course. Emrys and I have been married for three years." She made it sound like a century of boredom. "Go and show Bettrys around if you wish, Gordon, while I attend to tea. Emrys won't mind," Diana opened the door to add emphasis to her persuasion and they left the room obediently, without having taken a seat. This time through the back door of the huge, rambling house to the cobbled yard where they found themselves in the middle of the barns and outhouses. Beyond them Bettrys could see the dovecot.

"Can I look at the dovecot?" she asked. "Your mother told me there used to be a secret passageway from there to the beach. Did you ever find it?"

"Not true I'm afraid." Gordon smiled as disappointment showed on her face. But – ," he added with a hint of mystery, "I'll show you where there was one."

He led her across the grass beyond the barns, past the dovecot and stopped beside a low circular wall almost hidden in the tall grasses of the fallow field. There was a grating fastened with a padlock within the circle of bricks and far below was the glimmer of water. Bettrys found she was unable to look down the deep shaft without fear. This was one place she wouldn't bring little Cheryl!

Unaware that she could not see where he was pointing, Gordon explained: "Down there is a passage, probably fallen in now, where, so it's said, the smugglers used to bring their cargoes up to the farm, where they were hidden by the antecedents of Emrys Taylor."

"Lot of old nonsense if you ask me!" a voice said and they turned to see the red, shining face of Emrys Taylor. "Don't listen to him, young lady, talks a lot of old nonsense he does. Smugglers indeed! Most of the houses around here are new. The place was empty apart from my farm and Maldwyn's house." He held out a coarse, powerful hand. "You must be Bettrys. Where's the little one? We hope you'll bring her to see us?"

"Mam's minding her for an hour while I show Bettrys around the area, Mr Taylor," Gordon said. "Mrs Taylor has invited us to tea."

"Good. Good. I'll join you, shall I?"

Emrys was about five and a half feet tall with grey hair and a weather-beaten face in which dark eyes shone. His arms were thick and powerful, his hands coarse and surprisingly large. In all he gave an impression of immense strength. Like Ray Newbank, he was wearing jeans and a check shirt and, beneath it, muscles on his back rippled as he unlocked the grill on the well and heaved it easily out onto the grass.

"If you look down there, on the right, you'll see a bit of metal sticking out from the wall of the well." He put an arm around Bettrys and guided her to the circular wall. This time she made a greater effort to fight her fear.

The sensation when she looked over was the same as looking down from a high building. Sickness churned in her stomach and it took a few moments before she could cautiously try again to see where Emrys Taylor was pointing. Almost to the bottom of the shaft, ferns and mosses grew out from the rough surface, varying in type, each finding the place where it could tolerate the limited daylight. Almost hidden in the greenery, rungs of metal lead down the side to her right. Anyone using them would be able to look towards the dovecot and beyond that, the farmhouse, as soon as their eyes reached the rim. The water, glistening at the bottom, was like an eye fringed with luxurious lashes.

"I've been told – " and he gave a doubting grin at Gordon as he spoke, " – my father and grandfather used to tell me, there was a contraption down by there to divert the course of the stream so smugglers could walk dry-shod, through the tunnel from the beach."

"Is it still there?" Bettrys asked in awe.

"I've never been down to see, young lady and I don't think anyone else has." He turned to Gordon again. "Stories for the tourists, that's all it is, boy. If there is anything left of it, the metal will be too rusted to use and anyway, I keep the grill padlocked as the walls of the tunnel are bound to be unsafe. No one goes down there any more. One day I'll have it filled in. Best to avoid accidents before they happen than cry after they do."

Bettrys looked at him and wondered if the man was lying and if so, why. The padlock was not new but it had been recently oiled. And, on the rungs that led down the side of the well were scrape marks of feet. On three she had seen the distinct evidence that someone, recently, had used and deposited small flakes of mud on them, and several of the fern-leaves were bruised.

Good-naturedly teasing Gordon, Emrys strolled back with them to the farmhouse, where a young girl was placing the last plate of sandwiches on the white cloth covering the large kitchen table.

"Plenty of legends around the coast of course," Diana said when they had told her of their visit to the well. "What self-respecting village around here would admit to *not* having smugglers or pirates, or both? Good for the growing number of visitors, legends and the occasional ghost story. That old well hasn't been used for years and it's unsafe, so Emrys keeps it padlocked. The water from it goes down to the sea via your garden I believe, Bettrys."

They stayed for an hour, but all the time, Bettrys had

the feeling that Diana was impatient for them to leave. When at last they left the farm and walked back to the road, she unconsciously gave a sigh.

"She's a bit wearing, isn't she," Gordon said, closing the heavy gate after they had passed the farm-workers' cottages. "Kind enough though. She and Emrys haven't any children. She told Mam she can't have any and Emrys won't let her try to adopt."

"What happened to his first wife?"

"She left him and went back to town. Funny he should choose another 'towny' for a wife, isn't it? She spends more time travelling to and from town than she spends at the farmhouse."

"It must certainly be hard to adjust to life in an isolated place like this."

He looked at her, assessing her and wondering if he could say what was in his mind.

"What is it?" she asked, seeing his hesitation.

He didn't tell her that he hoped she would stay for ever. Instead he laughed and said, "Bit of a flirt she is, by all accounts. Rumours about a fancy-man abound. More than one, some think. That Leyton Newbank knows more about her than he should for a start!"

"The rumours are probably right," Bettrys laughed. "It must be like living in a glass tower stuck up there. I wonder that she can do a thing without everyone seeing or hearing about it! These houses on the lane are better than a guard of soldiers!"

"You'd think so, but the funny thing is, no one knows who her latest fancy-man is. Just that she meets someone. She's been seen going off in that Land Rover of hers and coming back starry eyed. She strides the hills wearing those jodhpurs and never gets on a horse. She'd never walk far in those boots, would she? Not made for walking they aren't."

"You old gossip, Gordon Howells!" Bettrys laughed.

"I know all that's going on round here," he laughed.

71

Bettrys wondered how he would react to Petal's suspicions that Colin Williams had been accompanied by Diana when he was almost pushed from the cliff, or to her own belief that Emrys Taylor was lying when he said the well was not being used. But she decided to say nothing.

"Now, in your capacity as know-all nosy parker, tell me again, who lives in the houses down below the road?" She waved an expressive arm down at the half hidden roofs below them between the road and the sea and looked at him curiously.

He coaxed her to climb up and sit on the gate they had just passed through and pointed first at her chimney, leaning at a slight angle. "Funny woman down by there," he said in a stage Welsh accent. "Wants to know all the ins and outs of everything she does. Proper ol' gossip she is for sure."

"All right, I deserved that," she laughed. "But I would like to know who lives here. Please?"

"The house close to the sea is our house, built on the base of a seventeenth-century house by my grandfather. There's a big cross on the front of the house which was used as a navigation aid to the incoming fishing boats years ago. Grandad was a fisherman from the time he left school, right up until – well, he's retired now. Mam, and my brother Pete live there with him as you know. My father died at sea when Pete was a baby.

"Behind that is the place I call home. Then there's the Coopers who, of course, you've met. Grandad's 'Moriarty' is Jake Cooper. Hates the sight of him he does. The Coopers have a son but no one knows where he is. If you're wise you won't ask. Gossip is, that Brynley Cooper is wanted by the police for some robberies round here and can't come home."

"Perhaps that's what's hidden in Carys Cooper's kitchen," she laughed. "Brynley Cooper's cache of jewels!"

"Jake has lost an arm, yet he makes a small living by doing a surprisingly varied number of odd jobs. He

72

looks after the smartest property on Yr Tro. Remember I told you about Frances and Jeremy Baxter? The posh couple from Swansea who own Costa Plenty? Only come at weekends they do and usually with a crowd. Weekend parties is what they use the house for. Costa Plenty indeed! They act as if they're the first to think of it! Daft they are, the pair of them," he added dismissively.

"The semi adjoining that of the Coopers belongs to Emrys Taylor's parents. Gareth Taylor, whose wife calls him Gar, moved out of the farm a few years ago. Couldn't get on with Diana, or so I believe. Old man Taylor calls his wife Petal. Gar and Petal. Rather a sweet old couple they are."

"I think that's as much as I can take in at present," Bettrys said thoughtfully. "So it's the Taylors who are farmers. Your family who were fishermen, the Coopers, also fishermen until Jake's accident, and the fancy pair from Swansea. What about the rest?"

"Holiday chalets. Owned by people who come during the summer holidays and occasionally during the Winter to do a bit of maintenance and that's about all."

They heard the sound of a fast approaching car and looked round to see the Land Rover coming towards the gate from the farm. They jumped down and opened the gate to allow Diana to drive through. She went past them without slowing and on to the road, turning left towards the village without saying thank you or even acknowledging them.

Gordon grumbled about her attitude as he pushed the gate closed, but Bettrys wasn't listening. She was wondering where, among the few families living on Yr Tro, she would find Cheryl's father. Or, whether she had chosen the wrong place altogether.

Gordon's young brother, Pete, was on the road, looking towards the village. As they walked towards him, the bus came rumbling along and he stepped forward. Without stopping, the bus slowed to allow the conductor to throw out a small bundle of papers which was expertly caught by Pete. Waving to Gordon and Bettrys, he pulled off the cord holding them together and set off to make his deliveries. The inexhaustible Potter left them and ran to follow Pete, extending his walk by another half an hour.

Gwen was sitting with Cheryl on her lap, reading a book to her, patiently pointing to the animals and making the appropriate noises to encourage the child to do the same. Seeing Bettrys, Cheryl began to jump up, then stopped and snuggled down again with Gwen.

"Oh, I see, got a new friend now. You don't want me," Bettrys teased and went to hug the little girl. "Thank you, Gwen. You've all been so kind to me."

"It's a pleasure," Gwen smiled. "We're here whenever you want us. You can trust us whenever you need friends," she added pointedly. But Bettrys only reiterated her thanks. The time for trust had not yet arrived. She needed to know more about everyone on Yr Tro before she opened up to anyone, even Gwen Taylor.

Gordon walked back with them, carrying more toys and books Gwen had found in her inexhaustible store.

"Bettrys," he said, as Cheryl ran on to open the door. "Can I ask you something?"

There was a slight pause before Bettrys nodded, but Gordon was beginning to get used to her hesitation. "Is Cheryl your child?"

This time Bettrys was silent for even longer than usual. She weighed her answer carefully. She hadn't given birth to Cheryl, but as there was no one else, unless she could find the child's father, then, yes, she did have full responsibility for her. So how was she to answer?

"All right, I'm sorry I asked. It doesn't matter anyway." He was afraid to ask if she was married, or was still in love with the child's father. He wanted the answer to both questions to be no, but if it was yes, then he'd prefer to remain in ignorance for a while longer.

As she poured water into the kettle ready for Cheryl's bath, she said, "Yes. She is mine."

He seemed satisfied by her reply After kissing Cheryl and hesitating, as if he wanted to part from her in the same way, he just smiled and left them. She felt momentarily guilty. She had lied and they had all been so kind. Running to the door she called after him, "Gordon, it isn't as simple as that. It's not what you think."

"See you tomorrow," he called back. "We'll go fishing."

Diana drove through the village, past the church, along narrow lanes with high banks on either side. Turning down an even narrower lane, she parked and waited. She had abandoned her usual jodhpurs and wore a sleek beige wool dress with a jacket of the same colour. The boots had been exchanged for high-heeled shoes. She still wore the snood over her fair hair but the hair itself was now beautifully curled.

She sat for a few moments until she saw a car pull up behind her. Then she got out and without bothering to lock the car, walked to the other car, an old Riley, and she got in.

"Any trouble getting away?" the driver asked.

"I managed it rather neatly," she smiled. "I invited a boring couple from the beach to tea. I was so casual about the time they spent with us, I'd have convinced Sherlock Holmes himself I had nothing to hide!"

The Riley bumped its way back onto the wider lane then a few miles further on, turned up a rutted cart track to where a small cottage, with wooden walls green with damp, was hidden in a hollow surrounded by willows and hazel and alder trees. Inside, the place was well cared for, sweet and airy. Near the chintz-covered couch was a tray on which there were two glasses and a bottle of wine. A fire glowed warmly in the stone hearth.

As Diana closed the door behind them, a man stepped

out from behind a weeping willow, boots squelching in the mud of a half-dried-up stream. He was still there a couple of hours later and he watched as Diana and the man left in the Riley to drive back to where her Land Rover waited for her.

Emrys wasn't in when Diana got home, her hair neatly brushed and hanging in loose curls around her shoulders. He came in a while later, explaining that he had been chatting with old Maldwyn and forgotten the time.

"Interesting old man he is," Emrys said. "Such a wealth of knowledge on the sea, and boats, and the ways of fish."

"Very exciting," Diana said dryly. "Quite rivetting!"

"Did you hear that Colin Williams almost fell from the cliff? Says he was pushed, but I reckon he was making that up to hide his stupidity at walking too close to the edge, don't you?"

He gave her a curious look that made her stomach curdle disconcertingly. He couldn't have guessed, could he? Then she smiled at Emrys and asked, "Well, do you like my hair? I've been to have it washed. I just can't face doing it myself. I haven't the patience to use a hand-dryer and anyway it takes for ever and then looks all frizzy and messy."

"It's lovely. You're lovely. The hairdresser is worth every penny."

"Thank you darling." She kissed him lightly. "Shall we go out for a meal tonight?"

"Why, are we celebrating something?"

"I'm sure we can think of something." She could hardly tell her husband it was to celebrate the return after several months of her lover. "Um," she frowned prettily, "my new hair-style?" Laughingly he agreed.

CHAPTER FIVE

The second night in her new home was unnerving for Bettrys. She had hardly settled under the sheets when she heard someone creeping past her window. She glanced towards the small bed where Cheryl lay sleeping, to reassure herself of her safety, then crept towards the window. The shadow of a man carrying a torch passed the faintly lit pane as he reached it, a thin beam threading ahead of his almost silent footfall.

Fear subsided as the soft sounds passed away. Someone coming home late and taking a short cut along the beach no doubt. Then she frowned. There didn't seem to be any reason for someone to cross through her garden to get to either the Coopers or to the road; the well used paths would have been more direct and far easier to find.

It was impossible to get back into bed and expect sleep but she didn't want to show a light in case the man out there was intent on mischief. Creeping around at night was hardly synonymous with being dangerous, yet there was something furtive about the crouching, careful walk of the unknown person. She shivered involuntarily and checked the sleeping child again.

Unable to get the visitor out of her mind, she went to the door. Perhaps the sound of the waves would soothe her and help her relax into sleep. She carefully opened it and looked out.

There was the sound of rustling, something approaching her through the low tangle of the flower beds. She was wishing she hadn't succumbed to the foolish whim to look out when she recognised the shape of Potter, strolling towards her. She welcomed him with relief. Surely he would have barked if the visitor was someone unknown to him? Satisfied, she patted and hugged the friendly animal, then closed the door and went inside. A cup of tea, she decided, then sleep.

She thought it would be sensible to close the window. That way she wouldn't be disturbed by the unusual sounds of the night. There would be animals strolling around besides Potter, and the trees creaking, branches touching the metal roof would have her in a constant panic, until she became used to it. She lifted the latch, but before she pulled the window to, she hesitated, her heart leaping in sudden fright.

Something was wrong. Not a sound this time, but the lack of one. The slow trickle of the stream falling down the rocks and heading towards the beach as constantly as the ticking of a clock, had stopped.

For a long time she lay there, unable to sleep, but knowing there was nothing she could do to investigate. Even if she were brave enough she could hardly leave Cheryl while she went out to look at the rock where the water fell. What would she see if she did venture out?

Perhaps on occasions it naturally stopped. Yet, hadn't Gwen told her it had never let them down? That it's source was utterly reliable? Perhaps the stream was used by someone further inland. But in the middle of the night? Sleepy now, her questions became less urgent. She decided to ask Gordon or his mother in the morning.

Tiredness was twisting her thoughts into lazy, unimportant imaginings, lulling her into gentle sleep, when she was again startled into wakefulness. The water returned with a rush, then settled into its usual steady flow.

The next morning Bettrys overslept. The sun was creeping through the thin curtains and changing the colour of the pale walls as she opened her eyes and stared first towards the small bed opposite. Cheryl was playing contentedly with one of her dolls, but she threw the doll aside and climbed out of her bed to greet Bettrys, obviously pleased that she had woken.

"Sorry, my darling. You must be feeling lonely with me sleeping like a useless chunk of driftwood!" She hugged the little girl for a while, then dressed her in the dressing gown she had bought her and went to prepare breakfast.

Although she talked to Cheryl all the time she worked, counting the spoonfuls of sugar she used for the grapefruit and cereal, playing a game and describing the shape of the spherical fruit, the rectangles of Weetabix, and the squares of toast as she usually did, her mind was restless with thoughts of the night's events.

As soon as they were dressed and the primitive kitchen tidied, she went to the house where Gordon and his family lived. Maldwyn Griffiths was up and busily at work, re-painting the large cross on the front of his house. He waved the wide paintbrush at her and gestured towards the open door then went on with his task.

Gwen was wiping flour from her hands she had been making pastry.

"Come in, Bettrys," she smiled. "Hello my lovely girl." She bent and picked up Cheryl, who snuggled against the motherly woman with obvious joy.

"Can she stay long enough to make some jam tarts with the left-over pastry?" Gwen asked Bettrys. "It won't take long and they love to help, don't they?"

While Gwen guided the enthusiastic young cook and wiped up the excesses of jam from the table, Bettrys told her about the incident of the previous night.

"The stream stopped, you say? But it never has. The people round here have often had to depend on it in past droughts and it's never let them down. You must have been dreaming."

"Can you stand up, close the window, open the door, pat Potter and make a cup of tea while dreaming?" Bettrys asked after a long pause during which she was thinking about what had happened. "I did all of those things."

"Dreams can be very real," Gwen said doubtfully. "But the stream doesn't stop, sure of that I am, ask anyone. And as for someone walking past, well, could have been anyone. A poacher avoiding the farm dogs perhaps? Or a late-night tryst? Plenty of that going on round here, specially in the summer." She washed Cheryl's hands and helped her place the baking tray in the oven, then added gently, "A strange house and by the sea, there's bound to be funny and mysterious sounds. Get used to it you will. I bet you'll sleep like a top tonight after all those disturbances. Now, let's fill the kettle and make a cup of tea to have with Cheryl's lovely tarts, shall we?"

Bettrys didn't mention her experiences to anyone else, not even Gordon, whom she saw later that day. Perhaps she *had* dreamt it, although she wasn't prone to unfounded fears or an over-active imagination. Tonight she would get to bed early and hope nothing would wake her.

She spent most of the morning working at her jewellery-making. After lunch, they went for a walk across the beach towards Ffynon Sands, where the sight of the springs bubbling up through the sand reminded her of the silence of the stream and made her edgy.

The day quickly became dull after the brief sun of the early morning and rain set in before they got back. Relentless rain, the sea lost in it, a fast-falling curtain, blocking out sight of everything beyond a few yards, hissing down in that steady way which seems set to continue for ever.

It was dark early and as she was tired. Bettrys went to bed at nine-thirty. At first she was unable to cut her mind off from the fear of hearing the prowler or becoming aware of the loss of the sound of falling water. The rain obliterated the fall of the stream but still she strained her ears for it, dreading it stopping. But sleep claimed her and when morning broke, brittle with brightness, she had not been disturbed.

She walked along the beach to gather driftwood for a fire and saw Mrs Taylor senior, shaking crumbs out for the birds.

"Saw that Diana visiting you," she called. "What did she have to say? Anything about Colin Williams putting his chalet up for sale?" She gestured with a sideways nod of her head and Bettrys saw the "FOR SALE" notice against the chalet gateway. "Bet she had nothing good to say about me and Gar! That woman could make a saint sound like a second Hitler!"

"Go easy, Petal," Gar admonished. "You don't help matters by your criticism."

"A couple of kids, that what she needs, keep her mind on home a bit more!" She smiled her naughty child smile and added: "There's an ol' cat I am. But my daughter-in-law riles me something awesome."

"Perhaps she *can't* have no children, you old fool!" snapped Gar.

"Old fool, am I? For that you can get your own lunch!"

"I can always tell when we're quarrelling," Gar sighed. "She refuses to feed me!"

"Well, wfft on her," was Petal's final word.

Gordon, an engineer working in a factory where motor cycles were made, designed special tools to make parts for the new models. He spent much of his spare time preparing a portfolio of photographs for a course he was taking at evening classes. When the weather was calm he often took the small motor boat down to the coast, past Ffynon Sands, to climb the cliffs and get pictures of the sea-birds that nested on them.

Coming back from such a trip, the boat phut-phutting gently on a calm sea, he recognised Bettrys walking along the sands, a rucksack on her back, and Cheryl walking beside her. Her long skirt was in peacock colours; purples and blues and greens, all glowing in vibrant display. She

81

had a way of swaying as she walked that Gordon found as exotic as the bird she had brought to his mind.

Potter saw them first and began to bark and whine, touching soprano in his eagerness to reach them and threatening to jump over the side of the boat.

Turning the tiller, Gordon headed for the shore. He shut down the motor and put the oars in rowlocks and rowed the last few yards, while Potter hung over the edge, still whining impatiently as Bettrys waited for them to land. Throwing off the rucksack, she helped pull the boat up onto the dry sand then said:

"You're early. Your mother said you'd be gone for hours."

"Forgot the extra film. I thought it was in my bag but it wasn't. Pity, there are a couple of choughs just beginning to nest and I hoped for a sequence of their progress. Their nest is in a precarious place but with a telephoto lens I'm getting some good shots."

He waded back to the boat and pulled out a biscuit tin. "Fancy some lunch? Mam's sure to have packed enough for three."

Bettrys patted the rucksack. "And I've brought enough for three so we should eat well."

Leaving the boat above the line of seaweed marking the height of the last tide, they walked towards the cliffs at the end of Ffynon Sands. There, leaning against a convenient rock, they sat and ate their lunch. Potter explored the crevices that were too small to be considered caves but which he and Cheryl found exciting.

"Are you settled in now?" Gordon asked as they packed the remnants of their meal away.

"It's not really comfortable but it's all right for the summer."

He hesitated, sensing as always how reticent she was to talk about herself, her past or her plans for the future. "Er, how long will you stay? Until the autumn?" She didn't reply and he went on nervously, "I hope so."

"I spent one whole summer in France," she said, not answering him. "Because of my tall, thin shape, at one of the hostels where I stayed I earned the nickname of Secretary bird."

"But you'll stay for the summer?" Gordon touched her arm, warm from the sun, gently insisting on a reply.

"I'll probably be here for a month or so," was all she eventually said. How could she say with any certainty where she would be at the end of the summer? If no one appeared who was likely to have been her sister's lover and Cheryl's father, she would have to move on, find another place called 'The Bend' and start her search all over again. She said none of this to Gordon. Instead she smiled and said: "Cheryl has found a friend in your mother. They were making jam tarts this morning."

"You made a big one for me I hope?" he called to the little girl. Cheryl stared at him and then nodded her head before running after Potter to explore another rocky fissure.

"Mam said you were disturbed by someone walking through your garden?" he said. "A poacher I expect. Emrys Taylor is always complaining about people after his game, not that there's much to steal these days. Not even rabbits, since he levelled the hill to build some holiday chalets. Didn't get permission, mind, so he killed them off for nothing."

"Did she tell you the stream stopped?"

"Never! Didn't think it ever stopped. Famous for it." He looked away when he said it and for a moment she wondered if he knew the reason. She watched his expression as she added,

"It stopped then returned with a heavy rush before settling to its usual flow."

Gordon frowned, his face showed nothing but puzzlement. "Sounds like something blocked it. A sheep fallen down perhaps? We can go and look if you like. The thing might still be alive and stuck down there."

Bettrys smiled at him happily, her sea-blue eyes sparkling with delight. "You believe me?"

"You must know the difference between dreaming and waking. Of course I believe you." He stood and offered her his hand to rise. "Come on, there's time now if Mam will look after Cheryl for an hour. Mr Taylor won't mind, specially if he thinks one of his sheep's in trouble."

Bettrys wondered how a sheep could have fallen through a grating, but she didn't argue. At least he was going to investigate.

He carried Cheryl and put her in the boat, then he pushed the heavy, unwieldy craft down the beach until it was bobbing free and weightless on the waves, before helping Bettrys and the anxious Potter aboard and clambering in himself.

Later that day they climbed the heavy gate leading to the farmhouse and called first to see Emrys Taylor.

"Diana's not here," he called, coming out of the cowshed where he had been preparing for the evening milking. "Gone into town for some supplies."

"Can we look at the old well?" Gordon asked.

"Again? What can interest you there?"

"We wondered if a sheep has fallen in or something. The water seemed to stop for a while then start again last night. Can we look?"

"Go ahead. Although I doubt anything will be down there. I keep the cover padlocked now it's unused."

"They had a water diviner here to find a well with a better rate of gallon per hour," Gordon explained as they walked past the dovecot to the well. "Clever they are, mind. Told them how many gallons per hour they could expect and the depths it would be found. It's pumped straight into the house now so there's no need for the well any more. The water there is regular but very slow, you see."

Leaning on the low wall they looked down into the

depths. Bettrys, as before, took her time before she could look down into the eerie shaft. There was nothing visible large enough to have held back the water.

On the rungs set into the side there were fresh marks and thin fillets of mud showed clearly on the third one down, as if a climber had changed the weight on his feet once or twice. This time Bettrys mentioned it to Gordon.

"Look," she said, "someone's been here recently. That's definitely mud from the instep of a shoe."

"And look here," he said in a low whisper, "the padlock has been snapped off, by something powerful, like bolt-cutters."

They decided to say nothing to anyone about their discoveries, although Bettrys wanted to show Emrys Taylor and let him deal with it.

"Just let's give it a few days," Gordon pleaded. "It'll be fun to do a bit of detective work."

"You could be hurt if you discover something going on that's illegal."

"Illegal? Never! Some boys having a bit of fun, that's all it'll be for sure. Just a bit of fun. I used the passage myself when I was a kid. Me and Brynley Cooper, we would sneak out at night with a torch and a candle and pretend we were ruthless smugglers. It's just a new generation of dare devils. But it'll be a bit of fun to catch them and have a laugh with them, won't it?"

"I can't get involved, Gordon. There's Cheryl. I can't leave her at night."

"Don't want you to. We'll use your place as the base for our enquiries. Just tell me if you see or hear anything more. Right?"

Bettrys nodded but she was unhappy about the whole thing. She wanted to do what she came here for and leave, without any more complications. Finding Cheryl's father was complication enough. Specially as she didn't even know his name and he most certainly did not want to be found.

"Where is Brynley Cooper?" she asked as they made their way back to the road. "Someone said he's in London."

"Mam says he's wanted by the police, but I don't know. I can't imagine Bryn as a desperate criminal, soft he was, and frightened of everything. Spiders, bats, crabs, the sea, and too scared of his dad to do anything daft." He grinned in the shadowy evening light. "I had to force him to walk through that rocky passage up to the dovecot. Up to our knees in icy water. Made him I did, thinking that if he faced one danger successfully he'd face others and defeat them."

"And did he?"

"Don't know." He shrugged. "He started chasing girls as soon as he realised he was male. Never saw much of each other after that. Handsome bugger he was. Hard to imagine, seeing Jake and Carys Cooper, but he was. Dark curly hair and eyes that were almost black. He had a skin that looked tanned, even in mid-winter and he was taller, by about six inches, than his dad." He winked then, his eyes catching the last of the light. "Handsome he was, but not as nice as me mind." He leaned towards her and kissed her gently, hesitantly. She accepted his kiss but made no move to prolong or repeat it.

"How could the water be stopped simply by someone using the well passage?" she asked as they approached the beach houses.

"I can't imagine, unless – but no, that wouldn't make any sense. Not after all this time."

"Tell me," she pleaded.

"Emrys said something about stopping the water, and I remember something – " he frowned, trying to force an unwilling memory to reveal its locked away secrets. "Only hearsay, mind. But apparently, years ago – I'm talking about the eighteen hundreds now, mind – when the stream was faster and deeper than it is now, there used to be a sort of flap that could be worked from the top of the well shaft and they used to close off the stream going through the well while the passage was used, then lift it and re-start the water when they were through. It must have rotted away years ago. Wood and metal wouldn't last that long."

"If it were replaced, what reason could there be to do that now?"

"None at all, unless someone used it as a short cut to the Taylor's game woods and didn't want to be seen by those in the farm cottages, or get his feet wet!"

"But then someone on the farm would have to work the flap, wouldn't they? You can't open or shut it from this end, can you?"

"Tomorrow, my busy little detective, I'll go in there and have a look." He stopped as they reached her door and, holding the handle, he kissed her again. This time, excitement made her respond and he looked at her in a questioning way before kissing her again.

There was a loud knock at the door when Bettrys was putting Cheryl to bed and, taking the little girl in her arms, she went to open it as the knocking began again, loud, imperious, urgent. She opened it to see Diana Taylor standing there.

"Hello, how nice to – " Before she could complete her polite welcome, Diana had pushed her way in and she stood in the tiny living room where Cheryl's clothes were strewn around the chairs, looking as if she was deciding whether it was safe to sit down.

"I'm just putting Cheryl to bed," Bettrys said unnecessarily. She pulled some clothes off the only comfortable armchair and asked, "Would you like some tea?"

"I'm intrigued by your search for dead sheep." Diana said with a shake of her head. "What on earth gave you the idea that a sheep got into the old well?"

"We saw straight away I was wrong," Bettrys said untruthfully, hoping to evade further questions. "The cover is firmly padlocked and there's not a chance of any creature larger than a shrew getting in there."

"But why – ?"

Bettrys smiled apologetically. "I had a strange dream and Gordon kindly indulged me by checking on it, that's all," she explained.

"Emrys is a good-natured man but he doesn't like people wandering over his fields. For one thing, summer visitors might think there's a right of way and that leads to unpleasantness."

"Oh, don't worry. I wouldn't trespass and in any case, Gordon asked permission before we went to look."

"I'm not being difficult," Diana said.

"Of course not. Stay and have a cup of tea."

Bettrys was puzzled by the visit. Diana stayed while Cheryl was bathed and dressed in her night-clothes, watching the child with interest, and she drank the tea, but once Cheryl was on her way to bed it was clear she was anxious to be off. Then, as she stood by the door, she turned back and said, "No need to tell Emrys I called. It's just that, well, he wouldn't tell you himself, afraid of being thought a bad-tempered farmer, I suppose, but he would prefer you didn't go wandering about. Right?"

"Of course," Bettrys smiled. "Thank you for telling me, I'll make sure I don't bother him again."

An hour later the door was banged on in a way Bettrys immediately recognised. She opened it to find a box on the doorstep containing a dozen eggs and a dish of cream.

Gordon was there when she answered a third knock a little later that evening. He carried a wind-up gramophone and some very old records.

"Mam thought Cheryl might like these," he said, putting the gramophone down on a chair. "They're Grandfather's, mostly old music-hall songs, but there are a few comical ones too."

They played a few, Cheryl's obvious favourite being "On The Good Ship Lollypop", and laughed at "When

Father Papered The Parlour", and the "Laughing Policeman", before putting them away and settling in front of
the wood fire to drink wine and talk.

"Diana Taylor called to warn me to keep away from
the well," Bettrys said. "She didn't specifically say 'stay
away from the well', but that was what she meant. I
wonder why?"

"You must have been mistaken."

"Gordon," she sighed. "I was 'mistaken' when I heard
the water stop and then start, and heard someone creeping
past the door. But there had been someone down that
well. Those pieces of mud from someone's shoe couldn't
have been there all that long. Rain would wash it away
or the sun would dry it until it fell off."

"Sorry. I believe you, I was just making my surprise
known in a clumsy way. Why can she want us to keep
away from the well?"

"Or the dovecot," Bettrys said. "Perhaps she meets her
fancy man there."

"Now you *are* inventing."

"Yes, I am," she smiled. "But it would explain her
behaviour, wouldn't it?"

It grew late as they sat and talked and at eleven o'clock
Gordon regretfully stood to leave.

"I'm tempted to stay," he said, then, as he started in
alarm, he added quickly. "I don't mean here, with you,
but somewhere around where I can listen to see if anyone
is around."

"Early April is hardly the time to sit out in a damp
garden listening for the trickle of water to stop."

"D'you remember what day you heard it?"

"Sunday."

"Then perhaps I'll try next Sunday. If it's a tryst –
old-fashioned word but you know what I mean, well, it's
likely it will be on the same day."

"You'll have to tell your mother. She might call and
wonder where you are."

"Not really. I often go out at odd times to photograph wild life."

Two days later Bettrys had a first possible clue to the person she was seeking. She had called to see Mrs Cooper to ask for a length of blue cotton to repair one of Cheryl's skirts.

"Give it to me, Bettrys, I'll fix that for you. No," she added as Bettrys protested. "Pleasure to do something for her. Call back in an hour and I'll have it ready for you."

The skirt was neatly, almost invisibly repaired, and waiting for her hung over the back of a chair when she called back later with Cheryl and Potter.

"You have a son, haven't you?" Bettrys said. "Brynley, isn't it? Gordon said he and Brynley were good friends when they were young."

"Works in London, he does. Something to do with transport, I'm not sure what. But he's doing very well by all accounts. He's got a car and a smart one, a black one, a Rover I think Jake said it was."

"I know London fairly well. What part does he live in?"

"Not far from Kew Gardens. Very posh it is. He's only got a flat, mind, but he'll get something bigger soon and then we can go and stay with him." She frowned. "Now, what was the place called?"

Jake came in then and she shut up as if she'd been shot.

"Dinner ready?" he asked, after greeting Bettrys and patting Cheryl's head.

"Just ready to serve," Carys said and scuttled out of the room as if embarrassed by her confidences. Bettrys noticed that the door was closed firmly behind her.

Brynley Cooper, who was the same age as Gordon, about thirty, was a possible candidate if he lived in the area around Kew. But how was she to see him, talk to him if, as she guessed, he never came home. And what

90

about the rumour that he was not in London but on the run from the police? Surely, having narrowed the search to this small stretch of beach, she couldn't be that unlucky?

Gordon didn't repeat his intention of spending Sunday in her garden listening and watching for the intruder to block the flow of the stream. Bettrys hoped he had thought better of it.

She put Cheryl to bed and at ten o'clock settled for the night. Putting the mystery firmly out of her mind, she went straight to sleep. It was more startling therefore to be woken a couple of hours later by the sound of a fight.

She threw on a dressing gown and as always, checked that Cheryl was safely sleeping, before opening the curtain and trying to see through the darkness what was happening outside. The grunts of men fighting was unmistakable; their bodies repeatedly banging against the thin sides of the house was what had woken her.

She grabbed a poker and, foolishly, a coal shovel, the only possible weapons, and cautiously opened the door.

"Gordon!" she called. "Is it you?"

There was a loud groan followed by the sound of someone running away. She raised the poker high and crept to look around the corner. She daren't go any further, not with Cheryl asleep in the house. When the figure of a man rose near her she held her breath and prepared to strike him but just in time, Gordon said, "Bettrys. Get inside. He's still here."

She threw down her primitive weapons in distaste. She might have hit Gordon, who was presumably there to protect her. "I heard him run off," she said. "Come on, you need help."

They went into the house and Bettrys turned the key in the lock. Before switching on the light, she listened to make sure there was no one out there, although Gordon's heavy breathing made it impossible to be sure.

The light revealed a shocking sight. Gordon's face was

covered in blood and his clothes were torn. In his hand was a short length of tree branch. She took a moment to calm herself, then said lightly, "I always hoped that when a man visited me at dead of night he'd have taken some trouble with his appearance. And, carrying a bunch of flowers, not a shillelagh!"

Talking in whispers to avoid waking Cheryl, Gordon explained that the water had stopped just as she had described.

"About ten minutes later a man came through the bushes and started to go into the passageway. He must have been waiting, listening. It's possible he was a poacher, but he didn't seem the type, besides, this isn't the time of year to kill pheasants and partridge, not with the young ones about."

"What d'you mean, not the type? What impression did you get? Age? Height? I presume it was a man?"

"Young, I think, and very strong," Gordon groaned as Bettrys bathed his face. "About eleven stone and perhaps an inch or two shorter than me. Nothing really to help me recognise him again. D'you think we should tell Mr Taylor?"

"No. There's no point. Best we forget all about it now. He'd have been discouraged by your catching him anyway."

"Perhaps you're right." Gordon's face was a technicolour nightmare and his eyes were closing with fatigue.

"You'd better stay here for what's left of the night," Bettrys said. She didn't want him outside with an angry man wandering about waiting to get his revenge.

"Your bed?" he asked hopefully.

"The kitchen floor!" she replied firmly.

"Next time I promise I'll bring flowers."

Bettrys didn't return to bed. She dressed and sat watching over Gordon. His nose and mouth had been injured in the brief fight and she was afraid to leave him in case of breathing difficulties.

She watched with wonder as the dawning light of the new day opened out in colours of unbelievable beauty. Gradually, the silhouettes of trees and bushes, and the skeleton of the old boat were revealed. She saw the blackness of the pre-dawn shatter as the sun on the horizon rent the night apart, bright and clear over the pewter sea. It was silent, not even a bird daring to disturb the magic of the morning. Then she became aware of the stream and she remembered. Some time during the night the stream had returned with a rush, then had settled into its gentle innocent murmur.

CHAPTER SIX

A pile of post arrived for Bettrys, posted on from the London flat. She searched eagerly in the wild hope of a message from Brett but there was only one letter, from Jonathan. The rest were advertisements, people wanting to sell her something. She sat down straight away and wrote back to Jonathan. She gave details of all that had happened and thought, re-reading it, that it sounded like a mysterious short story. She sealed the envelope and wondered what the next instalment would hold. She did not have to wait long to discover.

A few nights after the fight between Gordon and the stranger, she was woken by someone outside. It was close to the chalet and was clearly the sound of someone stumbling and falling. Branches snapped and there was the unmistakable sound of a man swearing. After a pause she heard him again, still muttering oaths. She glanced at the luminous clock and saw it was almost half past midnight. Going to the window and cautiously pulling aside the curtain, she looked out on a silvery scene in which she could make out little more than the trees and the outline of the sea. The sounds were softer but she guessed the man was approaching her chalet from the direction of the Cooper's. There was a wide path down from the road beyond Maldwyn's house, perhaps he was a stranger and had thought the path led somewhere other than the beach.

Keeping well down and peering over the sill, she watched as a figure moved towards her. It was as if he had seen her and was heading directly to her door. Her heart in her mouth, she remained mesmerised, then sighed with relief as the figure went around the side of the house. He was huge. At least six feet tall and looked as if he had the build of a sumo wrestler. Oh, how she wished Gordon had stayed.

He stood in the shadows, mingling with them occasionally as he moved from foot to foot with obvious impatience. Then the water ceased. The man walked away towards the place where the stream came out of the rocks, where the tunnel was almost hidden by fronds of ferns and covered with velvet mosses.

Without putting on a light, she made a cup of coffee and sat, waiting for his return. It must be something to do with Diana. Several people had referred to her having lovers. Well, for some reason this one must like wandering along underground passages! But no. It was ridiculous. At this time of night he could walk without being seen, across the fields to meet her at the dovecot, if that was their meeting place. Then she remembered the houses on the approach to the farm. Even agricultural workers were likely to have an occasional sleepless night. Leyton with his girlfriends, and that mother of his who looked the type to miss nothing of what went on. No one could walk up that lane and be certain of not being seen.

But walking along a passage underground? That was too fanciful for words.

Brynley Cooper left the clothes he had added over his sports coat and jeans on a natural shelf in the rock near the end of the passageway. He put the torch in his pocket and began to climb the rungs to the top. Below him the water trickled with hardly a sound. Stepping over the low wall he reached out for Diana and hugged her.

"My darling. How tired I am of all this. When can we tell Emrys and be done with it?"

"Soon, Bryn. Very soon." Together, they walked

towards the dovecot and, pushing aside the door, they went inside.

The corbelled building was still home to one or two pigeons, but it was relatively clean. They lay together on a blanket spread over the stone floor, and after sex had claimed, and then calmed them, Bryn Cooper said again, "How long do we have to wait? The villa in Marbella is all ready for us. All it needs is for you to tell me when we leave."

"You know my mother is terminally ill. I don't want to leave before she – "

"If I didn't know you better I'd think you were sentimental about the old harridan." He smiled in the darkness, touched her cheek with his lips. "But I know you too well."

"Yes, darling, it's the Will I'm worried about. Her money should come to me and we need it. But she's so eccentric that, if I leave Emrys, she is likely to change her mind and leave it to a charity." It was her turn to smile as she said: "It runs in the family, you see. Her parents were divorced, my father left her for a young woman whom he met in the amateur dramatics group. She's got it in her skull that divorce shouldn't be encouraged and has stated clearly that she will change her will should my marriage fail."

"She wouldn't though, would she? I mean, you're her only daughter. She wouldn't really leave her money to anyone else. A charity! Well, she just wouldn't." He leaned over and kissed her and as passion grew again, he whispered: "Tell Emrys, tell him tonight. Living like a troglodyte, hiding in mam's kitchen and under the stairs, having Mam believe I'm a desperate criminal wanted by the law, when in fact, I'm hiding from Emrys, who threatens to shoot me on sight! Then there's this crawling through the dark tunnel to the well. It doesn't suit me, my darling. It's time for us to move on, get out into the sunshine and – " Words were no longer possible as they became consumed with the need for each other.

In the chalet on the beach, Bettrys was once more lying on her bed. Sleep was proving hard to achieve. Twice she had risen, daringly opened the door and looked out into the chill, clear night, standing for a while to listen for some sound to reveal the presence of the intruder – which was what she now considered him – then returning to the warmth of her bed. She had seen a fox, trotting along the path, stopping to stare at her before continuing unalarmed on his nightly forage along the tide-line.

As at last she began to grow drowsy and thought that she would sleep, then the water returned with a sudden rush. She slipped out of her bed and went to the window. At first she thought he wouldn't come, but his huge shadow appeared at last and he walked cautiously back the way he had come, past her door.

As the stream began once again to flow at its usual level, she wondered who he could be. He must be local to go to so much trouble not to be seen. She had heard no car arrive or depart. But such a large man? Surely he would be easily recognised? Gordon was tall, but the only man as large as the intruder was Maldwyn, and she smiled at the thought of the elderly ex-seaman having an illicit affair. But who else was that size and living at or near The Bend? She had come with the somewhat futile hope of solving a riddle and found herself immersed in another. Exhausted, she slept.

Maldwyn Griffiths, at seventy-eight, was a fit and healthy man. He would probably still be working at least part time, had it not been for Jake and his accident. This injustice was his first thought every morning and his last at night. Jake had accused him of neglect, of leaving an untidily thrown chain around, and causing him to fall and break his arm so badly that it had had to be amputated.

He knew Jake had not been on board that day but he

couldn't prove it. One day, he promised himself, with the fervour and fitful repetition of a litany, one day he would discover just where Jake had been and the truth about how his arm was injured.

Because of the chimney sweep coming and Gwen needing his help moving furniture around, he hadn't collected his pension on the usual day. So it was a Thursday when he set off for his weekly walk into town. He strode out briskly, his powerful shoulders only slightly bowed with age and a lifetime of heavy work. His white hair shone in the morning sun, his thick eyebrows knitted together in a frown; he was deep in the thoughts that obsessed him. If only he could find out what Jake had really been doing that night.

What a waste of his experience to have to get rid of the boat he had sailed for most of his life and give up fishing. Now he was reduced to taking a weekly walk into town for the sole purpose of getting rid of his surplus energy and keeping his muscles from seizing up. Damn Jake Cooper. And his interfering wife!

The dog was following him. He didn't need to look around to know that and the expression on his face softened. Stupid animal. He knew it meant coming back on the bus and he hated that. He touched his pocket to feel for the spare lead he kept there in case.

The land on the side of the road to his left, away from the sea, was boggy. Cotton grass and rushes grew in a waving tide and a coot flew up, disturbing the air with its call and startling the dog. Beyond the wet area the fields rose and high above, almost in the shadow of the Taylor's farm buildings, he could see the tractor heading out beyond the hill to the fields, dropping down out of sight. He doubted whether Emrys could see him but he waved anyway and walked on.

The tide was high, the beach no more than a thin strip of grey mottled land separating the sea from the greenery of the road edging. Gordon's boat was riding the gently moving tide, and as he watched he saw his grandson wading out, trousers rolled up, to jump into it.

"Look what you've missed you damned fool," he muttered to the dog, as the road took them inland away from the coast. "You'd have had a better day with young Gordon. Don't you know he's got a day off?"

He went first to the post office and then for his usual pint. But he was early. He had mis-timed his walk and the Ancient Mariner was not open. Irritably, he walked on through the village and wandered along the quieter roads out on the other side. The road dwindled to a narrow lane and seemed, from the lack of signposts, to lead nowhere in particular, so he was surprised to see Diana Taylor drive past, a passenger in an elderly car. He raised his arm in greeting but the woman didn't turn back to return it. Maldwyn shrugged. She could please herself!

He walked back in a semi-circle through the fields and past the church and there he saw someone else he knew.

"Bettrys? What are you doing in the village?" he called. "Going back on the bus?"

"Yes, I'll see you there, shall I?" she replied, bending to fuss the dog.

"Unless Diana passes us on her way home. She's around here somewhere."

"It would be nice to have a lift," she said, looking around as if expecting Diana to appear on cue. "I've just been delivering some of my jewellery. I think I'll go into Swansea tomorrow and find a few more outlets. This isn't enough to keep me busy, or keep us fed."

"I know a few people in Swansea," he said with a chuckle, "but no use to you, girl. Fishermen and skippers of fishing boats, I don't think they'd want your fancy bits and pieces. Them that do wear earrings won't want any as fancy as yours!"

Gordon was waiting for them when the bus stopped above the scattering of houses on The Bend. Potter leaped at him, ecstatic with delight, and he fought him off and took Cheryl, leaving Maldwyn to manage the folding chair.

"I thought you'd all be on this bus," he said.

"Saw that Diana Taylor back of the village but she didn't come by in time to give us a lift," Maldwyn said.

As he spoke, a mud-splattered Land Rover dangerously overtook the bus as it pulled out from the side of the road. Diana squealed the brakes, causing the bus to stop suddenly again as she slowed immediately in front of it to take the narrow lane to the farm.

"Get herself killed she will, driving like a mad-woman!" Maldwyn grumbled. "Women like her aren't fit to be in charge of a vehicle!"

Gordon and Bettrys shared a grin and followed the old man down the path to the beach houses. "Go on with you, Grandad. You're only mad because you didn't get a lift!"

"Get herself killed. You mark my words! Emrys is a fool ever to have got tied to her."

Leaving Maldwyn to go on alone, Gordon went with Bettrys and Cheryl and helped her unpack her shopping. When Bettrys went into the living room she gave a shout of alarm and distress. Gordon ran to see what had upset her and found the room in a shambles. Someone had been there and given the place a thorough search.

All the small items and tools Bettrys used to make her jewellery had been thrown on to the floor. Books had been torn from their covers, the contents of her store cupboard, brought from the kitchen had been emptied onto the table and there were marks in the flour and sugar as if fingers had raked through in the hope of finding something.

"What on earth were they looking for?" Bettrys said in a bewildered whisper. "I haven't anything of value."

"Do you want to call the police?" Gordon asked, white faced with shock. "We oughtn't to touch anything if you do."

"Children. It must be a prank. Perhaps they thought the place was empty."

"Then you want to forget it? If so, let's get this mess cleared up. I'll go and get some brushes and paper sacks from Mam."

"No!" she shouted. "No, please Gordon, don't leave us. He – they – might still be around." She picked up the child and slumped into a chair. Covering the child's ears so she didn't hear, she said softly: "This place is beginning to frighten me."

"Come on, I'll take you to stay with Mam while I sort this mess. Tonight, I'll stay." He said it in a tone that brooked no argument and Bettrys didn't even consider trying to dissuade him.

After Gordon had replaced all the scattered items, Bettrys went through them, occasionally replacing something he had put in the wrong place but mainly just touching things, making sure everything was there. Nothing seemed to be missing. All the beads and silver wire, although thrown about, seemed to be there, and the money she had put in a tin to pay her rent hadn't been touched. It wasn't until she had checked for the second time and began to feel reassured, that she realised that something *had* been taken. The small wallet containing her family's marriage, birth and death certificates and all her exam papers, was gone. With them had been Cheryl's birth certificate and the one marking the death of her sister. Was she closer than she thought to the man she was hoping to find? Would the details on those certificates, with the dates clearly shown, be sufficient to make him move away again, where she couldn't hope to find him?

But wasn't she being melodramatic? Why would a man be afraid of a paternity suit and search for a birth certificate for a child he probably didn't know existed? Then she remembered that he wouldn't have been concerned if he had seen it. Eirlys had registered Cheryl as hers.

*   *   *

At Taylor's farm, on the following Tuesday, Diana and Emrys argued.

"I'll go where I please." Diana ignored what Emrys was saying and just repeated the few words in an aggravating manner that had the usually placid Emrys shaking with anger.

"You're my wife, for heaven's sake! If you won't share the work of running this place you at least owe me some loyalty! You're never here!"

"I'll go where I please."

"Wandering off all day and for half the night. What will people think! Friends enjoy telling me they saw you in town being driven who knows where by a strange man in a Riley car. Maldwyn said he saw you in an old car, then coming home, nearly causing an accident, driving the Land Rover. It isn't the first car you've been seen taking lifts in. You're hardly inconspicuous. You don't make any effort to be. People are laughing at me for heaven's sake. Don't you care?"

"I'll go – "

"Who is he, this latest fancy-man?" Emrys interrupted. "I forbid you to see him again."

"Don't be dramatic, Emrys. He's someone who gave me a lift while I was out for a walk, that's all!"

Through the open window, the rhythmic scraping of Jessie Newbank's husband Ray, cleaning the yard outside the milking parlour, could be heard. Inside, Jessie herself stopped her flying duster and listened to the argument between her employers.

Diana and Emrys stood silently for a time, the air between them bristling with unspoken anger.

"Why do you spend so much time out of the house?" Emrys asked, in a tone suggesting he didn't expect an answer. "Don't you have enough to do? Or is it me you can't stand the sight of?"

"You knew when you married me that I wouldn't settle down and be the dutiful farmer's wife and make jam and cook your meals . . . be a slave." Her eyes blazed, her face glowed with the heat of the argument and Emrys thought she was beautiful and desirable and – impossible.

"I'm not asking much, just that you be fair. I hate people taking me for a fool. I don't want you wandering off again, understand?"

"I'll go, where, I please," she reiterated with emphasis. Her full lips tightened with determination as she stared at him.

He wanted to hold her, kiss her, make love to her, and the impossibility of those things made the simmering anger inside him grow: an insidious weed with the ability to destroy. "No, Diana. Not any more you don't! I've had enough! Understand? Enough!" He raised an arm as if to strike her then, as she stared at him unafraid, and with such contempt on her face he wanted to cry, he lowered it and said: "Give up your men-friends or leave. It's up to you. I'm past caring which." He went out and, snatching the tool from a surprised Ray Newbank, worked furiously to contain his anger.

Later that night, when Emrys was snoring steadily in the spare bedroom, Diana stood up and reached for her jacket. She was fully dressed, even to her shoes. Without putting on a light she moved like a shadow down the oak staircase and out into the yard.

The night was dark, there wasn't even a glimmer of a moon but she didn't need a torch as she made her way to the well, then to the dovecot. Footsteps, stealthy but clear to her expectant ears, approached the door then, it opened, and she sighed as lips found hers and the man pressed her slim body against his own.

Gordon couldn't sleep. He was lying on Bettrys's couch staring into the darkness and wishing it was morning. There was an intimacy in sharing the same house with a desirable woman. The house was like an island keeping them isolated from the rest of the world with its inhibitions and conventions and disapproval. Knowing Bettrys was only yards away, aware of the flimsiness of the wall that separated them, he felt desire aching in him and wondered if she too was engulfed in similar thoughts and feelings.

There hadn't been a sound since they had settled to sleep, apart from the soft gentle sighs and the occasional shifting of Cheryl's position. He sat up and tiptoed to the open door. Peering around he saw Bettrys curled in a tight knot under the blankets. He didn't call her, not wanting to disturb her, afraid that his growing love for her would make him show his feelings too fiercely and too soon. He stood watching her for a moment: she was dreaming. She called out a name. Not his name but someone called Brett. He sighed and returned to his uncomfortable couch.

Hands behind his head, he stared up at the ceiling, where his eyes, now accustomed to the darkness, could just make out the shape of the single bulb. Then a beam of light crossed the ceiling and he darted to the window and crouched low, peering over the sill in an attempt to see who was passing.

He was too late, the torch had already passed the house and vanished from sight. He hesitated for a moment then grabbed his coat and carefully unlocked the back door. The first thing of which he became aware was the fact that the stream had ceased to flow.

At Taylor's farm, the door of the spare room opened a crack and Emrys listened intently. Then he walked down the stairs and went out into the night. The dog growled and he hushed it with a single word. Then he went to where the out-buildings ended and the fallow field began. He stood staring towards the dovecot then, backing into the shadows of the cowshed, he waited.

When he heard the whispered farewells of the couple emerging from the dovecot and walking towards the out-buildings he returned to the house. Almost twenty minutes later, when Diana looked in, he was in bed, giving the impression of being fast asleep.

"The stream stopped last night," Gordon said when Bettrys brought him in a cup of tea and Cheryl handed him a plate of biscuits. "It was silent for about an hour, then it flooded out before settling to its usual steady flow."

"At least you believe me now," Bettrys smiled.

Gordon rose from the couch, stiff and aching, unrefreshed by the few hours of sleep he had managed. Taking a biscuit from the plate he handed one to Cheryl and to Bettrys's surprise, the little girl said, "Ar-who," which Bettrys translated into "thank you".

"That's the first time she's said that," she whispered, not wanting to make too much of it and discourage the little girl from saying it again.

"Mam's spending time with her, Grandad reads to her, it all helps. Mam thinks she should be trying to say more than she does."

"Perhaps, although not all children repeat what they hear readily at her age. Maybe it's the unsettled life she's led. First with her sick mother, helped by occasional nursery nurses, then a series of bedsits as we made our way here. She was partly with me and partly with various child-minders while her mother was in hospital and – well, she's been moved about rather a lot."

"Her mother? I thought – "

"She's my sister's daughter."

"I see," Gordon said, although he didn't. "Can I ask one more question?"

"Of course."

"Why are you here?"

"I'm looking for someone. But please, Gordon, please don't mention that to anyone. I have a feeling that if the person knew who I was, then that person would disappear and I might never find them again."

He nodded. He couldn't help noticing her caution in

105

not giving away whether the person she sought was male or female. Talking slowly as she did obviously gave her time to think and be cautious.

"If I can help, you only have to ask," he said. "And – I hope it isn't a husband you're looking for!" He said it in a jocular way but there was a question in his eyes, which Bettrys answered.

"There's no husband," she smiled. "Not even a boy-friend."

He glanced at the letter addressed to Jonathan.

Jonathan Crawley was a friend of my sister."

"Someone must know you're looking for him though, how else can you explain the search through your things? It wasn't children, was it? We both know that."

"I don't know. But I hope it was just a prank. Don't you?"

"Come on, I have to get to work. See you tonight and, Bettrys," he held her arm and looked at her with anxiety in his eyes, "be careful, you and little Cheryl. I'd hate anything unpleasant to happen to either of you."

She smiled and assured him that she would indeed take care. He still held her arm and now, their eyes meeting in that unmistakable way, he leaned closer and gently kissed her. It was lightly done, but they were both shaken by it.

That night, Bettrys dreamed again of Brett. But the dreams were disturbing, forcing her into a wakeful anxiety. Each time he took her in his arms and looked into her eyes, his face frowned, became hard and cold, then faded and was transformed into the smiling, loving face of Gordon.

It was obvious that whatever was causing the stream to stop had become a regular Tuesday event. On the Tuesday of the following week, Gordon again stayed with Bettrys and Cheryl. On Bettrys's instructions, he did not tell his parents anything of the mystery that was beginning to shroud the small chalet rented for the summer. So he brought his camera equipment as a cover for his absence and hoped that his parents would accept his explanation of early morning shots of the choughs, and recordings of birdsong which, as the weeks moved inexorably on towards May, was approaching its best.

He slipped into the house after dark and, with Cheryl in bed, they sat beside the fire and talked. This time there was a discernible difference in the way they sat and talked. During other evenings there had been restraint, each knowing that the reason for Gordon's presence was for her protection and nothing else. Now the relationship had been changed by a loving kiss.

Bettrys was uneasy. Afraid of becoming involved before she had achieved her aim. Gordon was tense: wanting her, but he was afraid too. His fear was of moving too quickly or too soon, and spoiling the chance of developing a strong, loving partnership with this fascinating woman.

At midnight they turned off the light and sat quietly listening. The sequence was as before. The approach of a man, who flicked the torch on only briefly as he passed the corner of the house before disappearing again into the darkness. Then the cessation of the water and silence.

Allowing a minute to pass, Gordon followed, having previously told Bettrys to close and lock the door after him. She did so and waited in an agony of fear until he returned some ten minutes later.

"I'm sure whoever it is is using the passage through the well," he said, when he was once more safely locked inside the house. "I risked using my torch briefly and there were footprints. Large ones. A man's I'm sure. It's clear what's happening and I don't think we should investigate any further, do you? I don't fancy being beaten up by one of Diana Taylor's lovers, accused of being a voyeur!"

"Then you're sure that's the explanation?" She smiled her relief. "Thank goodness! I was imagining present-day smugglers and violent men bursting in and murdering us!"

"It's almost two o'clock. D'you want me to stay?" There was no ambiguity about his words as he gestured towards the couch with a hint of chagrin. Bettrys thanked him and brought the bedding he would need.

They talked long into the night, and later, heard the stream stop and re-start. It seemed of secondary importance to their talking. Bettrys explained about the man she had loved and who had left without a word when she had felt bound to stay and look after her sister. She was still cautious, watching her words and she deliberately did not mention her sister's unusual name. Gordon told her she had called the man's name in her sleep.

The postman brought a letter to Carys Cooper, telling her that "The Weekenders", as they called Jeremy and Frances Baxter, would be staying at Costa Plenty that Friday. She read the letter and made a mental note to buy the basic supplies for them as she usually did, and handed the note to her husband.

"I wish they'd give me more notice," Jake grumbled. "I haven't finished painting the kitchen windows yet. I'll have to do it today and leave what I'd planned until next week."

"Want me to do anything?" Carys asked. "Let anyone know your change of plan?"

"You could go and tell Emrys I won't be starting on whitewashing his barns until Monday."

"Right." Carys folded the sewing she had been working on and reached for a coat.

She was glad of the excuse to visit the Taylors' farm. Always a bit of gossip to be had from Jessie Newbank, the woman who did the cleaning. That Diana Taylor had caused Carys and Jake a lot of trouble a couple of years ago. So it was more than normally gratifying to hear that all was not well with her.

The quarrelling that went on constantly was local knowledge. Diana's "carryings on" were a gift to the small community, always game for a laugh and a bit of shocked excitement. Disapproval always made you feel good. Carys Cooper did her share of passing on the latest items: she didn't want anyone to guess just how much she and Jake hated the woman or why.

It was raining and the sea was barely visible as she set off up the path to the road. She had trouble opening the farm gate. It looked as if it had been damaged, perhaps by a car running into it. She tried to hold up an umbrella and re-fasten the heavy metal clasp, but gave up and dragged and kicked a stone to hold it temporarily until Emrys could get it fixed.

"Jake said to tell you he won't be up to start the white-wash until Monday," she called to the waterproof-covered figure coming out of one of the barns. "Jessie in? I thought for to have a chat."

Emrys waved vaguely in the direction of the door and went about his business, scowling to match the weather. Carys shrugged, he was in a right old mood for sure. She opened the door and called, and waited until Jessie appeared carrying the remnants of breakfast, on a tray.

Jessie, her husband Ray, and, on occasions their son Leyton, had worked on the farm most of their lives, and the running of the farmhouse, once in the hands of old Mrs Taylor, was now firmly in her own. That was one good thing about Diana. She didn't care enough to interfere.

"Come in and take off them wet things," Jessie instructed. "And wash all that mud off your hands. Walk up on your hands and knees, did you?" She was an elderly woman, with a heavy figure and long grey hair pulled severely back and tucked into a tight bun. She wore a wrapover apron almost covering a brown skirt, and thick woollen stockings on her sturdy legs. On her feet were soft, pink fluffy slippers.

She sensed Carys staring at the incongruous footwear and said, "Belong to her upstairs they do. I didn't wear my wellingtons and got soaked walking up the hill. Tell how little she does from these, can't you? As if anyone could do any serious cleaning wearing daft things like this." Having dismissed the stupidity of the pink slippers, she kicked them off and, in stockinged feet, went off to collect "the rest of her ladyship's dishes!"

With the ease of familiarity, Carys put the kettle on to boil and stood the teapot near it to warm. When Jessie came back she said, "Did you know the gate's broke?"

"Yes, she did it, as you might guess. Driving too fast and skidded on the mud last night. Woke me up she did, mind. And you should have heard her swearing. God knows where she was going at that time of night!"

Carys asked confidentially, "Things no better then?" She pointed a finger upwards. "Still not getting on?"

"Fighting every moment they're together. Not that they're together much! She's up half the night and sleeping half the day. What a carry on!" Jessie made the tea and said, "And there's him, poor dab, at his wit's end trying to deal with her. Best for him if she up and went, back to town where she belongs, like his first one did."

"Carrying on with some man who lives at the back of the village so I hear."

"Well, best we don't pass on gossip like that." Jessie's harsh features glowed with righteousness. "Gossip never does no good."

"Of course," Carys said, wearing her well-used look of disapproval. "There's enough talk without us making it worse. But she's been seen, mind. In some old-fashioned car so I believe. There's brazen."

"It's no use pretending, I suppose." Jessie sighed as if it were her carrying the worries. "Diana is no better than she should be and it's a pity he's got the burden to bear, poor man."

A shadow crossed the doorway, making the two women start. Then Emrys came in and asked if there was any coffee going. Jessie bustled nervously into the pantry and came back with a jar of instant coffee. If he had heard the women's conversation he gave no sign of it, but Jessie was unreasonably angry with Carys, as if she had been the cause of her employer's overhearing her remarks.

"Can't stop for long, Carys," she said briskly. "There's a lot to be done this morning, mind."

"I'm stretched for time too," Carys defended. "Only came with a message for Emrys, I did. Jake can't start the white washing as promised. I've got to go. I've a wedding dress to finish for next week. I can't stop for tea, sorry!" Pushing away the cup and saucer she had put out ready for her tea she stood up, replaced her wet coat and left. "Your gate's broke," she called back. "I can't shut it no 'ow. I've told you mind, so don't start blaming me if anything escapes!"

Emrys had overheard the two women talking and from the little that reached his ears he knew that Diana was continuing to add to the local gossip which was repeated and embellished with nothing less that delight. She was not popular and any excuse to criticise was treated like a gift from heaven.

Gordon was collecting photographs of the local wild-life for a slide show he planned to give in September. He wanted to capture scenes of the early explorations of a family of young foxes.

"If Mam will mind Cheryl, would you like to come with me?" he asked. "You have to be prepared to sit still and silent for a long time. I don't think I could find anyone more suitable to do just that," he smiled. "You're so calm and peaceful, Bettrys. I love being with you."

"Thank you," she smiled. "I'd love to come. But I'll have to be sure that your mother really doesn't mind. She has her often in the day and I don't want to be thought too casual with her kindnesses."

"Loves her she does. But I agree, you don't want to be thought a nuisance."

They were walking on the beach, returning from Ffynon

Sands, where they had picnicked and played games with Cheryl. They didn't even hold hands, content simply being together. Approaching the largest house on the beach, with the cross on its walls, they lifted Cheryl and carried her on their crossed arms up the steps, past the bench where Maldwyn usually sat, and into the house.

"Stay for a meal?" Gwen offered, poking her head into the small porch entrance, her face flushed and damp from the cooking. "I got a bit of sausage meat and I've made a pie."

"Before I do, can I ask a favour?" Bettrys asked. "I'd like to go and watch tomorrow night, while Gordon photographs the young foxes. And – "

Her hesitation gave Gwen the opportunity to nod and say happily, "She can stay with us and welcome. Lovely it is, having a child around and she's so entertaining." Then she frowned. "I'll stay with her at the chalet if you prefer, mind. If you don't want her to have any more upheavals that is?"

"I'll be happy if she stays with you," Bettrys smiled. "And, thank you for being so good to us."

That night, Gordon walked them home at nine-thirty and stayed to drink coffee. He didn't intend to stay long, but they talked about their day, and about how Cheryl was beginning to communicate with confidence. As the clock struck midnight he jumped up and reached for his coat.

"Sorry, Bettrys, love. I didn't intend to stop so late." He kissed her and it was another hour before he could tear himself away.

As he walked along the beach, back to his home, a figure was walking along the road above him. Diana had been to meet one of her friends and on the way home, the Land Rover had broken down. She had walked three of the five miles from town, carrying a bunch of flowers the man had given her. The card attached to them, on which "my love, to My Love" had been written, had fallen unheeded beside the road, as she had hastily pushed it into

112

her pocket and grabbed the flowers, before slamming the car door to begin her walk.

The following morning, a man driving along the empty road stopped to investigate and make sure there was no one in the vehicle. He picked up the card and read the words: "my love, to My Love". Thoughtfully, he put it in his pocket. As he started his car, he already had the glimmerings of an idea as to how he could use it.

He had sent his former wife away, given her the money to start a new life, lost the love of his children, all for Diana. It hadn't taken him long to realise he had been a fool. She showed him clearly that theirs was nothing more than a meaningless affair, frivolous fun. He had been a fool to believe her when she had promised that as soon as her mother died she and he would be together for ever. He fingered the card. Now the time had come to frighten her, make her give up the others and come back to him.

When he reached home, he looked again at the florists card, which he knew had come from the flowers he had seen Diana carrying, and considered how best to use it. Taking scissors, he carefully snipped away at the edges until he had only an ornate piece of card containing the five, handwritten words.

After more thought, he gathered together some newspapers and some paste. Searching sedulously for letters and numbers of matching size and style, he wrote a date, the tenth of May. The card and the message he stapled to a simply drawn map of Taylor's farm. He pencilled in the dovecot. Where the well was situated he drew a tiny cross. The cross he drew was not an X. It was the Cross of Calvary, used in churches.

And on graves.

CHAPTER SEVEN

The first of the season's parties was given by Francis and Jeremy Baxter in May. They paid young Pete Howells to deliver invitations to the local people and any of the chalet owners who planned to be there that weekend. The weather was not kind, there was a fine drizzle that gave a chill to the Sunday evening and those who turned up, arrived and remained, were ensconced in waterproofs and wellington boots.

"It's such a shame," Frances said, when she greeted Bettrys and little Cheryl. "We're usually reeeelly lucky for our first party, aren't we Jeremy?" Her voice was rather childish and Bettrys half expected her to miss out the "R's".

Bettrys had dressed Cheryl in a new, red, all-over rain suit, and wellingtons representing ducks and she carried a small umbrella. Bettrys had been tempted not to go when the weather seemed set to continue so drearily but the opportunity to meet so many of the people who lived, at least part of the time, at Yr Tro was too good to miss.

Gwen was there with Pete and old Maldwyn, and Gordon was planning to come when he had finished some work on his slides. Bettrys walked around holding Cheryl's hand and introduced herself.

They were an assorted bunch of characters as Gwen had already warned. Jessie and Ray Newbank from the farm were there with their son, Leyton, who appointed himself in charge of a fire which, surprisingly, survived the dampness and burned well enough for them to bake some potatoes – helped surreptitiously by Frances's micro-wave!

There were several who Bettrys had not yet met. There were the Kellys, in their early forties, always arguing. The Prices seemed older but were possibly not; their clothes and attitudes aged them, misleadingly. They arrived with a huge Great Dane puppy. The Normans, and the Thomases, who looked about fifty-plus, remained in a huddle, planning the long walks along the coastal paths they all enjoyed.

The Williamses were absent, their chalet bearing a For Sale sign. Colin had not returned since the afternoon when he had been almost pushed from the cliffs when he had been walking with a woman whom Bettrys and others suspected had been Diana Taylor.

Carys and Jake had not arrived by the time the potatoes and other hot food was ready, so Bettrys left Cheryl with Gwen and Maldwyn and went to call them. She opened the door into the porch and, as there was no sound, she went into the living room. Voices were heard coming from the kitchen and she tapped on the door and pulled it open just a crack. The door burst open against her and a furious Jake shouted at her for interfering in things that didn't concern her and accused her of being too inquisitive for her own good. Startled, Bettrys explained that the food was ready and made her escape. The Coopers did not show themselves then or later.

"Ashamed of their nonsense most likely," Gwen said, when Bettrys explained what had happened. "But perhaps they think you're trying to find out more about the accident to Jake's arm to help Dad. Not like Carys to be so melodramatic, mind. But Jake is a bad-tempered devil when he likes."

Diana and Emrys didn't appear. Petal defied Gar, and remarked to anyone who would listen that they were glad not to have to be polite to "that woman", for the sake of their poor dear son.

115

The Baxters had erected a caravan awning as a shelter and with the hot food and plenty of wine, the evening passed cheerfully enough, but by ten o'clock most had drifted away and Bettrys had taken Cheryl home to bed.

Gordon went with them but didn't stay. Bettrys seemed vague and uncommunicative. There was no way he could know that she was mulling over what she had learned about those who lived at Yr Tro and was trying to fit one of them into the role of her sister's lover.

Emrys was having difficulty holding back his anger. He had arranged to go with Diana to choose a new suit. There was an annual Summer Ball in May and he had decided that as well as a new gown for Diana he too should be dressed in something new. He had finished the chores, apart from bringing the cows back up from the bottom field ready for milking, a task he had delegated to Ray Newbank's son Leyton.

He was dressed and waiting at three o'clock but Diana had not appeared. When he called to say he was ready, Jessie Newbank told him, with what looked suspiciously like a grin, that, "The missus has gone into the village. For a walk, so she said."

Emrys waited until four-thirty. Then, getting into the old Morris that had once belonged to his first wife, he went to look for her. He drove fast and carelessly, using the horn to get people out of the way and hardly caring whether they did or not.

"Looking for Diana?" Jake said, coming out of the Ancient Mariner and seeing Emrys staring about, anger explicit on his red face. "She was in the cafe an hour ago, but she left the Land Rover and went for a walk, so she said."

Did he imagine the grin? Was it his temper and humiliation that made him believe everyone was laughing at him? It was common knowledge that Diana preferred other men to him. Why shouldn't they laugh? He would if the circumstances were reversed! But he had to try and stop the gossip before it drove him insane.

"I'm not looking for Diana," he lied, as calmly as he was able. "I know she's gone for a walk. She wanted me to go but as usual I was in the middle of something. No, it's the dog. He got loose and I was getting ready to go into Swansea and the old fool has wandered off. Bring him back if you find him, will you?"

"For sure," Jake said, doubting the man's words. Since when had he starting worrying for a dog who'd find his way home quicker than any human could? No, he was attempting to cover up for his errant wife. "What about Diana? Shall I tell her you're looking for her too?"

"I told you! Diana isn't lost! I know exactly where she is! I don't keep her on a collar and lead, she's allowed to go for a walk if she wants to!" Emrys got back into the car and drove home in even more irritable haste than he had come.

It was five-thirty when she returned. He was sitting in the chair beside the fire looking at the paper just delivered by Pete Howells. His voice was deceptively low as he asked, "Forgot we were going into town, did you?"

"Town?" There was a frown on her forehead as she looked at him, then it cleared and a look of dismay replaced it. "Emrys! Your suit! I did forget. I'm so sorry. I went for a walk around the back of the village, the bluebells are fully out in Mill Wood. I wanted to see them and I completely forgot. I'm sorry," she repeated and for once the expression was genuine. "I'll have a word with Leyton, see if he'll cover for you while we go on Monday." She turned to leave but stopped when he spoke.

"Tuesday," he said staring at her in a disconcerting way. "I want to go on Tuesday."

"Tuesday's fine." She met his gaze confidently.

"We could go to the cinema in Swansea and perhaps stay overnight."

"That would be lovely, Emrys. Yes, let's do that."

"What about your other arrangements? Your Tuesday meeting with one of your men friends. Wouldn't he be upset, you letting him down?"

For the first time Diana looked alarmed.

"What rubbish you talk sometimes. Been talking to that Carys Cooper, I bet! Loves a bit of gossip. And what she can't discover she makes up!"

"Get changed." Emrys spoke sharply. "Get changed," he repeated as she began to argue. "We're going visiting."

"Where? Who are we seeing? I have to know so I know whether to dress up or look the part of a farmer's wife," she said, defiance covering her alarm.

"Dress up, real smart, plenty of make up, do your hair loose and glamorous, like you should when you're going out with your husband."

Diana bathed and dressed in a summery dress and a short yellow jacket. She would have to wear wellingtons as far as the car; even with all the effort Emrys and Ray put in, the yard was never clear of mud. She pulled her hair from the slide that held it back from her face and allowed it to fall free. Her application of makeup was brief, but she put on slightly more than usual, concentrating on making her rather small eyes look larger, softening their expression of anxiety.

She was nervous of Emrys. He was obviously angry. She was angry with herself for forgetting their intention to go to buy him a suit. Today of all days, when she was in fact doing nothing more innocuous than wandering through Mill Wood admiring the bluebells!

With enforced gaiety, they called on Maldwyn Griffith and Gwen at Smuggler's Cottage, where Gwen made them tea and talked politely, if a mite curiously. Emrys was not a man to spend time on social calls without a purpose.

They dropped in briefly on Emrys's father and mother, Gar and Petal, who watched with some mistrust, expecting to hear that the cause of their visit meant something unpleasant.

Without having been told, Diana did what Emrys wanted. She played the part of a devoted wife. She was arm in arm with him as they arrived and left each house, kissing him in secret moments, but each time, making sure they were seen. She deferred to him whenever anything was discussed, not adding her own forthright views to disturb the amiable conversations.

At the Coopers, her tensions rose. Was this the real reason for the round of social calls? Did Emrys know that Brynley Cooper was back, and hiding in the small cupboard whenever there was a knock at the door and only going out at night? Did he know about Bryn's visits via the well and their love-making in the dovecot?

There seemed no evidence that he planned to create a fuss and demand to see the man the police wanted to interview. He greeted Carys and Jake, asked about business and seemed quite relaxed. He brought up the subject of the Summer Ball, the village's "highlight of the year" as he put it jokingly. "I want Diana to have the smartest and most glamorous dress there. She's beautiful and I want everyone to see her and feel jealousy," he said. He stared glassily at Jake and Jake laughed a nervous laugh and pretended to agree, muttering a pretence that he, like every other man in the area, already felt envy of him.

Looking around Jake saw that the colour that flooded his face apparently went unnoticed. He was relieved no one had been aware of his momentary discomfort. He poured and handed out drinks efficiently with his one arm but the tray trembled a little. For a moment there, he had been convinced that Emrys knew. The words had been lightly said, but had struck a memory of things best forgotten.

Diana played her part well, that of the modest wife, shyly accepting her husband's flattery. Then, to her chagrin, Emrys suggested that the fabulous gown should be made by Carys Cooper, who preened in her delight and offered to go with Diana into Swansea to choose the pattern and materials.

"I'll call for you at two o'clock on – let's say – Tuesday," Diana said breezily, avoiding Emrys's eyes. "Emrys and I had planned an evening out, but we can always go another day, can't we darling?" She smiled and said how exciting it would be choose a pattern and some cloth and watch it coming to life under Carys's skilled fingers. All the time, her anger with Emrys threatened to boil over. Shopping with Carys was not her idea of a good day out, or how she had intended to select her new gown.

Leaving a delighted Carys and a still-puzzled Jake, the round of social calls continued. Diana pleaded with Emrys not to go to Costa Plenty and the awful Baxters but Emrys held her arm tightly and harshly insisted they visited everyone.

At Costa Plenty, holiday home of Frances and Jeremy Baxter, they were greeted as if they were old and valued friends. The young couple were elegantly dressed in casual clothes. The material and style looked good but made it clear that the garments were for showing off their slim and well-tanned figures. Fran, as she liked to be called, was small and seemed to revel in being thought child-like. Jeremy, dressed in stylish clothes, that were almost feminine, acted the role of handsome protector to her girlish helplessness.

Here, it was Diana who was ill at ease. She avoided looking at Jeremy and Fran watched her with intense curiosity. When Emrys finally stood to leave, Diana almost ran from the place. When he handed them their drinks, Frances overheard him say, close to Diana's ear the one word, "Bitch".

Outwardly, the handsome young couple were eff-usive in their welcome, offering an assortment of drinks which, they said, had been replenished ready for their next Sunday evening party, to which they were both invited.

Horrified at the prospect of spending more time with the couple, and unable at this moment to pretend otherwise, Diana nevertheless looked at Emrys to answer for them both and to her almost visible relief, he shook his head.

"Sundays," he said with an adoring gaze at his scowling wife, "are special to us, even after being married all this time. On Sunday evenings we rarely go out, we encourage no visitors, but spend the precious time together.

Diana wanted to laugh. But, still playing the part she had been given, aware of Jeremy's inimical glance, she lowered her head as if in coy agreement.

When they eventually returned to the house, Emrys asked her to make him a sandwich. He took a loaf from the bread bin and placed it on the board. She threw it at him, followed it with the board, and went to bed.

The following morning, she sent a note via Pete the paperboy, to Carys Cooper, telling her that plans had been changed and she would meet her in David Evans, Swansea, at three-thirty. It would take the poor woman hours to get there by bus but that was a problem she had to sort out herself. There was no point in wasting the whole day.

On Tuesday she went into town early and spent the day exploring the shops. Whatever problems she faced in her life with Emrys, shopping was still great fun. There was an out-of-season sale on at one shop, selling bankrupt stock, and she browsed for an hour before choosing some good quality bargains.

She bought a winter coat for fifty-five pounds and a couple of dresses in fine wool for twenty pounds each that were a bit dated, but which, with the help of Carys Cooper, could be shortened and altered slightly to make attractive garments. There was an artificial rose on the front which she knew would come off as soon as she had the receipt in her pocket. With two heavy tweed skirts that would go well with her leather boots and jacket, she was well satisfied when she hurried to the small park, where she had arranged to meet Carys Cooper.

"Carys, my dear, I'm so sorry," she said effusively when she reached her. "I arrived late, then I got carried away with the bargains in the sale. Will you forgive me if we don't look at patterns and things today? I'm just not in the mood."

Without giving the woman a chance to disagree, she led the way to where she had left the car and drove her home.

Pete Howells was leaning against the closed farm gate. Potter sat on the empty paper-bag at his feet. Diana turned off the road, revving the engine impatiently, frowned and gestured to him irritably to open the gate for her. The boy must be stupid to stand there when it's obvious she was going to drive through!

"Open up, won't you?" she shouted through the window.

"I was asked to give you this, and to make sure it was not in front of anyone else, so I waited for you," Pete said. He handed her an envelope and she took it, then gestured again for Pete to open the gate, which he did. Without a thank you, she drove on up to the yard.

She went straight to her room and threw her various packages on the bed. She forced herself to open them all and display the contents before opening the envelope. She slid a finger in and pulled at the seal, then, after glancing out of the window to see whether Emrys was likely to come in, she pulled out the contents. As she unfolded them she smiled contentedly.

First there was the message, in his familiar handwriting, "my love – to My Love." Attached to it was a map, marking the old well with a cross. Funny, it was a cross of Christ, not an X marks the spot. There was also another page and this made her laugh with excitement and amusement. He had cut pieces from a newspaper to make up the message. What fun! She looked excitedly at the clock. The date was today, the time, midnight.

She hurriedly hung up the new clothes. She would show Emrys another time. Bargain, out-of-season clothes were trivial compared to the note. Now she must start dinner and then she'd bath and get into her night clothes and tell Emrys she needed an early night. Almost breathless with excitement she set about her tasks.

She wondered in weak moments why she needed other men. It wasn't a searing need of sex, she could have that within her marriage. She defined her need as a lack of loving and caring. Emrys frequently made her feel like one of the animals he needed to complete his little farm set! There was also the danger associated with the illicit meetings that gave spice to a life of boredom. Not danger of physical harm. Emrys would never hit her, he knew she would walk away from that without question. All that could happen if she were caught with another man was that the divorce, which she planned anyway, would come sooner than she intended.

She wondered idly how much longer she could stay at Taylor's farm. If her date that evening suggested it she would go with him. He, above all the others to whom she swore undying love, could persuade her. He had the means to give her the life she wanted, that would make her content. She glanced around her at the ancient walls that had sheltered countless generations of Taylors and felt nothing. She could walk out, leaving everything here, without a moment of regret. There was nothing here that was hers anyway. The furniture had been chosen by previous generations. She hadn't even been allowed to change the curtains.

After they had eaten, she lay in the warm comforting bath and day-dreamed of hearing the words she longed for. "Come with me, I need you. I can't go on any longer without you." She dressed slowly, hanging on to the dream, perfuming her skin and brushing her hair slowly and imagining his fingers running through it. Only a few hours and her life might have changed for ever. She knew she didn't love him. But he offered an escape from the life she was beginning to detest. She deserved better. Surely she deserved better than this?

It had been a mild day and the light hadn't quite gone from the sky when Bettrys took Cheryl and walked across the short length of beach to Smuggler's Cottage. She had called to see if the photographs Gordon had taken of the choughs had been developed.

As usual, Gwen took charge of Cheryl, and Bettrys and Gordon examined the photographs he had collected that day on his way home from work. They were better than he had hoped. The female was incubating and at their approach she had momentarily flown up and Gordon had manged to get a shot of three lightly speckled creamy-green eggs before she settled once again to her responsibilities.

There were others, one of the male landing close by and previous ones of the pair building the rather shabby nest of twigs and untidy grasses, which nevertheless was comfortably lined with wool in its centre cup.

When Bettrys went to find Cheryl to take her home, she found her sitting on Gwen's lap, repeating the final words on the lines of nursery rhymes chanted by Maldwyn and Pete. She shrieked with delight when she was applauded after the final one and held out her arms for Bettrys. "Bettis" she said proudly and Bettrys hugged her with delight.

"She'll soon be talking non-stop!" Bettrys said to Gwen, as Maldwyn carried the little girl down the steps to the beach. "Thank you." She smiled at Pete then at Maldwyn and Gwen, lastly at Gordon. "All of you. You've made her so happy, it's given her a family, for a while at least," she added, with a touch of melancholy.

"Nonsense, dear," Gwen said briskly. "Friends for always we are and never forget it. She really is a delightful child. We'll all miss her so much when you go back to – London was it?"

"London," Bettrys said. She couldn't evade the question, not with these generous and kindly people. "I taught art there," she added.

Mention of London brought Brett to mind and the usual lowering of spirits showed in her face. If only he hadn't left her, if only he were here, sharing the responsibility for her sister's baby, how much happier life would be. Jerked out of her reverie to see Gwen's kindly face expectantly waiting for a reply, she said, quickly inventing a lie, "I spent the last two summers in France. Walking, staying at youth hostels, and trying to improve my French. This year I thought to visit the land of my fathers. Although, my parents both left here before they were ten years old."

She laughed, a soft relaxed sound that was pleasant on Gordon's ear. He was shaken by how he dreaded her leaving. He had to persuade her to stay.

Gordon walked back with them, giving the sleepy Cheryl a piggy-back ride. At the door, he asked, "Can I stay a while?"

"I have to bath Cheryl."

"I'll help."

Once the final story was finished and Cheryl was in bed, Gordon stood hesitantly at the door. Bettrys sensed his need to say something and she was half afraid of what that something might be. It was time now for him to know exactly who she was, what she was doing and how she felt about him. All those questions and many more were on his handsome face. He looked different. Larger than usual, filling the small room with his presence. The artificial light threw strange patterns on his face and made his eyes shiny black like pitch.

She knew she would have to delay the discussion he wanted. Until she had discovered the man she was seeking, and told him about Cheryl, she had to keep her own council. Confide in no-one.

Before he had spoken, she said softly, "Not now, Gordon. I know you want us to talk, but please, not yet. Give me a little more time."

His shoulders dropped. Then he shrugged and smiled. The tension lifted from the room and he said lightly: "Stay, can I? I could do with a coffee." Without waiting for her reply he went to the kettle and fiddled about preparing the drinks. When he handed hers to her he said, "One day soon, can we talk? I mean properly talk. Nothing held back. Cards on the table." She sipped her coffee without acknowledging his remark and he went on, "You know I'm falling in love with you, don't you?"

"Gordon, I'm more than a little fond of you. But that isn't enough for – I don't sleep around. There was someone once, but that's over."

"Over but not forgotten?"

"Can we leave it for a while before we commit ourselves?"

"You can have all the time you want, as long as I know there's a chance."

She put down the cup and turned to him. Carefully keeping her arms at her sides, she didn't want to be thought a tease, she lightly kissed him. "Soon," she said. "Soon, we'll talk."

It was a quarter to midnight when Diana stepped out of the doorway and made her way, using the shadows when she could, to the well. There was no wind. The night was still and rather cold. She wasn't sure whether the man would come via the well or across the fields. On a Tuesday, the well was his usual route, but the mysterious note made her wonder if that had been altered. Something had changed or he wouldn't have written to her in that amusing way. Perhaps he had discovered a new and simpler route through Mill woods.

126

In case he chose the well, she removed the grating and hauled on the lever that closed the water supply and altered the course of the underground stream. It would eventually bubble up on Ffynon Sands. She was warmer after her slight exertions and she sat, with the jacket around her shoulders and waited.

She was facing away from the farm buildings in the direction in which her friend might come, walking over the fields, having left his car in a convenient layby. The footfall was so soft that even in the stillness of the night she failed to hear it. The first she knew was when arms, powerful arms in a waterproof jacket smelling of mustiness and stale misuse, pulled at her from behind and tried to force her over the low wall into the well shaft. It was so sudden she had no time to call out. It was then the fear doubled as she remembered that the grating was missing. There was nothing to stop her falling down the shaft.

She wanted to call to him, tell him to stop, that she didn't like horse-play. But there was no breath for words, no thought process to clarify what she wanted to say, only a fight for her life.

The man was behind her and she couldn't see him. He was heavier, more powerfully built than the man she had expected; the overpowering smell of mildew gave no clue of his identity. Not knowing who he was added to her terror. The struggle was almost soundless as she fought to save herself from falling.

The arms were terrifyingly powerful, gripping her in a hold like bands of steel. But this was no loving embrace. He was edging her nearer and nearer to almost certain death. Her wrists hurt as she pressed against the walls. Her knee was scraped painfully against the rough stones and she felt her strength receding. Breathing was difficult as panic prevented her taking air into her lungs. She was aware of her own and her assailant's gasping intakes of air. His breath was warm on her cheek.

He had intended only to frighten her then let her go.

He imagined she would cling to him, tell him he was the only one, that she loved him. She would promise never to see the other man ever again. He would drive away any remnants of desire for the other man with kisses, words and tender love. But everything changed. The fight became a battle in earnest. She wouldn't submit. She wanted to cheat him. To get away from him, struggle free before he could relent and ease her away from the edge, give her back her life. Her writhing body and muffled screams prevented him thinking of anything, except winning.

He wanted her to fall. Her fear and anger lit something in him that made him wish her dead. Then he would be free of his rival for ever. He would have won.

It was a loose brick that saved her. The man had succeeded in leaning her over the dark chasm where there wasn't even any water to cushion her fall. He was pressing down on her and she was kicking her feet trying to loosen his hold, while her hand grabbed the air in the hope of touching one of the rungs embedded in the side. Suddenly he slipped. A brick fell and touched the sides twice before landing far below them with a dull smack.

In that moment of distraction, she changed from weakened, defeated acceptance to fierce, hopeful strength. She managed to swivel her body round and using the man's body to lever herself up she grasped the top rung and heaved her body over the wall to safety. The relief turned to furious anger and she caught hold of the man's foot, sticking out from the wall and raised it. It was heavy. He fought against it but the fact that she had caught him off balance helped her. Relief and fury and her own near disaster contributed to her strength.

When the man fell, with nothing more than a grunt of surprise, she didn't look back, but ran into the house and sat on her bed for the rest of the night, trembling and sobbing quietly.

*   *   *

128

Gordon and Bettrys were aware of the water stopping but they took no heed, as they sat talking quietly and listening with amusement to some of the old records Gwen had lent them.

"It's Diana and her boyfriend again," was Gordon's only comment.

When he left, the water fall had still not re-started. He shrugged and kissed Bettrys chastely on the cheek. "Don't let it keep you awake worrying. She'll restart it as soon as lover-boy comes back through."

"I wonder who he is," Bettrys whispered. "Not that fancy-dressed Jeremy, is it?"

"No, he isn't here often enough. It has to be someone local, but who is young enough? If Brynley Cooper were home I'd be suspicious of him, mind. He had a bit of a thing for Diana when she first came. His father put a stop to it somehow. Don't know how. It was at the time of Jake's accident."

In spite of reassurances that the water stopping didn't represent danger, Bettrys only dosed, unable to relax completely into sleep. As the sun slowly awakened the day, she realized the flowing water had not restarted.

Wrapping Cheryl in a blanket, she went to find Gordon before he left for work. The light was sufficient for Gordon to peer into the crevice, but there was nothing out of the ordinary apart from a few snapped and bruised fern-leaves. The damp rocks with a green spread of mossy growth where the water reached gave them no clue to the absence of the stream.

"I'm going in," Gordon said.

"Don't!" Bettrys pleaded. "What if the water came back suddenly. It starts with a fierce rush. You'd be drowned."

"I'll listen carefully. In fact, I won't go straight through, I'll stop half way, where there's a sort of shelf. If all's well, I'll go on. Don't worry, I'll be all right." Smiling at her reassuringly, he told her to go inside and lock the door.

Taking out the torch he carried and, with his camera, as always, around his neck in case there was something to photograph, he disappeared into the rockface through the frilly collar of ferns.

The dark part of the tunnel was the easiest and he quickly walked, with shoulders bent, through the surprisingly sweet air of the natural tunnel. The first time he stopped to rest, straighten his back temporarily, and check on the shelf, he had reached half way.

On his right, about two feet above the water mark, was the shelf he remembered from when he was a boy and adventure had filled his days. There had been another nearby, more difficult to find but which offered complete concealment. One day, for fun he'd try and locate it again. He walked on, a little more cautiously, half afraid of meeting someone on his way back from what ever appointment he had kept, or assignment he had undertaken.

Light from above made the bottom of the well look uneven. It had changed since his last visit many years before. Stones had fallen by the look of it. He would have to be careful not to twist his ankle. Then, as he drew closer, he saw that the uneven pile was not stones. It now looked more like an abandoned mattress or some unwanted clothes, he thought with an irritated sigh. People are so lazy with their outworn things.

It wasn't until he stepped on the bundle to reach the first of the rungs that he realised firstly that the bundle wasn't wet, then, that it was the body of a man.

The man wasn't dead and he was torn between going back through the tunnel to reassure Bettrys that he was safe, and going to the farm, which was nearer, to raise the alarm. He decided quickly and climbed the rungs and ran to where Emrys was opening the doors of the cowshed. Buckets clanged hollowly in the early morning. Somewhere a door closed. There was the sound of Ray and his son, Leyton, talking softly and the gentle lowing of the cattle, all sounds so ordinary that for a moment Gordon wanted to go back to the well and reassure himself he hadn't dreamed the sight at the bottom of the shaft.

"Where did you come from?" Emrys asked, as he caught sight of Gordon. "I didn't see you come up the lane. Come out of the ground like a pantomime genie, did you?"

"Sort of – I – hell this sounds crazy, but you've got a badly injured man at the bottom of your well."

Laughing at first, Emrys was soon persuaded to walk to the well. As if humouring the young man, he leaned over; told Gordon to run and phone for an ambulance, before climbing down to see if he could do anything to help. The man was unconscious, near death.

Before Gordon was out of sight, Emrys ran with great urgency to the farm house. He took the stairs two at a time and panting with the sudden speed, said sharply to Diana, "You'd better make that bed tidy and insist you and I were together all night," he said sharply. "A body's been found at the bottom of the well and you'll be a likely suspect.

"A body? You mean he's – "

"Not dead, but by the look of him he soon will be. So, let's get our stories straight, shall we? Before the police come and start their questions?"

Bettrys waited in an agony of fear beside the damp bed of the stream. After half an hour inside the house she hadn't been able to stand the waiting any more. She couldn't leave Cheryl, so she picked her up and, still in night clothes but wrapped in a blanket, she carried her to Smuggler's Cottage and called for Gwen.

"It's Gordon. He went through the rocks to see if he could discover why the stream has stopped and – " she sobbed and then forced herself to speak calmly. "I'm sure he's all right, the water hasn't restarted, but he might have hurt himself. I want to go and find him, will you look after Cheryl for me, please?"

Gwen went back with her, followed by Pete, Maldwyn and a curious Potter. But before Bettrys had found a torch and steeled herself to step into the frighteningly dark tunnel, they heard a call and saw Gordon on his way down from the road, shouting, waving, assuring them he was all right. She ran to him and held him, before they walked back with their arms around each other, to where Gwen waited, with tears of relief in her eyes, to listen to his story.

"The man's arm is smashed, you say?" Maldwyn said later, when Gordon had told them all he knew. "A smashed arm was what Jake had, the day he said he had fallen on my boat and claimed enough damages for me to have to sell it."

"This man, whoever he is, has injured his head too, rather badly by what I saw."

"That might explain why Jake is such a pain!"

"Dad!" Gwen admonished.

"So close to home and I hadn't thought of it. But it's an accident that would explain Jake's injuries. And one that could have happened before. Perhaps, like this poor unfortunate, Jake was one of Diana's secret admirers who lost his footing on the well shaft."

"They think this victim might have been pushed." Gordon said quietly. "Imagine, Mam. Here in Yr Tro, we might have a murderer in our midst."

It was an hour before they heard any more. Then a policeman came.

"There's no sign of a body, Mr Howells," he said to a bewildered Gordon, "dead or otherwise, and the water flowing through that tunnel, well, there's little chance of finding evidence of one ever having been there."

"Why didn't I take a photograph!" Gordon said later. "The one time when a photograph would have been of some use!"

CHAPTER EIGHT

The police questioned everyone living on Yr Tro and many besides. Rumours were born, they swelled and exploded and were gone. Each family in turn seemed to be implicated, but much of the speculation fell on Bettrys as a stranger whose activities were little known, and Diana Taylor, whose activities were very well known.

It was not until the following day that the identity of the missing, presumed dead, man was announced. His car, a Riley, had been noticed beyond Mill Wood and an investigation led to the small cottage on the quiet lane where Diana had been a regular Thursday visitor.

Des Newton had sold second-hand books. The small cottage had one room and a large shed full of them, all meticulously sorted and labelled. Details of recent transactions filled a small desk diary and it appeared that most of his business, finding books for customers responding to advertisements in magazines, was done by post. The diary was neatly filled in with every daily event and it was easy to find all his most recent contacts.

But there was nothing to suggest a woman, and a woman was whom the police suspected. A woman, a rendezvous and a terrible accident. The woman nearest to the scene of the tragedy was Diana Taylor and Emrys swore she was with him all night.

"In fact," he assured the investigator, "we were still awake at one a.m., talking, discussing plans to go on holiday later in the year, around November."

The enquiries fizzled out but the questions remained

and the previously casual life on the beach changed, almost imperceptibly. Doors, always left unlocked were firmly fastened. Many had locks replaced and bolts added. Even Maldwyn, whom most considered fearless, insisted that Gwen saw to the doors and windows every evening, and the house once filled with sea-fragrant freshness felt stifling, with all the air and anxiety trapped within it until morning. The murder, or accident, had spoiled something very precious in the small community; they no longer had trust.

Two days later, Bettrys had gone with Gordon up onto the cliffs to carry some of the equipment he needed to do a series of slides on the flowers growing in the rocks. He had left her to climb down to a ledge and had been absent for more than half an hour, leaving her reading a book.

She had abandoned the book and was sitting gazing down at the beach below when she saw a boat coming into the shore. She wasn't certain but it looked like Gordon's boat, minus the outboard motor. As she watched, the man rowing it, stood and with the boat rocking dangerously, heaved a long object over the side to splash into the shallow waves. Abandoning the boat, the man walked swiftly up the beach to disappear under the cliffs below. From where she sat, the object looked like a roll of carpet.

Could it have been Gordon? There was something familiar about his walk and he was about the same height – so far as she could guess; her elevated position somewhat distorted the figure.

When Gordon finally returned she told him what she had seen and on their way home they went to investigate. It was a roll of carpet, but inside it was the body of a man.

This time, Gordon did take a photograph, and he waited beside the body while Bettrys hurried back to telephone the police.

Bettrys reported what she had seen, but did not mention

that at the time the possibility of its being Gordon had occurred to her, only that the man seemed tall and, from the way he rowed the boat, quite strong.

The questioning by the police was repeated several times, both individually and together, but they couldn't provide further help.

"They say that the last person to see someone before death, and the person to find the bodies, are the strongest suspects," Gordon said. "Thank goodness you were with me!"

But I wasn't, Bettrys thought with slight apprehension, you were away from me for more than half an hour!

One Saturday afternoon, Gordon and Bettrys were sitting at her window, with a sleepy Cheryl beside them. They had been out in the boat, recently returned by the police. Cheryl and Bettrys had played on the sands while Gordon had climbed up the steep rocks above Ffynon Sands to photograph the newly-hatched fledglings of the choughs. They had picnicked and enjoyed a bottle of wine and now they were languorously contemplating a lazy evening.

Unheard and almost unseen a man walked past. He was stooped as if trying to avoid being seen, and wearing what looked like an army overcoat and forage cap. Walking away from the other houses, pushing cautiously through the bushes, he turned as if heading for the road.

"Who is that?" Bettrys asked. "I've seen him passing here before."

Gordon shook his head. "He isn't one of the locals for sure. D'you think we should tell the police?"

"I think we should. If there's a stranger around here – besides me," she laughed, "then they'll want to know."

"Could you describe him?" Gordon asked doubtfully.

"I couldn't. So what use would our information be?"

"It was a man. Tallish. Dressed in army uniform." She shook her head. "No, I can't even be certain it was a man. The clothes gave that impression, but nothing more definite. I didn't see the face."

They discussed it for a while then decided that unless the mysterious person was seen again they would say nothing.

"It was probably someone just out for a walk. We do have a lot of visitors after all. We don't want to waste police time," Gordon said finally.

So it was startling a few hours later to see the man again. It was a man: this time they were both certain. He was fairly tall but his build was difficult to assess. The thick overcoat, which looked as if it might be too large, disguised him. Dusk was falling and the evening had taken the colour out of the trees around them. They saw him walk back from the direction he had previously taken, and enter the Coopers' house.

"It couldn't be the mysterious Brynley Cooper, could it?" Bettrys suggested. "If he's wanted by the police their close presence and frequent searches must be very unnerving."

"If he's there and hiding from the police he wouldn't budge, surely?"

"Carys Cooper *is* hiding something. They didn't want me there and Jake was almost hysterical at the thought of my looking into their kitchen."

Gordon frowned, searching his memory. "There's a door leading to the understair cupboard in there, but no one could hide in it. A policeman would find it with one hand in his pocket and his eyes shut!"

When Gordon left, Bettrys locked the door and as an added precaution, pushed a chair against the handle. The thought of someone who was responsible for the death of a man, even if it were not murder, was filling her lonely nights with fanciful imaginings. In her option, reinforced by discussions with Gordon and Maldwyn, the death in the well had been very like the attempt to push Colin Williams over the cliffs. Modus operandi, wasn't that one of the ways a killer was caught? She shivered, then gathered the things needed for Cheryl's bath and put aside thoughts of a mystery she didn't have the information to solve.

A knock at the door startled her and she was relieved to hear Gordon's voice.

"That man went into the Coopers' house! How stupid to think we shouldn't tell the police!" he said as she opened the door. "We thought it wasn't worth a mention, but he went straight through the porch cheeky as a bailiff! No parading up and down first, just straight in! Come on, we have to tell them!"

Jake was working on the chalet belonging to the Baxters, painting the red window sill of the porch. He looked up as Gordon and Bettrys approached him silently, Bettrys carrying Cheryl and urging her to be quiet as if it were a game.

"We just saw someone going into your house, Jake," Gordon whispered. "It must be a burglar. He passed us once before so perhaps he's done more than one house already! We couldn't see him clearly but he's no one I recognise from around here."

Jake lowered himself carefully from the steps, after asking Gordon to take down the tin of paint which he had hung on a convenient nail.

"You must be mistaken. This affair with the murder has unhinged everyone." But he dipped his hand in a bowl of soapy water and wiped it awkwardly, dabbing it on a piece of towelling stretched between bricks which Carys arranged for him each morning, and led the way to his house.

To Bettrys and Gordon he seemed noisy. He coughed once or twice and pushed wide the half-open door without any attempt at caution. Once inside, he walked through the house, downstairs first then treading heavily in his working boots, up the staircase and into each room.

"No-one to be seen and nothing disturbed. You must have imagined it. But thanks for keeping an eye," he said when he rejoined them. "I suppose we'll all be a bit edgy until this person is caught, won't we?"

"We did see him," Bettrys insisted. "It wasn't imagination. We definitely saw a man, didn't we Gordon?"

"Man," Cheryl said distinctly, as if to add weight to the remark.

"What about that place under the stairs?" Gordon asked and Jake looked at him as if about to hit him.

"What d'you know about that? Been snooping, have you?"

"Snooping? Bryn and I spent hours in there, pretending it was a space-ship or a racing car, you must remember us using it as our den?"

"Of course. I'm getting as jumpy as all the old women." He went into the kitchen and opened the door, poked his head inside then returned to them smiling. "Full of coats that'll never be used again, and bits of Bryn's bike and other useless stuff. I'll have to get it cleared out." After thanking them again, and ostentatiously locking the door, Jake returned to work and Bettrys and Gordon walked back to her house.

"I think someone is living in the Coopers' house, besides Carys and Jake," Bettrys said as she closed her front door. "Carys was most upset that day when I peered into her kitchen looking for her on the night of the Baxters' party."

"Mam's a bit like that, mind," Gordon grinned. "If she's been sorting cupboards, or doing a bit of baking and everything isn't in its place, she panics if someone comes and catches her in a mess."

"I can understand that. But Carys Cooper isn't that bothered about people seeing her living room untidy so why should she worry so much about her kitchen? It was all neat and tidy anyway. No, she seemed frightened. Her anger was edged with fear." She shrugged when she saw him smiling. "All right," she said ruefully. "I am a bit overwrought. Having an unexplained death on your doorstep isn't easy to cope with."

"Mind you, Jake did seem to be making a hell of a lot of noise considering we were hoping to catch a burglar, wasn't he? You'd almost think he was making sure he was frightened off."

People in the beach houses rarely closed their curtains. The death of the bookseller hadn't changed that. The view was of the sea and apart from anyone walking past on the lonely strip of beach, there was no one capable of looking in. Not that it was of much concern if someone did. The inhabitants went about their lives contentedly without worrying too much about others.

At eleven o'clock, when Gordon finally left, Bettrys felt less afraid. His being there had calmed her earlier fears, his sensible attitude and his reminders that the accident was over, done with, and the events did not involve her anyway.

Now she felt relaxed and unafraid of figures wandering about in the darkness. There was something very reassuring about Gordon and she was beginning to imagine a closer relationship. If only she could forget Brett; a new life beckoned.

Her life was a tangle, but the threads were already coming loose. She had to face the fact that Brett had never really loved her, that the time for loyalty was long past and she was free to begin to love again. She must accept also that her stupid idea of finding Cheryl's father was a hopeless cause. Once she could deal with these, everything would settle into place and she could begin to enjoy life once more. Too much time had been wasted on impossible assignments.

She stood on her doorstep for a long time, enjoying the peaceful night. It wasn't completely dark, a thin moon was giving only scant light over the water, but the white tips of the waves seemed to pick up and intensify the glow. Silhouettes of trees and houses became quite distinct as her eyes adjusted to the translucent light. There was nothing to fear in the darkness, she told herself.

Around her were people she already considered friends. She refused to think about the death of the unknown man. It had been an accident. She wouldn't let it spoil her time here.

The night time had been so different in the city. There, although it was brightly lit, it hid imminent danger from muggings and burglaries. Everyone rushed about in an impatience of money-making and success-seeking it seemed. Whereas here, people seemed to accept what they had and asked for nothing more, exchanging acquisitiveness for relaxed contentment. With the exception of the Baxters of course. The thought made her smile. They needed their new ornaments and beach furniture and the modern gas barbeque and a freezer full of exotic food.

The sky still showed a hint of blue, a cavernous cupola filled with dark velvet that was innocent of any fear. But fear stalked the one who had witnessed the fall from the wall of the well. Someone harboured the guilt of that awful moment, and had ruined the tranquillity of the place for the community for ever.

She didn't like leaving Cheryl, even for a moment, but reassured by Gordon's words, she nevertheless locked the door and walked towards the Coopers' house. Most of the houses were dark, their occupants in bed and asleep. From the Coopers' house there was a hint of light, as if from another room and diffused via the hallway to the room facing the sea. She stood for a moment, feeling guilty and, a little afraid of being watched herself. She would have no excuse and would have to admit to the inquisitiveness if she were confronted by an angry Carys, or Jake.

Standing where she could see into the room, she gradually made out the furniture and the fireplace with its armchairs pulled to face the now dead fire. Then, with a tightening of her heart, she realised that one of the chairs was occupied.

She stood transfixed and waited until the figure unfolded

itself from the chair and stood up. He was tall. Taller than Jake and head and shoulders above Carys. She saw him reach for a tray on which there was a pot of tea and what looked like a plate of sandwiches. The exiguous light from another room suddenly went out and Bettrys turned to go back inside. Then a light in the room itself was turned on and she saw clearly, the figure of the man.

She trembled in disbelief, unable to accept what her eyes were telling her, half believing she was on the edge of insanity. The light was extinguished almost immediately but the image was before her eyes like a dully developed photograph. The man was Brett, the man she had once loved, and whom she had left almost two years before.

Bettrys had to get away. She dressed Cheryl early and set off with the push-chair almost before it was light, and walked into the village. Potter was on the rounds with Pete Howells, delivering the morning papers, so for once she didn't have his company. She strode out fast, needing to tire herself and try and forget the sight of Brett, sitting in the Coopers' sitting room. She must have dreamed it. How could Brett, who lived and worked in London, be here?

Wherever she went, in all the shops and at the bus stop as she waited to return, everyone spoke of the death of the bookseller at the bottom of the well. Most thought Diana Taylor was involved. None could offer any facts to convince others, but with much head shaking and pursed lips, each believed emphatically that it was she who had enticed the man to where he met his death.

It seemed to Bettrys that talk of the bookseller's death would never die down. Having seen Brett last night in the Coopers' house, her mind had left the gruesome subject, so she added nothing to the discussions and arguments. He must be lodging there but she was so afraid he was implicated that she couldn't tell anyone what she had seen, not even Gordon.

Perhaps he was a relation? That would explain a lot. Small communities put great store on family loyalties.

Carys's determination not to allow anyone to enter her kitchen; Jake's efforts to warn whoever they had hidden, to make good his escape, after she and Gordon had seen him enter the house . . . it seemed to add up.

But why would they protect him unless he was in serious trouble? And what was Brett doing *here*? She had to try and talk to him. But how? She couldn't walk up to Carys or Jake and say casually, Oh, by the way, can I have a word with your secret lodger! She had to confront him outside the house and the only way was to watch for him on one of his nightly strolls. But first, she had to discourage Gordon from calling, and that was going to be hard to do.

He had developed the habit of stopping on his way home from work to spend an hour playing with Cheryl and, as the evenings became lighter and warmer, walking with them for a pre-dinner stroll along the beach, or up through the fields belonging to the Taylors.

The evening after Bettrys had recognised Brett, she tried to think of a way of telling him not to call for a while, and found it impossible. Unbelievably, he offered the solution himself.

"Bettrys, I won't be seeing you for a while," he began as he lifted Cheryl onto the farm gate for a ride as he opened it. She stared at him in surprise. Those were the very words she had been planning to say to him. He misunderstood her surprised look. "No, it isn't that I want us to see less of each other."

"Then why – ?"

"I'm going away, to a place near Cardiff. There's an extension needed to the electricity supply in a factory making cables. I'm in charge of the installation. It won't take more than three weeks and I'll be home on at least one of the weekends."

"I'll miss you," she said. The words were lightly said but at once she realised that they were devastatingly true.

He went on to explain what he would be doing but she listened with only a small portion of her mind. She

142

would miss him. Instead of giving her the opportunity to watch for and, hopefully, talk with Brett, she didn't want him to go. She tried to imagine spending every evening in the house without Gordon's comforting presence and she stared at him as if seeing him for the first time.

She tried to push aside the thought that she was falling in love with him. No, it was simply that she had become used to not being alone. It was going to be difficult to face the evenings without Gordon's visits to break up the long, empty hours. She was glad he was going. It was what she wanted. There was a task to involve herself with. She was just used to having someone around. It was nothing more than that.

Brett was gone from her life and she was free. The man she saw in the Coopers' house couldn't have been him, she told herself. It had been her silly, fanciful imagination. Thinking about him so much had made her mind flip and a stranger, whom she had not seen at all clearly, was transformed into his double. Logically, it was more likely to have been the missing and delinquent Brynley.

Brett had left her because they were unsuited and even if they met again, neither of them would want to revive something that was well and truly dead.

The argument going on inside her ended. A surge of happiness flooded through her. She touched Gordon's arm and stretched up to kiss him. "Gordon, I don't want you to go. I really will miss you," she said.

Ignoring the row of farm cottages with their windows like eyes, and the certainty that Jessie Newbank would be watching, Gordon carefully put Cheryl down and folded her in his arms.

"I'm glad," he said huskily. "You're becoming very important to me."

As they walked back down to the road it was getting dark, and something happened to disturb her happiness once again. A man walked along the road, silhouetted against the pale sea, and although he was bent, and dressed in thick, untidy clothes including what looked like a heavy overcoat – for which there was no need – Bettrys knew, this time without any doubt, that it was Brett.

Gordon had a lift to the town with Emrys Taylor and besides Bettrys and Cheryl, Gwen and Maldwyn stood on the road side and waved to him until the Land Rover was out of sight.

"Come back and have a cup of tea," Gwen offered. "I've made some biscuits with some stale old butter."

"Biscuit," Cheryl echoed and offered her hands for Gwen and Maldwyn to hold.

"Don't feel lonely, mind," Gwen said, when Bettrys was leaving Smuggler's Cottage. "We're always here if you want company."

Bettrys thanked her. Her emotions were in turmoil. She would miss Gordon, but seeing Brett again had disturbed her brief tranquillity. Her thoughts were so confused, the need to speak to Brett so great that she didn't need company during the day, in fact she deliberately avoided it. Time to think, sort out how she felt about Gordon, and how the reappearance of Brett would alter it. She needed solitude for that.

It was at night when the need for Gordon's presence was greatest. It was the time when there was a silence that was almost palpable, closing in around her, almost suffocating her, making her struggle for breath, so she had to open the door and stand for a while on the threshold and take deep lungfuls of clean sea-tasting air. When, half dozing, she was tormented by inexplicable sounds, and eerie shadows brought her to the edge of panic. That was when she missed Gordon most. Perhaps it hadn't been the beginnings of love but the need for another human being at a time when fear had made her most vulnerable?

Or was it Brett, still tormenting her with memories of their brief and wonderful affair?

She spent the next few evenings sitting in the dark

room looking out of the window, hoping for a sight of Brett. Days passed and she began once again to doubt her memory. She must have been mistaken. If he knew she were here he would come to her. It must be her he had come here to find. And, in a small community like The Bend, how could he not know?

In despair, determined to solve the riddle, she went to see Carys Cooper. Jake was working, cutting an overgrown hedge with a small bill hook, his single arm giving powerful strokes and neatening the edge with the taming blade with apparent ease.

She called and was invited to enter the small cluttered room leading from the porch. Carys was sitting at the table, tacking the hem of a white wedding gown with regular, rhythmical movements. Light from the overhead bulb touched the pearly buttons and produced rainbows and fire.

Around the room, on hangers hooked on the picture rail, were several more dresses. Three bridesmaids dresses in blue and a full-skirted white dress obviously made for a small flower-girl.

"Carys, they're beautiful," Bettrys said.

"There's a fitting tomorrow so you won't mind if I carry on with this, will you?"

"I'm fascinated to watch you," Bettrys replied truthfully.

The dark eyes behind the thick spectacle lenses darted between her work and Bettrys, keeping an eye on the hem of the gown on which she was working, warned Cheryl not to touch. She waited to hear what her visitor had to say with a patience that was hard to contain.

"Do you have a guest staying at present?" Bettrys began tentatively.

"No, Jake and I are not bothering this summer. He manages to earn a few pounds doing odd jobs, gardening mostly. And I have as much sewing as I can manage. With visitors as well it would be too hectic.

Why? Aren't you happy in the chalet them Griffith's found for you?"

"Very happy. It isn't for us," she smiled nervously, tensing herself to ask the question. "I saw someone I once knew and thought he might be living here, as a lodger."

"There's no one here except Jake and me!" Carys's eyes were like black holes, her emphatic reply leaving it difficult for Bettrys to ask further questions.

"But I saw, Gordon and I saw someone, it looked like a man I once knew, up in London. His name was Brett."

"Brett?" Carys laughed and Bettrys thought there was relief in those dark eyes, a slackening of tension in the thin face. "Brett, you say? What a silly name. Sounds like some filum star! Filum stars have names like Brett. No, you won't find no filum stars round here." She chuckled and turned the material to complete the neat stitching. "Brett. As if anyone round here would call their son Brett."

Three days later, while Bettrys sat at the window in the dark, listening to some old records Gwen had sent for Cheryl, she saw him. Running out and forgetting for once to lock the door, she ran after him as he made his way up to the road. She reached out and touched the coat but he had heard her and he ran harder, long legs eating up the ground. As she rose to the level of the empty road there was no sign of him. He had obviously hidden in the bushes but she felt disinclined to spend hours searching. Instead, she said, "Brett? Brett? Come out and talk, please. It's Bettrys. You know me. You can't have forgotten, not in two years." She waited for what seemed an age but there wasn't even a rustling of grass to reveal his presence. Hurt, and a little angry, she returned to the house and the sleeping child.

Determined to wait until he returned, she sat at the window watching the night brighten with the almost full moon, and darken again. She woke stiff and disappointed.

She had to go into town that day, to deliver an

order of earrings, intricately designed brooches made with beads and some more expensive pieces made with citrine, aquamarine and lapis lazuli.

After packing up all she had to take, and writing a list of items she needed to buy, she went to see Gwen.

"Have you ever been to London?" she asked, hoping to illicit the information of others who had.

"Me? Never been further than Swansea," Gwen laughed. "Always too busy." She turned to Maldwyn who was reading a book on sailing. "You went once, on some outing or other to see a show and got drunk on the way home! Didn't you Dad?"

"Damned waste of time and money," Maldwyn grumbled, then went on to describe some of the memorable events of the day as if it had been yesterday. Intermittently grumbling, he made them see London through his eyes, as an exciting place and the one day he would never forget. He enjoyed it but would never admit there was any place as perfect as his own on Yr Tro.

"It's Gordon you want to ask about London, mind," he said as he bent his head once more to his book. "Lived up there he did, for a few months in – " he looked at Gwen and asked, "when was it, last year some time?"

"Longer than that," Gwen said. "There's forgetful you're getting, Dad. It was almost two years ago. There for about six months he was. He came home in the September he did, middle of the month. I remember he was home for his birthday on the fifteenth."

"Oh, nearly two years ago, was it?" the old man said. "He was damned glad to be back, I remember that, for sure. Looked far from his usual happy self. Yes, I remember that. Unhappy for weeks so we wondered if he was ill. Some girl I expect it was."

The words gave Bettrys a jolt. Her sister had been happy with her unknown lover, until she realised she was expecting a child, then her man friend whose name Eirlys refused to tell, had left her. It would have been at the beginning of September two years before. It must have been Gordon or he would have mentioned living in London to her, surely? Forcing her voice to sound calm, she said, "I have to go into Swansea tomorrow, to get some things I need for my jewellery-making."

"We'll have Cheryl, shall we? Better be here with us than traipsing around on endless buses." Bettrys didn't refuse. She needed time to consider this latest and most unwelcome piece of news.

Sitting on the bus, listening to all the lively chatter going on around her, she felt isolated and lonely. Gordon might be Cheryl's father. He was in London at the relevant time. He had returned home a couple of weeks after her sister announced the news of a pregnancy, distressed about a woman. The thought made her feel sick and she wished herself anywhere but on this bus slowly wandering around the villages on its way to the city of Swansea.

Brett had unbelievably re-entered her life but was determined not to meet her. If only he would talk she might be able to sort out how she really felt about him. Everything was a mess and she was tempted to abandon her search for Cheryl's father and go back to London. Find a flat, find a job, any job, temping would do. She had to do something that would keep her busy and free from thoughts about Brett and Gordon. She had been let down by both. That must mean she was unlovable.

What was she doing here anyway? What would she say if she did discover the man who had been her sister's lover through those summer months? All she could do would be to present him with the facts. He would probably deny any responsibility and she would go back to London with nothing changed.

She thought of the people who lived on The Bend, trying hard not to accept the possibility that the man she was seeking was Gordon. Surely he wasn't capable of leaving someone to face having a child all alone? If he were, then she was best putting as much distance as she could between them. Better face the harsh fact she was unlovable rather than become involved with a man who could do that. Determinedly, she turned her thoughts to others who lived in The Bend.

Several of the chalets had not yet been occupied so it was possible the man she wanted had not yet arrived. Of the ones she had so far met, there was no one who could possibly be the one she was looking for. Jake was hardly the type to have an affair with a young woman and she couldn't see her beautiful sister with a man as old as their father would have been anyway! Emrys Taylor didn't seem likely either. He had enough trouble with his wife!

Carys and Jake's son Brynley was a possibility so far as age, but he was far away. So even if he were the one, there was no chance of meeting him.

There was Jeremy, the handsome and wealthy owner of Costa Plenty, husband of Frances. She didn't think he would have been her sister's type. Besides, if she landed this in his lap she would be ruining two lives without any benefit to either her sister or the child.

Pete Howells, at twelve, was too young by several years! So, that left Gordon, a possibility she did not want to contemplate, even though Gwen had told her he had been in London during the relevant time.

She bought the items necessary for making her jewellery and wandered through the smart shops to spend a few idle hours before her bus left for the journey back. After completing her shopping, she still had a couple of hours before the bus returned so she went into the large and fascinating Swansea market, situated not very far from the site it had occupied far back in history. The attractive and varied stalls sold everything from books, cards, clothes, carpets, jewellery, kitchen ware; through Welsh wool and woollens, holiday gifts. Cockles, mussels, lava bread, and on to the ordinary foodstuffs of meat, fruit and vegetables, many grown locally, and displayed so temptingly. She

149

managed to take an order for some of her necklaces and earrings at one of the stalls, then, at the small cafe near the bus stop, she ordered tea and a scone.

She had just settled herself into a corner seat when a customer came in and she automatically looked up. Gordon looked startled, then smiled, and came over.

"Fancy seeing you here!" He leaned over and kissed her.

"What a surprise," she echoed with an edge of doubt. "Aren't you working today?"

"I am. Well, I should be, but I had the chance to come here to collect some parts we needed. Are you getting the three-thirty?"

"I was," she said with a smile, "but there's another two hours later!" Suspicion still filled her mind, but she was unable to resist spending a little time in his company. Perhaps she would discover something further about his time in London.

The beach was not far from the centre of the town and they crossed the sand-strewn road at the slip, where the red Mumbles train had once run, filled with cheerful passengers riding the six mile trip from The Terminus to Mumbles Pier. They walked among the early summer visitors, hand in hand. Gordon continued to bless his good fortune.

He bought them each a cone and they leaned against the sea wall that had been warmed by the sun, and talked.

"Your mother told me you were in London for a while," she said when their immediate news had been exhausted. "What part did you stay in?"

"All over," he said vaguely. "I had friends in Wimbledon, and Southall, and for a while, I lived near Victoria."

"Do you know Ealing?" she asked.

He frowned and then shook his head. "I don't think so. But I don't know the districts very well."

"Why didn't you tell me you'd been in London? You know I lived there."

"I don't know. It was almost two years ago, I hardly think of it now." He frowned and his expression was of honest surprise at the question.

She looked at him and tried to decide whether or not he was truthful or just good at lying. Then he smiled and said, "When you go back, I'll visit you and you can show me all there is to see."

"My sister was the expert. She was a guide to some of the famous buildings when she was a student." He asked her sister's name but Bettrys was evasive. She wanted to keep as much information about her sister to herself as she could.

"Your name, Bettrys. It's just occurred to me that it's Welsh for Beatrice. Were your parents Welsh?"

"Yes. Although they both moved from here when they were young. They were killed while they were on holiday more than ten years ago."

"Don't go back," he pleaded. "Stay here with me, where you belong. We'll go and fetch your sister if you like. You, your sister and Cheryl can make your life at Yr Tro, with Grandad, Mam, Pete and me."

"I can't – "

"'Can't' can change his mind easily. 'Won't' takes a bit longer!"

"My sister is dead," she said.

"What on earth happened? She must have been very young? Not another accident? You poor love, what you've gone through."

"She killed herself. She discovered she was pregnant and when her boyfriend left her, she – well, she drank you see. The drink plus the pregnancy and the birth of Cheryl, it was too much for her. Too much for *me* was her last thought. The thought that made her kill herself I believe. She overheard us discussing what a burden it was, and, she jumped under a train."

She was trembling. She hadn't spoken so coldly about it all before. She had been watching his face, trying to find

151

guilt there, wanting him to be innocent but dreading that he might admit to being Eirlys's lover.

"You've borne this alone, haven't you?"

"I've been trying to find the man, give Cheryl a name and at least the possibility of a family." She looked at him and as their eyes met, his deepened into a frown.

"You think I might be the man? All the questions about London, and Ealing? What do you think I am? You believe I'm capable of walking away from a girl when she's in trouble?"

"I'm sorry, I *don't* think you're that sort of person. It was only when I learnt yesterday that you were in London at the time. I thought you might not have known. I thought – Oh, Gordon, I don't know what I thought."

"You were upset? At the thought it might be me? Does that mean you care?" He kissed her and his lips soothed away unhappy memories. His arms holding her close to his beating heart felt so right. He must be why fate brought her on her fruitless chase. What did it matter if she failed to find Cheryl's father? There was plenty of love in the world for one fatherless child to share.

Time passed in a haze of happiness and they had to run to get the five-thirty bus, on which Bettrys sat oblivious of the chatter around her, no longer lonely or isolated, except by inner happiness and confidence for the future. Gordon might or might not be a part of her future, but Brett was the past.

Gordon was the here and now. Brett was forgotten, already a distant, unhappy memory. She faced a five mile walk from the village or an expensive taxi ride, but today she didn't care.

Stepping down from the taxi she was humming to herself. She chuckled like a child as she slipped and almost fell on the cement path from the road down to the beach. Glowing with happiness, her green-blue eyes sparkling, she pushed open her door and threw her packages down on the floor. Before going to collect Cheryl she would unpack her shopping. She looked towards the grate, half wondering if she would light a fire. There, sitting in the solitary armchair, was Brett.

CHAPTER NINE

Bettrys stared in disbelief as Brett rose from the chair. Her muttered, "Hello," seemed about the most stupid word she had ever said but she couldn't think of another. She just looked at him as if her eyes were playing tricks, her mind was creating a fantasy, her dreams finally confusing reality with wishful thinking.

Her body responded to him in an instant. She was filled with a deep sense of joy, and relief that he was back in her life. At that moment she didn't know how or even why, but the sight of him, standing there in her small room, was a promise of fulfilment. Freedom from loneliness. The emotions Gordon had brought were immediately forgotten.

Brett was as attractive as she had remembered: no fantasy was required to embellish his slim figure and aristocratic stance. The months of separation were forgotten in a moment, together with all her pretence. She still loved him as much as the first time they had met. The dark hair, the sharp, slightly flared nose and the lean, chiselled chin and, those devastatingly beautiful eyes.

"What are you doing here, Bettrys?" His voice, harsh and angry startled her out of the feeling of joy and relief and she gave a cry.

"Brett! It's been so long," she said finally. She wanted to run to him and feel his arms holding her, washing away the long absence, but his face was cold, and the low, angry voice said,

"Why have you come looking for me? Don't try and

pretend that child is mine. That won't work. You and I were never that committed."

"Committed?" She frowned at the word.

"I want to know why you're here."

"I came – " she was about to tell him about Eirlys and Cheryl but something, the look on his face perhaps, stopped her. "I'm having a holiday, that's all. But Brett, what are you doing here? Why should you think I followed you? I had no idea this place existed until a few weeks ago."

"How very strange." Sarcasm made his lips curl and the handsome face lost much of its charm. Instead of looking at the man she had loved for so long she was looking at a stranger. Even his voice was different, with a hint of lilting Welshness.

The sudden kaleidoscope of emotions made her weak. She fumbled behind her for a chair and sank gratefully into it.

"I have to go and fetch Cheryl," she whispered. "Will you wait here? I won't be a moment." Her legs shook as she stood, then he stepped across the room and roughly pushed her down again.

"Tell me why you're here!"

"Brett! Why are you so angry? I didn't know I'd find you here. It was just a whim that brought me to this place. Something my sister said once."

"So, you did come to find me?"

Confused, she stood once again and made for the door. This time he didn't stop her, but instead, called, "Don't tell a soul I'm here. D'you understand?"

"Why should I?" She paused at the door and looked back at him, scowling, filling the room with his anger. "On the other hand, why shouldn't I? No one here would worry about my wanting us to meet. We parted a long time ago, when you were off to Greece, remember?"

"I'm – I'm in a bit of trouble. Just don't mention that you know me, all right?"

"I've never heard of anyone called Brett," she said, and she hurried out of the house before he saw that tears were not far away.

Gwen saw at once that something was wrong, but Bettrys made the excuse of bus-sickness and went straight home. She pushed open the unlocked door and found the room empty. There was only the faint scent of his aftershave to convince her it was not part of another dream.

While Gordon was working in Cardiff, Bettrys had been concentrating on finding work. The more she saw of the area the more she wanted to make it her home. Teaching jobs were non-existent, and she thought that, while she waited for something better, work in one of the village shops would be interesting. She saw two advertisements in the post-office window and applied by letter. One was already taken, and the other, at the gift shop where she sold some of her jewellery, asked her to call for an interview. As she was already known to them it was, she hoped, only a formality.

She was less happy about staying on in Yr Tro since the shock of seeing Brett. Although, since that surprising and disturbing visit, she hadn't seen him again. Every time she entered the house she half expected him to be waiting for her. In the evenings, when Gwen, or Maldwyn or on occasions, Diana Taylor, called it was always Brett she expected to see.

Early one morning a knock at the door revealed Carys Cooper. The day was gloomy, it having rained most of the night, and Bettrys had not yet dressed. She sat with Cheryl, coaxing the little girl to eat breakfast. She invited Carys in, apologising for the untidy room, then noticed that the woman carried a suitcase.

"Not leaving, are you?" Bettrys laughed when Carys carried the case inside and put it on the table. "Don't tell me you are fed up with living on Yr Tro?"

"I had a bit of a sort out, found some oddments of material and I've made these for Cheryl." Opening the case, Carys brought out dresses, and slips, and jackets and a beautiful winter coat, trimmed and lined with artificial fur. "And don't offer to pay me, they are presents and you're welcome. If you like them," she added hesitantly.

"Carys! Like them! They are beautiful. Oh, what can I say? Thank you. You must let me pay you, they're worth pounds!"

"Well, asking you to leave so sudden like we did, I felt a bit guilty about that. I must have made you feel very unwelcome. It was just a family matter, nothing to do with you at all."

"I wasn't offended. Giving us a room even for a couple of days was a favour. I knew it wasn't really convenient. Thank you so much for these lovely clothes. We'll have to go out somewhere all dressed up, won't we, Cheryl?"

"Dressed up," Cheryl repeated.

Laughing, Bettrys put the kettle on to boil and invited Carys to stay for coffee. The woman seemed ill at ease and when they sat nursing their drinks, Bettrys asked, "There's nothing wrong, is there? I mean, I don't want to pry, truly I don't, but if I can help – ?"

"You've met my son."

"Have I?" Bettrys frowned. "Sorry, I don't remember. Gordon has introduced a few of his ex-schoolfriends from time to time. But I don't remember your son. I thought he was working in London."

"You don't have to pretend with me. He told me he'd been to see you."

"Brett." She whispered the word.

"Brynley, but most call him Bryn."

Again Bettrys frowned. "Bryn?"

"He said he was waiting for you when you got back from Swansea the other day. I just wanted to warn you that he really is in trouble. Dangerous trouble. If you care for him, and he said that you and he were once more than good friends . . . " The dark, shrewd eyes behind the thick glasses stared at her over the beaker she held to her lips. "Well then, if you and he were – friends, you must help for to – to keep him safe."

"I don't understand." Bettrys spoke slowly, puzzled by the two names.

"You don't have to. Just keep quiet about having seen him. He hasn't been home for months. That's all we need for to say."

It was still raining, that steady, almost silent, curtain that darkens the air and brings evening in the middle of the day. Lifting the collar of her old macintosh, Carys stepped out into the sombre day and was quickly swallowed up in the gloom and the dripping bushes that surrounded the houses and chalets.

After Carys Cooper had gone, Bettrys stared at the beautifully made clothes. It was all so confusing that she wanted to bundle everything she owned into the suitcase standing open on the table, catch the next bus out and never look back. It seemed the only thing to do.

Later that day she did catch the bus, deciding it was too wet to walk, having no proper protection for Cheryl. She took the old push-chair, macs to cover them, and took the midday bus to the village. As the rain continued to fall steadily, making the few shoppers scuttle from one doorway to another, she held Cheryl under the protection of her own waterproof and stood outside the gift shop. Her intention was to cancel the interview for the job of assistant, running the small gift shop part time with the owner. She had been clear in her mind when she left the house. Now she hesitated.

There was something wrong with this place. The happiness of the first few weeks had been shattered. Gwen and Maldwyn were the same friendly people, but Yr Tro was no longer sweet and clean and innocent.

Gordon could conceivably be Eirlys's lover and the father of Cheryl. Brett, bursting back into her life and

158

bringing brief hope, frightened her. His handsome looks hid something unpleasant. He was not Brett Cavendish but a man called Brynley Cooper and he was part of the unease that filled the Cooper's house. Diana Taylor exuded unhappiness and was suspected of being responsible for a man being killed: a death that might not have been an accident. Such a small community, so many secrets.

All these thoughts spun wildly in her head as she stood at the doorway of the gift shop in the pouring rain on the dark glowering afternoon, cuddling Cheryl. Why was she even hesitating? She must leave, and before Gordon returned from his three weeks in Cardiff. Seeing him again, allowing her attraction for him to confuse her even further, made no sense at all. She had to get away. Forgetting Gordon and Brett and all the rest, that was the sensible thing to do.

But she wasn't in the frame of mind to be sensible. Some devil inside made her want to stay and see what developed. Whatever was behind it all, it was not connected with her. She and Cheryl were in no danger. They were outsiders, onlookers in whatever was happening at Yr Tro. Her curiosity refused to give way and she stepped inside the shop and accepted the job she was offered.

She saw the Land Rover belonging to the Taylors passing as she came out of the shop. Diana Taylor was driving, just visible through the windows that streamed with rain in the increasing downpour. She wished briefly that the woman had seen her and promised her a lift home later.

There was a small cafe which served snacks and hot drinks not far from the church and walking as quickly as she could, she went there, unfolded herself and Cheryl from their protective clothing and ordered tea and cakes. Talking to Cheryl, smiling at other customers, some of whom admired the child, others complaining in an automatic way about the weather, her thoughts were so busy that suddenly she jumped up in alarm, realising they had missed the bus.

There was either a two-hour wait for the last bus, which came from town and headed back to the depot, or a walk through the now furiously pelting rain. Two hours after the few shops had closed was not a cheering prospect. But there was no choice, she would have to wait. She couldn't walk home in this.

A charity shop was still open, and she went there to shelter while she decided where they could spend two hours. On a stand near the door she saw a plastic hood and cover that might, with a bit of encouragement, fit the push-chair. With the assistant's help she fixed it so Cheryl was safe from any further soaking, bought a couple of extra blankets to make her comfortable and warm, and set off to walk.

It was five miles. After two of them she felt that he had made a mistake. Every inch of her was wet. Her feet sloshed about in her boots, making them ache with the effort of trying to keep them still, the rain approached her on a wind she had not been aware of, bringing the rain slashing into her face.

To add to her dismay, a wheel of the push-chair came loose and she had to tilt it as she walked to prevent the wheel from pulling them off course. Every muscle in her body ached. If she were to stay here she would definitely need a car!

Occasionally a car would pass and each time she hoped that it might be someone she knew, but they only brought yet more water spraying over her. The push-chair was one in which the child faced her and Cheryl luckily, seemed cosily content.

Bettrys's long hair channelled water past her collar, soaking her cotton top. She soon felt chilled and clammy around her neck and shoulders. This had not been a good idea. Better she had phoned the gift shop instead of going in on such a dreadful day. But there had been an air of unease that had forced her to get away from The Bend for a while.

Lost in the silence, broken only by the hiss of the rain, the sound of an engine made her groan, expecting another muddy shower and she stopped as if to lessen the effect. A Land Rover overtook her and she recognised the number plate. It was Diana. How unkind that she didn't stop. The farm vehicle would hardly suffer from a couple of wet passengers, and she must have recognised them.

To Bettrys's relief she saw that the car was indicating and slowing down a short distance ahead. The heavy vehicle came to a slow, cautious stop, and Bettrys hurried forward, thanks already expressed as Diana opened the driving door, stepped out, crouched against the rain, and waited for Bettrys to reach her.

"Get in the front, I'll throw the push-chair in the back," she said briskly. "Hurry up! I don't want to end up as wet as you in return for the favour of stopping!"

Bettrys strapped herself into the passenger seat, with Cheryl beside her. She thought about the uncharacteristic behaviour of Diana getting out and putting the push-chair in the back, rather than waiting for Bettrys herself to do it, but she didn't comment. She was too relieved to be out of the foul weather and being taken swiftly home.

"What on earth have you been doing out with that child in this weather?" Diana demanded in her forthright manner.

"I had an interview, for a job."

"She should have been left with Gwen Howells!" she said sharply. She glanced in her mirror, adjusted it so she could see into the back of the vehicle. Bettrys thought at first she was checking on the safety of the push-chair, then realisation came. The reason Diana braved the pouring rain to help her with the push-chair, and she smiled.

"You're staying then?" Diana said. "What can you possibly find around here to keep you?"

"I don't know. Perhaps the novelty of such a small, quiet community after the anonymous bustle of London." She turned her head as she spoke as if addressing the pile of sacks in the back. "There's such an open honesty about the people of Yr Tro, wouldn't you say? Everyone exactly what they seem?" She glanced at Diana, who tightened her grip on the wheel but didn't reply. "Perhaps," Bettrys went on, "if this is a taster," she tapped the window referring to the relentless downpour. "Perhaps I'll change my mind after a winter here," she smiled widely, aware of Diana's unease. Just then they went over a dip in the road and the push-chair moved. Bettrys stretched to look around and make sure it was safe.

Diana's urgent, "Leave it! It can't do any harm!" was revealing. The anxious expression on her face, and the way she glanced in her mirror as if to look behind them, convinced Bettrys she was right; someone was hiding under the sacks. It had to be something important to explain Diana getting out and facing the rain to put the push-chair away.

For the rest of the journey they discussed Bettrys's new job and her hope that one day she would either be able to return to teaching or start her own nursery school. Diana tried to show interest but she was increasingly tight-lipped, nervous, and Bettrys was amused by the woman's anxiety. This gave a new meaning to the expression "playing gooseberry"!

So she was having an affair with Brett, or Bryn. The realisation that she didn't particularly care was heady excitement. She no longer cared! He was a cheat and a liar. Diana was welcome to him. She felt a bubble of excitement inside that threatened to explode. She wanted to sing. Laugh. Defy the rainstorm and shout her happiness aloud.

Instead she said, "Oh, I wish Gordon were home. I feel like celebrating." Diana thought she meant the job, but she was thinking of the release from undeserving love.

At the top of the path leading down to the houses on the beach, Diana again jumped out to take the push-chair out of the back of the car, even though Bettrys protested there was no need. Bettrys clutched Cheryl, got as close as she could to the tail-board and called, "Bye, Diana and thanks. Bye, Bryn, I hope you haven't been too uncomfortable!" For once in her life Diana was left speechless.

She had hardly removed Cheryl's outdoor clothes and slipped on her dressing gown when the unmistakable banging on the door heralded the arrival of Diana.

"Come in, the door isn't locked," Bettrys called, reaching for matches to light the fire. She smiled a greeting then watched as the flames licked higher and higher through the criss-cross lengths of wood and began to reach hungrily for the coal.

"We have to talk," Diana said. "He – you know who I mean, is in danger."

"Put the kettle on, will you?" Bettrys felt that for once she was in command of a conversation with Diana Taylor. She smiled as Diana did as she was bidden, then handed her a jar of drinking chocolate. "It will help warm us all up," she explained.

When Cheryl was comfortable and settled at the table with some biscuits, Diana said, "Someone is trying to kill Bryn."

"The same man who pushed the bookseller down the well?"

Diana started as if she had been struck. "No – I – yes. Oh how do I know!" she snapped angrily. Then more calmly, "Bettrys, I'm afraid for him."

The amusement of the last hour faded and Bettrys asked, "Do the police know?"

"Well, that's the trouble. The police are looking for him regarding some other matter, so we can't go to them. That's why we're being so careful not to reveal his presence."

"Hiding in the Cooper's house, isn't he? And you think the police don't know? Carys Cooper would give the game away the moment they asked her. She isn't exactly

163

poker-faced, is she? If I guessed there was something odd about her behaviour then the police most certainly would!"

"He moves around. I help. At first it was so he wouldn't face untrue charges, and a possible prison sentence. Now, well, I think someone in my past is jealous of any friends I make and is likely to attack them."

"Sorry, but I find this hard to believe. And even harder to swallow is your – and his – refusal to go to the police. What's a couple of months in prison compared to a threat of being attacked and possibly murdered? It was murder, wasn't it? The man in the well shaft? Although the police haven't said, they think it was murder, don't they?"

"That one was an accident."

"Sure of that, are you?"

"I'm not sure of anything. I wish I knew who it was. I can't think," Diana sank deeper in her chair, suddenly less confident, more approachable.

"You said 'that one'. Have there been that many?" Bettrys asked.

"Bryn thought you might be looking for him, helping the police. He thought he was going out of his mind when he saw you wandering into his mother's house, when he had last seen you two years ago in London. Why are you here? Why are you looking for him? He swears he didn't tell you about this place, and it's too much of a coincidence for you to have casually chosen this out-of-the-way spot to have an extended holiday."

Bettrys was longer than usual replying. She had to be careful. Some instinct prevented her from trusting Diana and Bryn. Bryn, or Brett as she had believed him to be, had proved that dishonesty came as naturally to him as swimming did to a fish.

"You knew him in London. He told me about that," Diana went on, "but you must have taken a mild friendliness for something more. You did follow him, didn't you? Did you think he would fall into your arms and reward

164

your diligence? Well, he won't. He's mine. As soon as we get free of this police matter he and I will be leaving, starting a new life, probably in Spain, far away from this damp, cold place. Ask him. He'll tell you."

"There is the small matter of Emrys, your husband. Or is he going with you? A *ménage à trois?* What a fascinating prospect!"

"I met Bryn soon after I married Emrys but I already knew I'd made a mistake."

"Then why was he in London and you down here?"

"Bryn's father found out and thought his son shouldn't 'mess with married women' as he put it. He tried to stop it and there was an accident and – "

Suddenly, unexpectedly, Bettrys made the connection.

"And Jake pretended the accident had happened on Maldwyn's boat and made the man penniless? I expect that was Bryn's idea too, he does have an exceptional capacity for fraud, doesn't he!"

"It's that *well.* I'm beginning to believe it's evil."

"Oh, come on," Bettrys said quietly. "You must be depressed if you're starting to blame inanimate objects for human frailty!"

"He really does love me."

"Yet there are others?"

"I suppose I lack faith that things will eventually turn out for us. Bryn doesn't know about the others. He doesn't know that Des – the bookseller, was coming to see me."

"What a complicated life you lead."

"I've always lacked love. I think that's what I've been searching for."

"Oh, and in which book on psychiatry for the beginner did you find that?" Bettrys was being deliberately hard. If an ex-lover were really on the rampage, then Diana shouldn't move from her husband's side.

"You think I'm a fool, don't you?"

"I think you are as great a liar as Bryn, or Brett as he called himself when he and I were together."

165

"What? How dare you!"

"Diana, I don't know what game you and he are playing, but if he were in danger of even a rap over the knuckles from his mother he would be unable to keep quiet. What's the real story?"

Diana stood up, a blustering anger on her face, but she didn't say a word, she just left, slamming the door behind her.

It was the last week of Gordon's stay in Cardiff and on Friday evening he would be home. As she began to prepare Cheryl for bed, she decided that on Friday evening she would tell him everything.

She prepared a meal for them and bought a bottle of his favourite wine. There was no fridge but the water in the stream was almost as good and she placed it under the shallow fall, where the water dropped before wandering past her chalet.

A chicken, bought from the Taylors, was roasting in the oven, potatoes and parsnips browning around it, and on the fire, the water waited for the vegetables she had chopped in readiness.

Cheryl was in bed by seven o'clock and every moment that passed after that, Bettrys expected a knock at the door to announce his arrival. At eight he still hadn't arrived and she went to stand at the doorway to listen for him.

She shivered in the chilly evening air, and had a feeling of déjà vu as she stretched out to catch a glimpse of him walking along the beach towards her. Just like she had once waited for Brett, in London. Perhaps, like Brett, he wasn't coming back.

It was as she stood there listening with increasing dismay that she became aware that the water in the stream had stopped flowing. Someone was again using the well as access to the Taylor's farm. Her heart increased its beat as the sound of someone scrambling through the bushes reached her ears and instinctively she darted inside and closed the door. Peering through the crack she saw a figure, dressed in heavy oilskins passing close to the door. His face was deep inside a sort of parker hood and she couldn't even see if the person was male or female. The bulky clothes gave no clue to the build, only the height was undisguised. He was almost six feet tall and she had the uncomfortable impression that it was Gordon. It was only later that she realised that the man had been carrying her bottle of wine!

She was trembling as she took the chicken out of the oven. She put the over-cooked meal on the table and stared at it with dismay. She checked several times that the door was locked and decided that she was becoming neurotic and paranoid. What had made her think the man was Gordon? The facts were that he was of similar height and was wearing clothes like those Gordon wore for his photography expeditions. That wasn't enough to convince a normal person, she told herself. This place was beginning to get to her so she saw villains at every turn. Blaming Diana's visit, to make herself feel better, she undressed, washed and went to bed.

At eleven-thirty, she had just put aside her book and snapped off the light when there was a cautious knock at the dor. At once, all her fears returned. She said softly, "Who is it?"

"It's me, Gordon." The voice was low, little more than a hiss. "I'm sorry, darling, I missed the bus and had to walk. I'm longing to see you."

With a sob of relief she unlocked the door and Bryn burst in.

"Bettrys, you've got to hide me, there's been another death at the bottom of the well."

CHAPTER TEN

Bryn was wet and streaked with mud from his shoulders to his shoes. Bettrys was unable to speak; the shock of seeing him after his pretending to be Gordon made her dumb.

"Can I take off these wet things? I'll tell you what happened, but please, get me a hot drink and a change of clothes."

"A change of clothes? Where would I get men's clothes from at this time of night? Why don't you go home, it's only a couple of paces. Why come here and why trick me by saying you were Gordon. Where is Gordon? Is he in trouble?"

"I saw that the water had stopped and I went along the tunnel to see if Diana was – "

"Entertaining a friend?" Bettrys finished grimly.

"I thought – well, I know she isn't exactly conscience-driven and – there was a huddled figure at the bottom of the shaft. A torch shone on the floor, flickering, as if the man had dropped it. I – I doubled back and fell a few times in my haste."

"Why here? And why didn't you get help if someone is injured? Why didn't you go home?" Bettrys insisted in frustrated anger. "You say a man's lying at the foot of the shaft and you haven't sent for help? Why for heaven's sake?"

"Damn it all! Why d'you ask so many questions?" He took off his jacket and threw it on the floor and followed it with his trousers. He wasn't wearing a tie but he loosened the collar of his shirt and stood there with a towel taken from the fire guard, rubbing his dark, curly hair. There was a wildness about him that, in the past, Bettrys would have found irresistible but now, she only saw an unreliable, weak and cowardly man, trying to take advantage of a previous affair that had ended without even a proper goodbye.

"D'you know your questions used to drive me mad when you and I went out together? Always questions! Just get these clothes spread out to dry and stop waiting for detailed explanations. First things first for heaven's sake!"

"No." She had reverted to her normal quiet and slow tone. "No, I haven't any obligation to help you and if the police are interested in your whereabouts you'd better leave at once because if you don't go now, this minute, Brett/Brynley, or whatever you're calling yourself this week, I will go to the Howells and call the police myself."

"You wouldn't!"

"Try me." She picked up his trousers and threw them at him. Then she went into the bedroom and picked up the sleeping child and began to walk towards the door. She couldn't leave Cheryl alone here with this man. Her heart leapt at the thought of what might happen. The little girl might wake and be frightened by her absence, at the very least.

Bryn hesitated, standing, leaning slightly, as if unable to make up his mind whether or not to stop her by force. Then there was a knock at the door loud enough to sound like Diana.

"If that's your Diana you'd better answer it, then you can both leave together." She stood calmly waiting.

"Come in," she called when he didn't move. "It isn't locked."

The door was pushed open and Gordon stepped inside, a welcoming smile already fading as he looked at her, then at the half-dressed Bryn.

"What's this?" he said coldly. "Am I interrupting something?"

"He came for a change of clothes, or so he said. He's just leaving." Bettrys went and stood beside Gordon, a tacit reminder that she was with him and not the interloper. Gordon continued to stare at Bryn.

"Oh, I'd better introduce you two," she said sarcastically. "This is Brett, someone I once knew in London. This is also Brynley Cooper, Diana Taylor's brave lover. Bryn, or whoever he is, is also the instigator of the scheme to cheat your grandfather out of his boat by claiming negligence when Jake fell, not on the boat but down the well shaft!"

"What rubbish." Bryn hopped about on one leg in his haste to re-dress himself. "Talk about imagination. A woman scorned and all that, eh Gordon?"

The door was ajar, Gordon not having recovered from his surprise enough to close it. A further knock was followed by the entry of a policeman.

"Excuse me Miss Hopkyn, but I wonder if you can help us?"

Gordon turned to face the constable, Bryn curled up facing the fire and Bettrys walked away and replaced the still-sleeping child in her bed.

"Now," she said as she re-entered the room. "How can we help?"

"I wonder if you noticed that the water in the stream has stopped?"

"I did notice, about nine o'clock it would have been."

"Has it stopped before, I mean since the death of Mr Des Newton. The bookseller," he added as the name made Bettrys frown.

"I think so, but I can't say when or how often. I might not have noticed. Why?" She couldn't help glancing towards Bryn as she asked the question.

"No reason. I shut it off myself and I just wanted to know if it had been noticed."

"Oh, well I hope I helped you."

"Yes, thank you, Miss Hopkyn. I won't disturb you further. I wouldn't have bothered so late, only seeing the light and hearing voices like – " He left without appearing to notice either Gordon or Bryn, but Bettrys suspected that his visit was not as innocent as it seemed.

"You'd better tell Gordon what you told me," Bettrys said when Bryn was fully dressed again in his wet clothes.

"Nothing to tell," he muttered. "I thought I saw a body at the bottom of the well shaft but it must have been that policeman, that's all."

"And you came to involve Bettrys in your game of hide and seek with the law. Very considerate!"

"I thought it was another body, Gordon. Damn me, I didn't half move fast back down that tunnel!" Bryn smiled, trying to make Gordon laugh at the vision, but Gordon just stared coldly.

"So not only did you fail to help a possibly injured man, you brought the danger here, to Bettrys. Very noble!"

"You don't understand."

"I understand that you're a coward and a cheat. You always were, even at school, but I never dreamed you'd cheat my grandfather out of everything he had. You and that father of yours."

Bettrys could see from Gordon's face that a fight was imminent and she opened the door wide and asked Bryn to leave.

"You two can settle your grievances somewhere other than my living room, with Cheryl sleeping close by," she said and her quiet tone and the mention of the child calmed Gordon sufficiently for him to allow Bryn to leave.

"Gordon, I planned a better welcome than this." Bettrys pointed to the ruined meal, and he took her in his arms. For a time, Bryn and his troubles were forgotten.

Much later, with their arms around each other, watching as the flames of the fire died down and disappeared, Gordon asked, "What's been happening?"

"I cooked a meal, then, when you didn't come, I settled into bed. Bryn knocked at the door, pretended to be you so I would let him in, and – "

"I mean before all this. How do you know Bryn? Why did you call him Brett? I thought Brett was a previous love?"

She told him the whole story then. About the brief affair with the man she then knew as Brett Cavendish and their breakup when her sister was ill. She told of her sister's drinking and her difficult pregnancy. She talked about the birth of Cheryl and the death of Eirlys, but being very careful not to mention her sister's name. She also explained about the young policeman who had loved her sister but who had been pushed aside for some mysterious lover. And of her own arrival at Yr Tro in the hope of finding him.

"Was it you, Gordon?" she asked quietly. "You were in London that summer and I traced you through the few clues my sister left me, to here, The Bend." Again she was careful not to mention her sister's name. "There are so few people here," she went on. "And none of the right age who were in London at that time. It must be you."

She looked at him, anguish burning inside her for the end of her search and the failing hope that Gordon was not the one to have callously left her sister ill and in difficulties.

"People come and go here. It's a holiday place and an area where people come and stay briefly between other, more permanent homes. A shifting population, hundreds of people could give this as an address and only days later have moved on.

"But you were in London then?" she insisted quietly.

"Yes. And I knew a few girls, but there wasn't anyone special, certainly no one who lasted more than a couple of weeks. Believe me, Bettrys, I wouldn't have left someone I cared about like that. How can you think it of me? And I certainly didn't hide from anyone the fact that I lived here. I'm rather proud of the place and love telling people about it. I'm not secretive, and I'm not hiding any guilty secrets."

"Secrets abound in this place," Bettrys said sadly.

"But not between you and me."

"Not any more."

It was very late and Gordon stood, preparing to leave. Then they heard the sound of voices, calling, shouting. Opening the door they saw powerful torches throwing their beams up into the night sky and bringing slashes of colour to the surrounding bushes.

"Now what's going on!" Gordon said.

"Well you might ask!" An angry voice shouted close by and they saw Carys Cooper and Jake, coats thrown carelessly around their shoulders and carrying storm lanterns. "Gone again he has and it's your fault, coming here nosying around and getting the police onto him. He's innocent. And they're trying to blame him for all sorts. Now you'll get him arrested and he'll never get out of their clutches."

"You'd better come in," Bettrys said, stepping aside for the sobbing woman to enter.

"Why did you give him away? He told me you loved him once. Funny sort of loyalty this is!"

"The police called and saw him here. It was nothing to do with Bettrys," Gordon said. "Now, tell us what's happening."

"He walked into the porch and a policeman was waiting for him. Come from your house he had and was waiting for him. He got away somehow but they'll soon get him. There's nowhere to hide him now they know he's here."

"If he's innocent then he'll soon convince them," Bettrys soothed dishonestly.

"What d'you mean, *if?*" Carys Cooper's mouth all but disappeared in an angry grimace.

*   *   *

He washed his hands energetically as if wiping away the

173

deed. His eyes were tranquil although his hands moved so furiously. He looked a happy and contented man. He knew what he was doing was right. When Colin Williams had evaded him and escaped with his life he had wondered for a while if he had been mistaken, but when Des Newton fell down that well without his assistance he had known, deep in the very spirit, that it had been a sign for him to continue.

She was the wicked one, Diana, but he must let her live, make her suffer, knowing she was the cause of the men losing their lives. That was her punishment. He might have to kill the girl, mind, he thought dispassionately. If Bettrys got too close to the truth then, to save himself, he might have to make her one of the victims. He didn't want to. She was a lovely girl and the baby shouldn't be an innocent sufferer. But, he shook his head sadly, he had to complete his given task and if she had to die, then there was nothing he could do about it.

Bryn wasn't caught, and although the police were in the area for several days, he wasn't seen. The Coopers' house was searched regularly as were the other houses on The Bend, even the empty ones. It was Gwen and Maldwyn who answered the questions about the occasional occupants of "Costa Plenty".

"Costa Plenty, that's the Baxters. Nice enough young couple. They haven't been so often this year, mind. Business keeping them busy so they tell me." Gwen explained. "But I reckon it's all these murders and accidents have put them off. It's hardly the place to come to have fun, now is it?"

"They let everyone know when they're around! Parties and fireworks and bonfires, just like a gang of kids," Maldwyn said disparagingly. "Deprived when they were small, I reckon. Making up for all the things they weren't allowed to do then, that's their excuse if you can believe it! Daft, the lot of them."

Three days later, as evening began stealing the colour from the day, Gwen was sitting with a sleeping Cheryl while Bettrys sat on the cliffs and sketched the sea, the few boats lying at anchor and admiring the last of the light. A moon was already in the sky, bright as a balloon in the darkening evening. It was something Bettrys had often wanted to capture and the weather seemed perfect.

She was settled comfortably in a shallow depression on the cliffs above Ffynon Sands with only a sketch-pad and a selection of pencils. She would add colour later, memory aided by the few words added to describe shades and tones.

Gordon was at work, an evening job, in which the factory had to be shut down. So she was surprised to see his boat. The light was fading fast but she was almost certain it was his, even though the evening was distorting both the colour and the shape. She was about to stand up and wave but hesitated. If it was Gordon, he would know where she would be and he would wave or call. The figure in the boat did neither.

Her heart increased its beat as she realised that the man guiding the boat puttering into the quiet bay was not Gordon. The indistinct figure, although dwarfed by the distance and the angle of her sight, nevertheless seemed too heavily built and ungainly for Gordon. But who could it be?

She watched as the man scanned the area with binoculars, sweeping back and forwards along the beach and the cliffs. She pressed lower into the soft grass, as the glasses spun towards where she lay, afraid that even her small shape would be visible to the man's thorough and cautious examination. Then, when he seemed satisfied, she watched with horror as he lifted a long limp package over the side of the small boat. The small craft tilted a few times, corrected itself but finally, as the package was at last manoeuvred into the shallow water at the edge of the waves, the boat over-balanced and turned turtle. In

175

the still silent air she heard a curse, then the man picked himself up.

The light was fading fast now and she could hardly make out what he was doing. It seemed as if he were unrolling the long package, and the covering, whatever it was, was tucked under his arm. He walked up the beach and disappeared below the level of her view.

The tide had just turned and there was that restless, unsettled movement as the mysterious, magnetic pull of the waters changed from flow to ebb. The boat wallowed ungainfully as the small choppy wavelets disturbed it, but her eyes hardly left the long package which lay still. She had the frightening feeling that it was another body, deposited on Ffynon Sands in the same way as before, and again, while Gordon was absent . . .

Shadow around her, once benign, now appeared to threaten, the shape of low bushes seemed to loom towards her, intent on forcing her to stay. Telling herself she was a fool to allow imagination to control her, she hastily packed her few belongings. She walked, ran, slithered and fell down the steep path and along the beach to where Maldwyn sat in the early darkness with two of his friends, on the seat outside Smuggler's Cottage. She was afraid she would be implicating Gordon, and before he had been given an opportunity to explain where he had been. But how could she not tell? The body – if it were a body – might still be alive!

When they had listened to Bettrys's breathless account of the scene on Ffynon Sands, they telephoned the coastguard. An hour later, they were told that the body of a man had been found, apparently drowned. If Bettrys had not seen the body dumped from Gordon's boat, it would have been presumed to have been a tragic accident.

Jake was taken to identify his son and came out crying with relief that it was not Bryn, but Leyton Newbank, the son of Ray and Jessie, who worked for the Taylors and lived on the track leading to the farmhouse.

Later that day the police found the mud-splattered clothes of Bryn abandoned in the tunnel leading to the well. Gordon Howells and Bettrys were questioned about the last time they had seen Brynley, but were allowed to go home.

"It's strange how everything seems to involve the Taylors' farm and that well, isn't it?" Bettrys said, as she and Gordon walked back down the path from the road to the beach. "Could Leyton be another of Diana's men-friends?"

"If he was then this puts Bryn in danger. It seems that someone is trying to wipe them all out!"

"Don't say that." She shivered, the shock of what she had seen still fresh in her mind. "A lover's revenge, that's what Diana had suspected. But really Gordon, that's too fantastic for a place like this."

"No place is immune from murder. Some of the most beautiful places have a grisly past."

"Change the subject, or I'll be having nightmares!"

"Well, think about it, love. That second-hand bookseller, Des Newton, for a start. He and Diana had been meeting regularly, hadn't they? And there was Colin Williams who came here often without his wife. He was attacked and almost thrown over the cliff. He was sensible, mind. He hasn't been back since! But if he had, and if the murderer had succeeded, then it wouldn't seem so fantastic, would it?"

"The police weren't told about that, were they?"

"No, the man wanted to avoid his wife finding out. I don't think he'll be straying for a while."

"D'you think we should tell them?"

"If I'm right and there have been two murders and an attempt at another, it's a very different picture from one accident and one unexplained death. Hearing about the near accident might make them revise their thinking and catch him before another man is killed."

"You don't think – oh, Gordon, I'm afraid."

177

"You've no need to be. Nor have I, if I'm correct in my guesswork. Thank goodness I didn't succumb to her charms!"

"What if the man takes revenge on me for telling the police? If I hadn't told them what I saw they would have thought poor Leyton Newbank had borrowed your boat and had an unfortunate accident."

"Try not to think about it, love. There are enough policemen around the area for you to feel quite safe."

"Will you stay?" Bettrys asked, when she had collected Cheryl from the Howells and brought her back to the chalet.

"On the kitchen floor?" he asked.

"In my bed," she said holding him tight. "I don't think I want another night alone in this house, ever."

"You are sure? I mean, I don't want you to think you have to pay for my protection. I'll stay anyway if it makes you and Cheryl feel safe. Potter and I will guard you both, with no strings attached."

"I'm not just making use of you," she said. But doubts filled her mind and showed in her frightened eyes.

"Then I'll stay, but on the kitchen floor, me and Potter sharing a sleeping bag. Another night, when all this has calmed down, then we'll make a separate decision about your bed, all right?"

It had been a long day and when Bettrys had read a couple of stories to Cheryl and put her to bed, she was overcome with tiredness. Gordon made them a meal and at ten o'clock, feeling utterly exhausted, she went to bed. Drained by the events and the worries they brought about her own, and Cheryl's safety, she nevertheless found sleep impossible. Hours passed as she fidgeted and fought with her pillow in the hope of finding a position conducive to sleep.

She couldn't shut off her thoughts from the unbelievable knowledge that there was a murderer wandering around, and, more unbelievable still, that it might be Bryn/Brett.

In the early hours of the morning she switched on a torch and crept into the kitchen to try and make herself a drink without disturbing Gordon. Potter's large eyes gleamed in the light of the torch, but the sleeping bag was empty. Gordon was not there.

She found him standing outside the door, staring up at the sky. "What's the matter?" she asked anxiously. "Did you hear something?"

"Only you, incessantly moving about, obviously as unable to sleep as I."

"Gordon," she whispered, "come to bed."

She was woken by his kiss and opened her eyes to see Cheryl sitting up in bed clutching her favourite teddy, and Gordon, wearing only a shirt, holding a tray of tea and biscuits.

"I could get used to this," she smiled lazily.

"You will, my love, you will," he said, handing the little girl her drink and a bottle for her teddy, before lifting her in and settling her between them in the bed.

He left soon afterwards, to return to his own chalet and get ready for work. At eight o'clock, Bettrys heard the toot of the horn as his friend who gave him a lift called to collect him on the road above. Suddenly the place seemed hollow and empty without him. She knew that she was beginning to need him for more than the occasional hour or two. There was a gap in her life and Gordon was the one to fill it.

It seemed strange that Bryn had not been found by the police. They suspected him of murder. Although Bettrys found that impossible to believe, that someone with whom she had been so intimately involved was capable of the ultimate violence, their theories had a certain ring of truth. But in spite of the evidence, and his previous dishonesty, she and Gordon still believed that he was a possible next victim rather than the murderer. Either way, there would be no freedom from fear until he was in custody. If he used her as a haven as he had on the night he had seen the policeman at the bottom of the well shaft, she would be in danger, whatever the truth of it.

"Why don't you come and sleep here," Gwen suggested one day when she and Cheryl were sitting in the neat kitchen drinking fresh lemonade. The weather was warm; stifling once away from the beach, and Bettrys had just finished her first week at the gift shop.

"There's no need. I'm quite safe, really. I just get moments of panic, when I imagine someone outside staring through the window and deciding how I'll be killed." She made a joke of it but her laughter was false, as Gwen knew very well.

"Look, come and see the small bedroom which Gordon used to share with Pete when they were all home. It isn't very smart, mind, but you can treat it as yours, come and go as you like. I'll be on hand to mind Cheryl too," she coaxed. "Not that you'll fancy going out on the cliffs at night again for a while!"

Bettrys discussed it with Gordon and they agreed that, until the murderer was caught, Bettrys and Cheryl would make their home with the Howells at Smugglers Cottage. The small chalet was close up and when all their belongings had been either removed or packed away, the building returned to its unused, uncared-for state. A basic, cold, artificial home where people could pretend for a while that they belonged and were happy. Bettrys felt she never wanted to go inside it again.

With Cheryl becoming even more a part of the Howells family, Bettrys relaxed and tried to forget the awfulness of the deaths in the small community.

"I think I know where Bryn is hiding," Gordon told Bettrys one day. They were sitting on the beach making a sandcastle for Cheryl, after Bettrys had finished her day's work at the shop, while Gwen was making them an evening meal.

180

"Then you should tell the police," Bettrys said at once. "He could be killed. You could get him some protection by informing on him."

"Let's go and see, shall we?" After making sure they wouldn't be late for the meal and leaving Cheryl happily helping Maldwyn gather some driftwood, he led her to the entrance to the tunnel.

"It isn't far inside," he said, as she hesitated. "We found the place when we were kids. It's only a shallow gap but a grown man can slide in and not be seen from below." He heaved himself up and grasped hold of a protruding rock and hung there panting a little. "Not so easy as when I was ten years old!"

The top of his body disappeared, there was a moment's silence that made Bettrys believe he had disappeared for ever; then he poked his head out and waved at her.

"Come away, Gordon, please. I'm frightened."

He wriggled out and landed beside her again. He hugged her to reassure her and said, "I was wrong. He isn't in there. The place is empty and unused. Perhaps he's forgotten it. Damn. I was hoping to persuade him to go to the police himself." Looking up, the entrance to the hidy hole was impossible to see, yet Gordon assured her it was large enough to hold several men.

The funeral of Leyton Newbank was a sombre affair with the parents pale-faced and silent. They seemed bewildered, confused by the loss of their son. A funeral of their child was a day they never expected to see. Bettrys went to the church with Gwen, Maldwyn, Pete and Gordon, and noticed that Diana was not there. Emrys sat alone beside some of the people from the village.

Police enquiries continued and the search for Bryn seemed unabated. There were occasions when The Bend seemed to be completely occupied by men in uniform. The stream ceased flowing twice and although Bettrys no longer lived at the chalet alongside, she heard about it and wondered if the police were still hoping to find Bryn hiding there. The rocky shelf which Gordon had checked, high above the level of the water, was a perfect hiding place, but on reflection, it was unlikely that Bryn would think it a safe place for long-term concealment. The tunnel and well were searched daily by the police.

With summer at its height, the gift shop was busy and besides the three days she worked there, Bettrys spent several hours each week making jewellery to sell at her various outlets. She was not earning a lot of money, but life was easy and expenses here on Yr Tro were low.

When the weather was dry, they spent most of their spare time outside, either sitting on Maldwyn's bench or playing just below the house on the sand. They never walked as far as Ffynon Sands, but Gordon went there on occasions to photograph the sea birds. His boat had been recovered relatively unharmed and, after the police had examined it, it was returned to him, but Bettrys would not go out in it. The boat, like Ffynon Sands, had been irrevocably spoilt for her.

Stepping off the bus one evening after work, loaded with shopping from the local supermarket, she had began to walk down the path to the beach when Brynley appeared. The trees and bushes were in full leaf and in the dappled shadows she was unaware of his presence until he spoke.

"Bettrys, can you come to the chalet tonight? Make an excuse of wanting to check that everything is safe." Leaving her gasping in surprise and unable to reply, he disappeared into the greenery and there wasn't even the sound of leaves rustling to reveal his presence.

"No!" she shouted into the silence, and Gordon, walking up to meet her laughed and asked if she were arguing with rabbits.

"No, I – " she shook her head and waited until they were safely inside the Howells's kitchen, and she had greeted

182

Cheryl and handed the bags of food to Gwen, before she told him.

"Bryn! It was Bryn! He was hiding in the trees and he asked me to meet him at the chalet tonight," she said in amazement. "He didn't give me a chance to argue, that was why I shouted at him."

"I think you should go," Gordon said.

"What?" Gwen, Maldwyn and Bettrys spoke in chorus.

"I'll be with you of course, but I think you should go."

She sat down and stared at him. "Gordon, in a small community like this loyalty is strong. I can sympathise with that. There's almost a family feeling between the people here. But Bryn's a wanted man. I know to my cost that he is a charmer and has a way of making people believe him. But we can't flout the law in such a casual way. You all think that if he hasn't been caught, then you, as neighbours, should protect your own, avoid involving the police, give him a second chance. I can understand that. But the police are looking for him and it's our duty to help them. And, he might be in danger." She looked at Maldwyn and displayed her trump card. "It was he who persuaded Jake to cheat you out of your boat, Maldwyn." He just nodded. He knew that much himself. She threw up her hands in despair. "Oh, what is it about this place! There have been two deaths and a near-accident. We have police wandering about like other people have ants and you're asking me to meet Bryn and listen to what he has to say?"

"I'll be there. I'll follow him and find out where he's hiding, then, then we'll tell the police."

"Why not tell them now? Let *them* meet him?"

"He'd know. He wouldn't turn up. He has a sixth sense that one. But if he saw you going there, then we stand a chance of catching him. I want him caught." Gordon's face was stern. Maldwyn's too.

Gwen stood up and put an arm around Bettrys. "I think he might be right, love," she said quietly.

That night, Bettrys made her way to the chalet. She waited until dawn, shivering in a chair beside a sluggish fire. But he didn't appear.

CHAPTER ELEVEN

The elderly Taylors, Petal and Gar, were sitting outside their small home. Gar was reading the paper just delivered by Pete Howells and Petal was peeling potatoes intended for their lunch. Although it was early, not yet seven-thirty, there were several people walking along the beach. The Prices with their ungainly but adorable Great Dane puppy, who pulled them along as if they were riding a sledge; the Kellys, arguing as usual as they gathered a few pieces of wood for their evening bonfire; Stella and Cyril Norman, in a huddle with the Thomases as they held a fluttering map and discussed their day's walk along the coastal footpath.

Bettrys left the Howells' cottage, where Maldwyn was sitting with his morning cup of tea, and, with the push-chair held awkwardly under her arm, walked past the Taylors towards the path and the road.

"Where you two off to today, then?" Petal asked in her high-pitched, frail voice. "Shopping, are you?"

"I'm going to the library but if you want anything from the village, I'll be back on the two o'clock bus," Bettrys offered.

"There's early you're going, love. We haven't had the eight o'clock news yet, look."

"I'm going to see Diana first," Bettrys explained. "I haven't spoken to her for a while and I wanted to see if she's all right."

"Diana? All right?" Gar lowered his paper and looked at her over his reading glasses. "That one's sure to be all

185

right! Knows how to look after herself she does." There was clear disapproval in the old man's voice. He shook his paper as if wishing it was his daughter-in-law. "Never does no work. Never even gets her hands dirty. D'you know she never cooks our Emrys a meal if she can help it! Fills that freezer with convenience food, would you believe! Wanders around meeting her fancy men and embarrassing our Emrys. *she's* all right! It's our Emrys who needs a bit of sympathy, being married to that flighty piece!"

Bettrys was startled. Although the old couple must have known about Diana's behaviour ever since she came to Yr Tro, this was the first time she had heard Gar openly disapproving of her. Perhaps, she thought, I'm beginning to be accepted as a local!

"I'll just pop in and say hello," she said hoping to avoid a discussion on their daughter-in-law's wayward lifestyle. "Is there anything I can bring you from the village?"

"Yes, some writing paper," Petal said firmly. "There's a letter I have to write see, and – " she was firmly hushed by her husband. "A letter," she repeated, then bent to continue preparing the vegetables, her small, bony hands swift at their task.

Diana was in her dressing gown when Bettrys reached the farm house.

"Coffee," she announced. The single word was not a question, more a demand. She took a cup and saucer from the huge Welsh dresser that filled one wall of the kitchen and brought it to the pine table. She glanced at Cheryl. "Would she like a drink?"

"Ask her," Bettrys smiled.

"Would you like a drink of orange juice?" Diana said sharply to the child and hearing the tone and not the words, Cheryl buried herself in Bettrys's skirt.

"You ask her. I'm no good with children," Diana said irritably.

"You've never wanted any?"

"Of course I wanted children. Don't be stupid!"

Startled, Bettrys said, "I'm sorry, but as you've been married twice and – I thought – "

"I had a child when I was fifteen. The child is past her own fifteenth birthday, yet there isn't a day when I don't think about her. An infection led to an operation that put paid to any more." Diana banged the coffee down in front of her visitor, a firm end to the conversation.

"I'm going into the village, walking, as it's a pleasant morning. Is there anything you want?"

"Nothing you can buy in the shops." The unhappy woman sipped her drink and looked into the corner of the high-ceilinged room as if examining a private vision.

"Have you thought of adopting?" Bettrys dared to ask. "If you really want a child, there are problems getting a baby, but there are children badly in need of love and care. You have lots to spare, I think."

"You're the only one to think that."

"You scare people away."

"Stupid lot around here don't understand anything that isn't spelt out in words a one-year-old can follow."

"One-year-olds can follow a lot more than you'd think."

Diana turned to look at Cheryl, who was sipping her drink from the beaker Bettrys had filled with the orange juice. "Would you like a biscuit?" she asked, this time in a calmer voice. Cheryl smiled and held out her hand.

"Daa do," she said, and Bettrys translated the sounds as "thank you".

"Someone said Colin and Betty Williams were in the village a few days ago. Their house is still for sale. Perhaps they are going to use it." Bettrys imparted the information casually but the effect on Diana was electric.

"He mustn't. He wouldn't come back. He wouldn't be such a fool!"

"Because of the near accident, you mean?" Bettrys remembered Gordon saying he thought the incident was connected with the murders. "You think it was not really an accident?"

"Of course it was an accident. Stupid fool trying to climb cliffs without proper equipment."

"He told Gordon he was sitting on the top, not climbing." She hesitated a moment then said quietly, "Gordon thinks he was another murder victim who fortunately escaped. Something ties these men together, Diana, is it you? Did you know these men – know them well?"

Diana did not reply. She turned away from Bettrys and stared again at the corner of the room. Her breath was fast; Bettrys did not know whether to expect tears or outrage and anger. Then Diana turned and picked up the empty coffee cups in a dismissive manner. It was clear that Bettrys had outstayed her welcome.

Bettrys sighed inwardly as she stood to leave. Really, Diana was so prickly, so impossible to befriend, she seemed unwilling to impart the slightest hint of what she thought and felt, yet, Bettrys felt she understood her a little better after that brief visit. She was more certain too that whatever the impression she gave to others, Diana hated the life she was living. She was a deeply unhappy woman. Perhaps she used men the way her sister used drink – and men too, as a substitute for alcohol's mind-deadening oblivion.

Walking back past the houses on the rough farm track, Bettrys saw Jessie Newbank and stopped for a brief word. The woman was still distraught and Bettrys failed to find words to comfort her. How can you ease the pain of losing a twenty-four-year-old son? The son's having been the victim of murder made it even more difficult.

She offered to bring anything Jessie needed from the village, added some knitting wool and some black cotton to her list, and went on through the gate to the road. Potter was waiting, looking hopefully at her, half turning as if expecting to be sent home.

"Come on, you might as well come with us," Bettrys called and the dog danced around, understanding her invitation, before taking up position of guard and leader, a few yards in front of the push-chair.

It was Friday, one of the days on which Bettrys did not work and the day when the holiday chalets on Yr Tro began to fill for the weekend. On the way to the village, she saw the Baxters towing a trailer with a boat. Frances leaned out of the window and called, "Party, Sunday evening, will you come? We'd reeeeelly love to see you." Bettrys waved acceptance, shouted her thanks and walked on. The parties were hardly exclusive, everyone was invited as long as they brought something to swell the supplies of food and drink.

As she approached the first of the village houses, Bettrys stopped and looked back before crossing the road. A car was approaching fast and she saw in her brief view of the driver that it was Diana. Strange, she thought, if she was coming into the village she might have offered me a lift. Then she decided generously that Diana hadn't known at the time she had called on her. Something must have happened to make the journey necessary and urgent. She wondered idly if it had anything to do with her mention of Colin Williams.

Having finished her shopping and chosen the library books, there was an hour to wait for the bus back. Potter was bored with waiting around, his bright eyes looked at her; he was hoping for something more interesting, before he had to get on the jerky bus.

"Come on, we'll go to the fields for a run." Turning away from the temptations of the cafe, where fresh cakes and coffee beckoned, Bettrys walked past the church, along a narrow path to where a steep field led up, around the village, and to Millfield Wood. With the dog running excitedly ahead, she bent to unfasten Cheryl's reins from the push-chair and give her a brief freedom, when she heard a commotion that startled her.

From the woods at the top of the field she saw a woman running, screaming, and recognised Diana Taylor. Not knowing whether to run to help her or grab Cheryl and flee from whatever had frightened the woman, Bettrys stood petrified until Diana saw her and called.

"Get an ambulance! Get the police! There's been another – oh my God, Bettrys, he's killed him. Drowned him in a stream."

All nervous energy gone, Diana sank to the ground, her legs unable to support her. Turning the little girl away and pointing foolishly to a book she had hastily taken from her basket, Bettrys tried to distract the child from what the woman was saying, while at the same time trying to persuade Diana to explain what had happened. From Diana's fraught expression, bulging eyes, the high colour on her cheeks and the jumbled-up words that made no sense, Bettrys thought at first she had been drinking.

"It's Colin Williams," Diana groaned. "I was upset. I had another row with Emrys after you'd gone. I was walking towards the wood when I saw – I saw him lying on the ground half hidden by rubble from a fallen wall. It's true what Gordon thinks. Colin *was* attacked. He and I once – Oh, Bettrys, what am I going to do? Someone I know is doing these things. Someone I must have loved." Her face distorted and she was violently sick.

Bettrys helped her to clean herself, then said, "Walk back with me to the nearest shop and we'll call the police. I'll stay with you, but please, I know it's difficult, but please try and stay calm. I don't want Cheryl upset, she's only a baby." Diana was trembling but once the worst of the weakness had left her, she stood and, leaning on the push-chair, began to do as Bettrys suggested.

"It must be Bryn," Diana mumbled as they retraced their steps back past the church to the centre of the shops. "There's no one else it can be. He must be insane."

"Don't talk about it now. Wait until the police have a few facts." Bettrys went cold at the thought of Bryn's being capable of murder, but she held her feelings in check and tried to soothe the woman. She was relieved when the

190

policeman arrived, and she was no longer responsible for Diana, who was close to hysteria.

By the time the police had interviewed her, Bettrys had missed the bus and after a few more minutes spent going over what she had told them, she was taken home in a police car, Potter barking at every dog they passed, enjoying his privileged position to the full. She went straight to Gwen and Maldwyn and told them what had happened.

"Where is Bryn? I can't understand how he's avoided the police all this time," Maldwyn said. "Not that I think he's a killer, mind. But he is wanted by the police and if he isn't the killer, Gordon is probably right, he's in danger of being the next victim."

It was almost time for Gordon to come home from work and while she waited, Bettrys delivered the wool to Jessie Newbank and the writing paper to Petal. On impulse she went in to look at the now empty chalet of which she was still the tenant. As she opened the door there was a smell of smoke and for a moment she foolishly thought she had left the fire burning all this time. The brief and idiotic thought had made her step into the living room and there, sitting on the armchair as she had found him once before, was Bryn.

"Bryn! What on earth are you doing *here*?"

"Managing to keep one step in front of the police."

"You ought to go to them. There's been another death."

"What?" He stood up and stared around him as if expecting the murderer to jump out of the walls. "Who? When? How did he die?"

Bettrys wondered if he were acting, or if the news really was a shock.

"It was Colin Williams." Bettrys looked at him, trying to judge whether or not he was genuinely surprised. She knew how good an actor he was and doubted the surprise was genuine. "Don't you think you ought to give yourself

191

up and tell all you know? It seems that all Diana's ex-lovers are being wiped out one by one. You are one of them, aren't you?"

"Once she and I were close, yes, but not since I met you," he said, his eyes softening into love.

She stared at him, almost laughing at his audacity.

"Really! D'you think I'd fall for that line? I might have been gullible once, letting you cheat me out of two hundred pounds, but I've learnt a thing or two since then."

"Who is he?"

"Who?"

"The father of your child. Loved him too, did you? You aren't that much different from me, are you? I've been working it out, it couldn't have been long after you and I parted. I don't blame you," he said magnanimously. "Life is for living and all that. Although your pretending you were leaving me because of your sister's illness was cruel and dishonest."

"Cheryl isn't my child. She belonged to my sister."

"Oh, I see." He stared at her thoughtfully for a moment. "So you're still the prim little miss, are you?" The words were bland but the tone was insulting.

"It was true, and you left me, remember. Because I had to delay our trip to Greece. Well, it doesn't matter anyway. I'd have outgrown you soon enough anyway."

He continued to stare at her in frank admiration and, something else – could it be invitation growing in those dark, fascinating eyes?

Then he said, "Yes, I think I can see that she isn't yours. She's more like Eirlys than you, smaller and chunkier, not long, lean and elegant like you, Bettrys." He smiled then and stretched out his long legs in a languorous way. "Come here, I think we can slowly gather up the threads of where we left off, don't you?"

"Go to the police and tell them what you know."

"Oh, I don't think so. Let them find the killer before

they find me. I don't want that lot landing on my head! Best I keep out of their clutches until the case is solved. I think I could enjoy being hidden for a while, if you'll be my jailor and bring me sustenance each evening."

Bettrys turned to leave and he darted out of his chair at a speed that frightened her. "Not a word about where I am, Bettrys. All right?" He turned her in his arms and kissed her hard and without pleasure. "My beautiful ice-maiden. But I've shown you the pleasures of a summer thawing, haven't I?" He released her and gave a quiet chuckle, and she hurried out and closed the door after her. She ran back to the Howells, wanting to see Gordon, but he was still not home.

"Called us to say he'd be late," Gwen explained anxiously. "Seems the police went to the factory and wanted to ask him some more questions.

They heard a car and Potter barked excitedly. Bettrys ran out and along the beach and up to the road, where Gordon had just stepped out of a police car. Bettrys surprised him by the intensity of her welcome. Bryn had given her an uneasy feeling. He seemed untouched by the deaths. Could he be responsible for them? Had she really once been in love with a man capable of murder?

They all discussed everything that had happened and Gordon told them he had told the police his thoughts on the murders. Everyone was subdued by the newest in a series of frightening events that had ruined the relaxed mood of Yr Tro.

Bettrys had the chill feeling that something else was about to happen. She shivered uncontrollably as she tucked Cheryl in and climbed into bed herself. She was glad to be sharing the Howells home but was worried about Gordon, alone in his small chalet between them and the road. Whatever was happening, it was far from over. She felt it strongly and no reassurance from Gordon or Gwen could ease her fears.

It was not until late that night as she lay unable to

sleep, thinking about Brett who was really Bryn, mulling over their odd conversation, that she realised he had said about Cheryl being more like her sister, Eirlys. How had he known? He had never once called at the flat. So far as she knew, he and her sister had never met.

It suddenly made sense. Eirlys's man-friend hadn't come to the flat either. It was too much of a coincidence for the two men to be that coy about being introduced to a sister! It must have been Bryn! He could easily have met Eirlys and, when the plans to spend six weeks in Greece had fallen apart, he and Eirlys could have quickly arranged an alternative. It might even have been arranged at the time he issued the invitation to Greece – his intention to bid her farewell would have been made easy by her own decision not to go. She thought disconsolately of how she had spent that evening waiting for him to arrive to say goodbye – and to return her money. The rejection so long ago was still a painful memory.

It wouldn't have taken much planning once he had decided to take Eirlys on a fun-week to Brighton. Meeting somewhere away from the flat, the drive down, booking into an hotel, the whole thing given added excitement by the knowledge that Bettrys had been replaced by her vivacious sister. Eirlys would have been taken in by his apparent wealth and certain charm, as she had.

Then the more devastating thought hit her like a punch on the jaw and made her head spin. Brynley Cooper must be Cheryl's father! It was he who had driven Eirlys back to drink and drugs, and caused her death!

She wanted to get up, there and then to face him with it. He might be in her chalet, or in the tunnel leading to the well. Unseen by any one searching for him unless he wanted to be found. She only had to go creeping about, calling his name. He would be vain enough to come to her. She tensed herself as if to rise then fell back among the covers. She was afraid. The night, once so pure and sweet-scented, a curtain giving rest and peace from the busy day, had become a threat, a veil behind which evil men hid poised, ready to strike.

Tomorrow she would tell Gordon what she had learned. Together they would find Bryn and *make* him tell them the truth. Then she remembered it was Saturday and she would be working at the gift shop. Well, a few hours more wouldn't matter. And she had to talk to Gordon first. This was not something she could do alone. As soon as she got home, she and Gordon would discuss it and then she would persuade Gordon to go to the police and tell them where he was likely to be. He knew about the murders. She was sure he knew.

By nine o'clock on Saturday morning, as she opened the gift shop for business, it was already too late. The police had received a letter, stating that Brynley Cooper was hiding in the well shaft, high on a deep, almost hidden, rocky shelf; or one of the Taylors' sheds or, the chalet rented by Bettrys Hopkyns.

Two dozen policemen had combed the area, the previously unnoticed shelf was searched but no trace of him was found. Gordon came to the shop and soon after, the police arrived and she was interviewed. She told them everything she knew and much of what she suspected.

"I went with them when they looked for the deep shelf in the rocks," Gordon told her after the police had gone. "They didn't find him but there was a bundle of clothing there. A heavy overcoat, parker jacket, thick seamen's boots and two quilted gilets."

Gordon frowned as he told Bettrys of the find. "If they were worn by a slim man, they would make it difficult to run and move easily, although they could be quickly discarded. And, from a distance they'd make him look completely different, cumbersome, overweight and perhaps give the impression of someone much older. What d'you think?"

"I think," she said with a shiver, "that Bryn is tall and thin, and clever enough to have thought of it."

195

On Sunday, while the police scoured the area for sight of Bryn, arrangements for the party on the beach went on as planned.

"It might seem hard and unfeeling," Frances said, when Bettrys was on her way back down the path from the bus that evening, "but Jeremy thinks we should carry on as normal. This is our dear little holiday haven after all, and these people are reeelly our dear friends."

"I don't know," Bettrys hesitated. "It would seem callous to me, with so many unexplained deaths."

"I've been up to see Diana and Emrys and Emrys insisted that they come." She smiled her childlike smile. "Even the Coopers are coming and their son is wanted for questioning or whatever they call it. Pleeeease, Bettrys, come with Gordon and bring Cheryl and help us to forget being frightened for a few hours."

"Are you frightened?" Bettrys, unkindly, thought the young woman incapable of sufficient imagination to be scared.

"Well, yes. Of course. It's all a bit close to home, reeeally, isn't it?"

"You mean because it's happened here, on Yr Tro?"

"And because of Jeremy's previous – well, you know."

"I don't know," Bettrys said. "I've only lived here since Easter, remember. What about Jeremy and – " She made a wild guess, "Jeremy and – Diana?" She saw at once from Frances's expression that she had guessed correctly.

"She was his first wife you see. At least, not his wife, not reeeally."

"Diana was married to Jeremy?"

"You won't tell Jeremy I've told you, will you? He doesn't want it discussed. They weren't reeeally married remember, so there's no need for the police to know."

Bettrys ran down the path and into Gordon's small chalet above the house where his mother lived.

"Gordon, we have to talk to the police again. Did you know that – " she stopped and gasped with shock, her hands, having dropped her bag on the floor flew to cover her mouth. Standing at the bedroom doorway was Bryn.

"Don't mind me," Bryn drawled lazily. "I'm your ex, remember. You and I, we're in the past, Bettrys. I'm not likely to be embarrassed by you two falling into each other's arms."

"Bryn came to ask how the police know about that space in the rocks," Gordon said, tensing up at the man's abrasive remarks.

Bettrys thought at once of the writing paper Petal had asked her to buy, but she didn't mention it. "Go to the police," she said flatly.

"I will, my dear, when this murderer is caught."

"You could be next," she said with greater urgency.

"And would you care?"

She moved and stood closer to Gordon, a reminder that he was the one who mattered.

"I think you should go," Gordon said. "If the police find you here we'll all be in trouble."

"Thanks for the food." Bryn patted his pocket, bulging with sandwiches and chocolate." He blew a kiss towards Bettrys, winked at Gordon and stepped out of the door, disappearing silently and swiftly into the bushes.

"He's enjoying it!" Bettrys said.

"There was always a bit of the dare-devil in Bryn. Even at school, he would 'mitch' lessons then hang around the school hoping that teachers would see him, yet, although half the class would know what was going on, he always managed to avoid being caught. Danger is the fizz in his lemonade, the boost, the sharp edge he always needs to make the ordinary bearable. Life for him has always been too ordinary."

Gordon smiled in spite of the seriousness of the situation. "He always had the sort of boyish looks that attracted the girls – and appealed to their mothers! He let down the tyres of the headmaster's car once. He persuaded his mother to say he'd been ill and in bed all day, yet he'd been walking around and had even held the end of the girls' skipping rope during the lunch hour!"

"Did you know that Jeremy was Diana's first husband?" Bettrys asked when she was sure Bryn had vanished. "Frances said they were not exactly married, perhaps they were living together and using the same name. I don't know, she's very vague at times. But if there was any sort of permanent relationship, then he is in danger too." She thought for a moment then added, "He must be aware of what could happen. If three of Diana's ex's have been killed, he must know the risks."

"But this party tonight, it's still on. Why does he come here if he knows he's in danger of being the next?"

"I doubt if anyone would actually believe that he was about to be murdered, not here in a quiet place like Yr Tro. And if Frances has been told not to tell anyone, perhaps he feels safe enough to continue with the pretence that Diana and he are strangers."

"I don't want to go to the party. *I'm* afraid, even if he is not!"

"But we will go, won't we?"

"I suppose we must. I expect there will be plenty of policemen there."

"Sure to be. They'll be watching and listening and hoping for a breakthrough."

"I wish them luck. The sooner this is over the better for us all." She frowned then and said anxiously, "What if they pick him up now? They're bound to be watching every house. Food you've given him will be in his pocket. Oh, Gordon, you could be in serious trouble."

"I took the precaution of giving him a pack of sandwiches I bought in Swansea."

The troubled look did not fade from her face. She looked up at him as she began to walk down to Smuggler's Cottage to collect Cheryl. "Gordon, you know where Bryn is hiding, don't you?"

"There are several places he uses. I've told the police

and they've missed him. That much I'll do, but I won't actually grab him, tie him up and call the police, or walk him into custody. If he were charged with murder and he's innocent, well, I couldn't cope with that. Friends are hard to treat like villains."

"Yes," Bettrys said with firm disapproval, "and that's why so many murderers stay free and kill again. And again."

"He wouldn't kill anyone. I have to give him the chance to stay out of police hands until the man is caught."

"You're wasting police time. Until they talk to Bryn, they won't be looking for anyone else!"

"Why don't you go to the police and tell them we've been talking to him, that he's been given food from my pantry?" He looked at her and then nodded. "It isn't easy, is it?"

"All right then, how would you feel if he were the next victim?" she asked.

"Hell, I'd rather not think about that!"

CHAPTER TWELVE

The mood at the Baxter's party was brittle. Everyone seemed to be trying to pretend that it was a normal, mid-summer evening and they had a few carefree hours ahead of them. The music playing encouraged the Kellys' to dance but they soon gave up as no one else joined in. Beside the regular inhabitants of The Bend, strangers were present. No one said so, but everyone knew that they were police, sent to keep an eye on the group, to listen and watch for something to lead them to Brynley Cooper.

The Normans and the Thomases, more casually dressed, having abandoned for once their walking gear, were pestered by the Prices' puppy, who seemed capable of escaping from whatever hurdle they built to keep him inside their chalet. The Kellys chattered loudly, their attempt to appear normal and partyish sounding instead anxious and on the point of panic. Henry Kelly had put on a party hat but it did not amuse; it only embarrassed him and others, and after a while he threw it down, where it was eaten by the puppy. There was some uneasy laughter as the dog was dragged back to the Prices' chalet, and the barrier replaced.

The air of unease made the lively dog a nuisance rather than an excuse for laughter. The music seemed tinny and artificial and Frances, standing beside the music-centre selecting tapes, wondered how she would keep the guests happy until it was time to eat. "Perhaps," she suggested to Jeremy, "we could eat a bit sooner than we'd planned?"

"No. The charcoal won't be hot enough until nine-thirty." He tipped more wine into the punch she was carrying. "Hand around a few more drinks and encourage people to dance. Don't stand there dithering, get out there!" His sharp words startled her. He was as tense as the rest of the group.

"Love you," she said brightly and tripped out into the evening sun, a smile pressed firmly on her pert and pretty face, and tried once again to be the perfect hostess.

She topped up glasses and chatted to each one as she made the rounds, glancing back from time to time to see if Jeremy had come out to help her. "Reeeally," she said to Carys and Jake, who sat in a corner not far from their own front porch, "You'd think this was a funeral rather than a summer party." She blinked eagerly at Jake, "Come on, Jake, let's see you and your little wife showing the others how to enjoy yourselves."

Obediently, Jake stood and offered his right arm to Carys. He walked to where the space had been cleared for dancing on the rough sand. The music was low and rather slow and they seemed at odds with the rhythm. Then the tape clicked off and another rhythm, fast and insistent, flowed over the group. The volume was raised and Frances avoided looking towards the veranda, where, she guessed, Jeremy would be glaring at her for her stupidity and her dull choice.

"That's more like it, isn't it?" she beamed at the Prices, who were considering whether or not to dance. "Come on," she encouraged, "show the rest how it's done."

There seemed, for a brief moment, the possibility that things would liven in spite of all the difficulties but the arrival of Diana and Emrys cooled the atmosphere once again. Diana was wearing her usual jodhpurs and strong shoes. Her hair was tied back in an untidily fastened bun. She lacked the usual pullover and wore a fawn and green blouse, shirt-like and ordinary, her only concession to the evening gathering. Frances and the others guessed the couple had been quarrelling and also guessed that Diana had not wanted to come. She walked to the veranda and helped herself to a drink, hardly looking at Jeremy, who glanced at her then walked away.

Leaving her husband, Diana walked to the Prices' chalet and fondled the ears of the puppy.

Frances bustled around trying to persuade others to join the dancers but it was with relief that she saw Bettrys, Cheryl and Gordon walking towards them, followed by Gwen and Pete. Slowly, unwillingly, walking in their wake, was Maldwyn and the ever enthusiastic Potter.

"Thank goodness! You two will get these slow-coaches moving, won't you? Jeremy's disappeared. He's probably starting to get the meat ready for the barbie." She glanced at the veranda then and saw that Jeremy was standing watching her. "Keep the music lively, darling, Gordon and Bettrys are here." The music stopped and the heavy beat of a Motorhead record filled the air. Gwen went to hand the Howells' share of the meat to Jeremy, who took it with hardly a word.

Gordon picked up Cheryl, who was wearing one of the dresses made for her by Carys, and danced with her in his arms, while Bettrys coaxed a stranger, whom she guessed was a member of the local constabulary, to dance with her.

Everyone seemed wrapped up in their own thoughts. The music and the efforts of Frances to get the party off the ground failed to liven their spirits. Bettrys confided to Gordon that she thought it was the presence of the police.

"I thought so at first, but the mood seems to be coming more from Jeremy. He's glaring at Diana and at his poor wife as if he wants to kill them both!"

"Perhaps the Taylors weren't the only couple to have a row this evening."

Potter barked near the blocked entrance to the Price's chalet. The puppy barked back and Potter replied more and more loudly and was rewarded by the Dane puppy flying, like some toy donkey, over the barrier and running off with him to explore the bushes for rabbits.

The music continued, the dancers moved around in the sand but there was still an air of tension, as if all present were waiting for something to happen. The dogs had disappeared and if the Prices knew, they pretended not to, being in some way held to the ill-at-ease group around Costa Plenty.

The sun disappeared with a sudden blaze and darkness fell on the beach-party. Frances looked for Jeremy to ask him to light the coloured lights swinging gently in the evening breeze but she couldn't find him.

"Oh, reeeally, Cheryl," she scolded, pretending to talk to the little girl, but meaning her words for Bettrys and Gordon. "I don't know what's the matter with your Uncle Jeremy tonight. He loves these parties in his little house on the beach, but today he seems to wish himself somewhere else!" She went into the house, switched on the coloured lights and those on the veranda, then searched the rooms. When she re-appeared she called to Bettrys, "He isn't anywhere to be found. Now isn't that odd? What could he be thinking of, wandering off in the middle of his party?"

"*His* little house on the beach, and *his* party," Bettrys said to Gordon as they sat and drank a cup of coffee. "She always refers to everything they own as *his*!" After they had eaten their fill, and more coffee had been offered by Frances, playing the perfect hostess in the continued absence of her husband, Gwen and Maldwyn said their goodnights and left, whistling without success for Potter and the Dane puppy. Maldwyn went with them carrying the almost sleeping Cheryl. He was unable to disguise his relief that the evening was over.

"Bloody waste of time. We'd have been better off watching the box. And more comfortable too," he grumbled. "There's us standing out in the cold; miserable, bored, being fed with indigestible chunks of bread and meat, and the host vanishes! Shows he has a bit of sense, mind, missing his own party!"

Gordon glanced at Bettrys and felt a churning fear.

"Where *is* Jeremy?" he asked. "God, don't let him be another victim." Holding back his rising panic, he approached the policemen who were also preparing to leave and asked, "Seen Jeremy, have you?"

"It's all right, sir. He felt a bit sick and has gone to bed. He didn't want his wife to tell you all and break up the party."

Gordon sighed with relief. "For a moment I began to think – "

"Sorry you were worried, but we're keeping a very careful eye on this place. A very careful eye."

"Thank goodness. Everyone is edgy. I hardly expected them to leave the safety of their homes to come here tonight," Gordon said.

"Safety in numbers, and they needn't be anxious about going home. Every house has a guard on it. Go home to your little chalet, Mr Howells, and sleep sound." The policeman smiled in the darkness, his face a shadow lit only by the remains of the fire reflecting in his eyes and on his white teeth.

Gordon turned back to the dwindling group around the bonfire and called, "Goodnight everybody." This seemed to be the signal for others to depart and the Prices went in search of their delinquent dog and the Coopers drifted back to their house with yawns and a polite "thank you". Gordon looked for Bettrys and she had disappeared.

"Bettrys?" he called. Then he went back to the policeman and asked if he had seen her go.

"She went off following the path behind Costa Plenty. Collecting glasses I think she was."

"That was the idea," Gordon frowned.

* * *

Bettrys was wearing one of her long, flowing skirts, this

time in colours that Gordon described as dull mud and sludge green, and which Pete approvingly called desert camouflage. When she left Gordon, put down the glasses she had collected, and walked towards the chalet of which she was still a tenant, she thought no one had noticed her go.

She did not intend going inside the silent building, certainly not on her own, but curiosity led her to check if there really was a guard on every property on Yr Tro. An empty building would be a likely place for Bryn to hide. He seemed able to slide through the policemen with the slightest ease of a ghost. She wondered if he were there now, having failed to turn up the night he had asked her to meet him, would he expect her to go there under cover of the party, hoping she wouldn't be seen? Was he the murderer, watching as she moved around in the dark and waiting for a chance to complete the next stage of his campaign?

Her heart began to race in an uncomfortable way. There was something hidden in the night that spelled danger and even the presence of the policemen didn't make her feel safe, so why was she wandering around in the dark on her own? She wanted to reassure herself that Jeremy was safe. As a woman, if their reading of the murderer's motives had been correct, she was in no danger herself.

Forcing herself to move on, she passed behind Costa Plenty. The house was very dark at the rear. The bonfire, the decorative lights and house lights blazed at the front. She glanced up at its dark, looming shape as she slid through the shadows. She had to see for herself that Jeremy was alive and safe. She had to climb up and look in through the larger of the two back windows.

The place had been built to enjoy the views. Only the main bedroom and the small bathroom had windows at the back, facing the sloping ground which lead up to the road. The curtain had not been carefully drawn. There was little likelihood of anyone looking in; Yr Tro was such an isolated spot.

Bettrys climbed onto the water butt and as her eyes peered above the sill, she saw that the bed was empty, the covers thrown back and Jeremy was standing at the doorway of the room. He was fully dressed and talking to Jake. How had Jake got there? She had seen him wish the constable goodnight and walk home with his wife!

She could hear a policeman close by, talking on his radio, presumably telling his superiors that the party was ended and the inhabitants of Yr Tro were on their way home. She slipped down, intending to find Gordon and tell him what she had seen. It probably meant nothing, but the secretive way they had met made her think the police should be told.

She wondered vaguely about her intention of telling Gordon before the police. Tonight she suspected everyone. Gordon hadn't been completely honest with the police when he was asked to help find Bryn. Perhaps he knew more about what was going on than he had told her? Had he reasons of his own for helping Bryn? Could it be simply friendly loyalty? And would that apply if the friend was suspected of murder? Yet, she had to trust him.

Where was Bryn? She couldn't believe him capable of the act of murder. She had been in love with him, had shared the most intimate relationship for a few short, wonderful months. Love is said to be blind, but surely she would have known if there was that ability for violence. Could he have been planning all this while she had slept beside him? She knew he was far from the charming, easy man he had appeared to be. Was he something far worse? Fear made the small of her back feel vulnerable, chill. She feared, deep down, that Bryn was the man the police were intending to catch. So why was Gordon helping him?

Perhaps Gordon's attempts to clear him were for her sake? She would have to face the fact that she had made love to a man who had murdered out of jealousy. Did he believe that keeping Bryn from such a charge was important to her sanity?

Concerned now with getting back down before she was seen, she couldn't concentrate on finding the logic of it. She just knew that she needed to tell Gordon before talking to the police.

She felt for the ground with her foot stretched downwards; she seemed higher that she expected to be. Her toes touched and she carefully lowered herself to the neatly trimmed grass. A rustling sounded as something approached and the Dane puppy bounded through the small garden, certain of a welcome, convinced everyone loved him, pushing her against the wall in his enthusiasm. Then a shadow eased away from the wall and a voice whispered urgently, "Bettrys, my love, you have to help me!"

"Brett."

"Bryn, but you can call me what you like, only get me away from here. The place is surrounded by police. I have to get away."

"Bettrys?" She could hear Gordon calling for her and she pulled away from Bryn in relief.

"I'm here, Gordon." She ran, pushing through the shrubs, the dog leaping around, showing his pleasure at finding her. In her haste she fell against bushes, caught her arms on thorns, tore her skirt, but was unaware, imagining a thousand demons chasing her through the darkness.

Then she was back to the artificial lights, where Frances was dousing the fire, and saying, "It was reeeally nice of everyone to come."

The last bottles and cups and glasses were being carried towards the veranda by the Kellys. And there was Gordon, standing staring towards her, big and strong and so important to her. Relief and love showed on his face. She was grasped, held and she felt safe.

"It was Bryn," she whispered under the cover of his

embrace. "He's over by Costa Plenty and wants me to help him get away."

"I'll go. I'll pretend to search for Potter."

"The Dane was there. He frightened me but I didn't see Potter," she said.

"Better camouflaged than you are," Gordon smiled.

"I'll come with you."

"No, best I deal with it alone, in case I'm caught helping him."

"I don't want you to leave me. There's only one policeman left that I can see, and he's on the balcony drinking coffee with Frances."

Arm in arm they headed towards the Howells' cottage, waving goodnight to the Kelly's and Frances, then they disappeared into the bushes and made their way back to Costa Plenty. They stood hidden in the shadows and waited. They saw the policeman leave after making sure Frances had locked her door, then saw him go to stand near the road, obviously waiting for his relief to arrive. A slight rustling in the undergrowth made them look down expecting to see the ever hopeful Potter join them in the expectation of a late-night stroll. But it was Bryn who appeared.

"Can you distract the policeman while I make it to the tunnel?" he whispered. "It's cold and I'd love to sleep by that bonfire. But I think I'll be able to sleep without disturbance in the tunnel. They've already looked along there twice this evening. There are dozens of them," he complained as if they were an irritating swarm of wasps.

The policeman came down the path at that moment, his sharp ears had heard something.

"Go out and meet him, Gordon," Bettrys whispered. "Take Potter and tell him you're taking him for a last walk." She pushed him and he stumbled so there was only one thing to do and that was what she had suggested.

Behind her, Bryn slipped away and headed on silent feet to her chalet and the opening where the stream left the rocks. He'll get wet feet, she thought with a shiver, there's no Diana to change the course of the water, but he'll be safe enough for a few hours.

She didn't move, her clothes blending in with the night. She was frightened, the night was closing around her, claustrophobia made her sweat in spite of the chill of the night air. She forced herself to stay, she had to give him enough time to enter the tunnel and climb up into that narrow fissure in the rock.

The sound, when it came, was so slight that she thought it must be something as small as a field mouse. Then it came again, louder this time and she froze. Someone was following Bryn. She didn't think of the most likely possibility, that it might be a policeman. Some sixth sense told her danger threatened. Danger not for Bryn but for Gordon.

Her thoughts and opinions were like a switchback out of control. Bryn was the killer and threatened Gordon, then he wasn't the killer and he had to stay free until the real murderer was caught. Then conviction returned that he was in fact the guilty one and was following Gordon! Gordon, while believing he was helping, was interfering with the murderer's plans! The switchback came down with a bump on the positive belief that Bryn was the killer. And he was moving stealthily after Gordon!

All these thoughts flew through her mind in seconds. Slowly, fighting back the need to scream, she followed the silent figure. She had a torch in her right hand and raised it as if to use a weapon. She passed the remains of the old boat in front of her chalet. The blackness was intense. A hand came from behind and knocked the useless weapon from her grasp. A hand covered her mouth, stifling an incipient scream. An arm gripped her tightly; the man's body pressed closely against her back.

"Move," a voice said almost conversationally into her ear, "make a sound and you and that boyfriend of yours are dead."

It wasn't Bryn. She didn't know whether the revelation was a relief or not. If it had been Bryn she might have been able to talk to him, persuade him to be lenient. With a stranger, why would he care? But who was it? The voice was familiar but in her terrified state she couldn't recognise it. That it was the killer she had no doubts. The knowledge that she was literally in the hands of a man who had killed three times, possibly more, made her muscles soften into liquid and she felt herself falling.

"Don't faint. I have little patience with weak women. Walk. Slowly and with no noise. Make a whisper of a sound and it will be your last." He still spoke almost casually, the matter-of-fact tone making the words incongruous and almost a joke. But the hand across her face was no joke. Or the realisation that she was alone with a man capable of murder.

She was pushed towards the back door of her chalet. The door was not locked and without easing his grip of her he forced her inside. The door closed quietly. The man stood with his back to it, holding her against him.

"You shouldn't have come to Yr Tro," the voice behind her said, almost sorrowfully. She couldn't reply. She wanted to say, let me go and I'll never come back, but the hand across her mouth made it impossible.

A torch shone briefly into her face and she heard the muffled sound of struggles coming from somewhere to her right.

"It's Gordon," the voice told her. "He and you have been a nuisance. But you won't be any more. Tonight will see the end of my quest and you won't be able to irritate me any more."

Quest. The word sounded strange. More fitting to medieval times. Was it a sign of derangement? Was the man who was holding her insane?

Close to her she heard the movements and grunts of someone trying to free himself. A moment of greater fear, then she knew it was Gordon and she relaxed, willing him

210

to do the same. There might be a chance of getting away, but this was not it, and a brief illusion of compliance might put their captor off his guard.

It seemed an age before anyone moved. Gordon had been forced into keeping still by the warning of what might happen to her. The man continued to hold her and the stillness was as unnerving as the first moments of capture. What was he waiting for? What did he intend? Then Bettrys realised who was holding her. The hand over her face smelled faintly of soap, a soap she had used recently, when she went into the bathroom at Costa Plenty to wash her hands. The man holding her and Gordon prisoner was Jeremy. And he had been the "husband" of Diana. In an unexpected movement she pulled free of the hand across her mouth and said, "It's Jeremy!"

Jeremy drawled casually, "He knows."

The hand was holding her again, roughly. She couldn't breathe easily through her nose. Her rasping breath sounded deafening. The hand pressed into her flesh so her teeth were cutting the inside of her mouth. She tasted blood. Jeremy spoke again.

"If you promise not to make a sound, your mouth will be uncovered." Eagerly, Bettrys nodded.

She felt the man behind her twist sideways then forwards, forcing her to follow his movements, felt rope pass around her and knew she was fastened firmly to the stove. Then she heard Gordon's muffled voice say, "Darling. Are you all right?"

Her "yes – " was lost in Jeremy's demand for silence.

They were pushed forward, then down to the floor, so she and Gordon were sitting side by side, their back against the cold metal. To feel him close was such a relief, even though he was obviously tied like herself to the stove, that she felt tears fall, and a great lump swell in her heart. "Oh, Gordon," she whispered, before she was kicked roughly and told to hush.

Time passed in eerie silence, Bettrys began to shiver as

the chill metal and the cold of the empty building began to seep into her body. When Jeremy spoke again it was startling, as if she had been woken from a strange sleep.

"I think it's safe to talk." Jeremy almost whispered the words. "First of all, where is Bryn? I want him. Now."

"Miles away if he has any sense!" Gordon said. "There are more police round here than inhabitants. And that includes Emrys's sheep!"

"Try again." The softly spoken words paralysed Bettrys. The two short words held such unbelievable menace. Why couldn't Gordon just tell him and let Bryn take his chances? But when Jeremy leaned closer to her and asked the same question: "Where is Bryn?" she shook her head and said, he had no idea.

"Why do you want him?" she dared to ask. "Are you a policeman? He's wanted for robbery and fraud, isn't he?"

"I want him. I don't care about robberies. I want him for ruining my wife's good name."

"Your wife? Frances?" Gordon frowned.

"Diana! She's my wife! She might be married to Emrys, but she's still my wife!"

There was a movement at the door. Nothing more than a slight movement of air, a change in the blackness. Bettrys held her breath.

Then the door swung open and a man entered. Jeremy swung round and his torch shone into Bryn's smiling face.

"Looking for me, Jeremy?" Bryn asked.

"You're next on my list," Jeremy said, all pretence at calmness gone. In the thin beam of light from the torch, Bettrys had seen a length of rope hanging on Jeremy's arm. "Welcome to the party, Bryn," Jeremy almost purred. "I've savoured you until last."

"Let those two go. I won't try to escape. Here," he offered his hands, pressed together as if in prayer. "Tie me up if you wish, but let them go."

"No one goes until I tell you what I think of you, you bastard. You started Diana's misery. You gave her a child!"

"Sorry my friend, but you've got that wrong. It wasn't me, I'm hardly old enough if you stop and work it out."

"You were old enough all right! You pestered her, took advantage of her innocence. You persuaded her into having an affair."

"Sorry, but that's rather a laugh. She taught the art of loving to half of the village!"

Jeremy's hand lashed out and slapped Bryn's face. Bryn grabbed the man's arm and there was a struggle, half seen in the light of the fallen torch, terrifyingly close, the two men filling the small room. They tripped over Gordon's legs as they moved around the room, pushing and hitting out at each other, falling against Bettrys one moment, the next clawing at each other like animals on the floor.

Then the room was filled with people; lights flooded the dark night, flickering at first like a freak storm, and uniformed police separated the two men. Each was handcuffed to an officer. It was Jake who entered first behind the police, and he who untied them. His single hand efficiently releasing the knots. It was in that small chalet that they were told the rest of the story.

Brynley and Jeremy, together with their escorts, sat against the wall, the handcuffs a strange addition to their summer clothes. They were waiting for cars to come and take them into custody.

Jake and Carys came, ignoring the police demand to keep away, followed by Gwen, carrying Cheryl, and old Maldwyn. Others stood on the dark beach outside, waiting for some explanation. Frances had learned that her husband was under arrest and pushed her way through the crowd. She sat, trembling, beside Bettrys and Gordon. Her eyes were red and she looked half her age, like a schoolgirl caught out in some misdemeanour by the head. Bettrys felt deeply sorry for her.

Hand in hand, after reassuring themselves that Cheryl was safe, Bettrys and Gordon sat in the odd gathering, and listened. Maldwyn stood, leaning forward on his stick, glaring without any attempt at disguising the fact that he did not like sharing a room with Jake. Gwen smiled reassuringly at Bettrys. Carys was holding back tears and Jake was stiff with unhappiness, his eyes swollen with disbelief at what had happened to his son.

It was Jake who began to explain.

"I suppose the whole thing started with Diana," he said with a glance at Jeremy. "Diana was brought up by an elderly aunt. Her parents fought their way through the first five years of her life then they separated, each promising to come back for Diana when they were settled. Neither of them ever did. She was a lonely child who wandered around by herself, sharing time between groups of friends but never really belonging anywhere.

"When she was little more than a child herself, she had a baby. She was only fourteen at the time and refused to terminate. She ran away from home. It was Jeremy who found her then and looked after her. They had the child adopted and Jeremy and Diana stayed together until she was twenty. Then she left him."

"Who was the father of the child?" Gordon asked.

"Ray Newbank."

"You don't mean that – "

"No, Leyton Newbank wasn't her son." Again Jake glanced at Jeremy.

"Leyton Newbank was one of Diana's lovers, that was why he had to die," Bryn explained. "The child was a girl and was adopted by someone who lived in Cardigan. They have never met."

"Jeremy couldn't cope with her leaving him," Jake went on. "They had never lived as man and wife. He, believing she was still too young, too innocent in spite of the baby. She found someone else and left with only a brief note to thank him for his care."

214

"He loved her, did he?" Bettrys asked.

Jake nodded, glancing at the policeman who was taking down in shorthand all he said. "All he wanted was for her to be his wife. He just waited too long. She thought it was only a caring love he felt for her so she found someone who treated her like a woman, and went with him. The affair didn't last though and there were several other brief relationships before she married Emrys.

"Jeremy found her after she married, and bought a chalet here on Yr Tro. He seemed content for a while to just watch over her and make sure she was happy. Then he found out about her affairs and decided he had to kill them all."

"Our affair was only fun," Bryn explained, with a half smile at Jeremy. "We talked about a lasting love, of how I had a house waiting for us in Spain. She pretended that her mother was on her deathbed and she had to wait until she died. It was all a game. Diana is like that. Pretence is all she understands."

"Perhaps if she found someone who really loved her – " Bettrys said sadly.

"He did," Bryn said, gesturing with handcuffed hands to Jeremy. "Fat lot of good that did her!"

"We've suspected him from the start," the detective sergeant said. "But having Brynley Cooper wandering around, wanted for other offences seems a good cover. If he wasn't under suspicion there was the chance of him slipping up."

"Or murdering again!" Gordon gripped Bettrys's hands more tightly.

"Then Bryn was helping you all the time?" Bettrys said.

"We accepted his assistance, unofficially you might say. He was wanted for fraud, cheating unsuspecting ladies out of their cash. It seemed more important for us to catch a killer."

Maldwyn turned to Jake, the rage of years in his old

215

eyes. The shaggy eyebrows meeting in a thatch that didn't shadow the fury. "Now, Jake Cooper. While we're telling all, let's have the truth about your accident, shall we? You weren't on my boat the day you fell and shattered your arm. Where were you?"

Jake looked at Carys and she nodded slightly, giving her permission and approval.

"I fell down the well-shaft," he said. "The accident didn't happen on Maldwyn's boat."

Light gleamed in the old man's eyes. "I knew it!" he said with an air of satisfaction.

"It was for Bryn we did it," Carys said sadly. "We didn't want to cheat you. But he was in debt and had to have money. It was our only chance of helping him. He's our son," she added in pathetic explanation."

"What were you doing in the well?" the detective asked as the constable quietly turned to a fresh page of his note-book. "You aren't telling us that you deliberately threw yourself down the well to get money for your son?"

"I was trying to stop Bryn meeting Diana. No good she is, she's caused nothing but trouble since the day she was born." He moved as Jeremy threatened to jump on him. But Jeremy was securely held. "Couldn't leave any man alone. Flirting came as natural to her as breathing." He gave Jeremy a defiant glare. "She couldn't help herself."

"Poor dab," Carys was quietly crying.

"I was at the top of the well, following him, hoping to persuade him to come back with me, when Bryn leaned over to restart the water and his sudden appearance made me lose my footing," Jake explained. "Bryn saw at once that I was badly injured and we dreamed up the plan to claim compensation. He carried me home, sent for the doctor and while I waited, he went to Maldwyn's boat and loosened one of the stanchion posts." He glared at Maldwyn and added defiantly. "The wood around them *was* rotten and they could have gone any time!"

"So to pay your son's debts you made me bankrupt – "

Maldwyn began to shout, but he was hushed by Gwen as the door opened. A policeman announced that the cars had come to take the prisoners to the station. A still doggedly cheerful Frances walked up the path beside Jeremy. Insisting that "It *will* be all right. Reeely it will, Jeremy. How can I possibly manage without you. It must be all right. It's all a mistake."

"Poor dab her too," Maldwyn sighed.

When Jake and Carys had seen Bryn taken in another police car, they sat talking for the rest of that night, talking round and round the situation, then falling into reminiscences about when Bryn and Gordon were children, what hopes they had had for them, how they had dreamed of them achieving wonderful things.

Bettrys went to stand outside to watch the sun come up with its promise of a new and better day. Maldwyn and Gwen sat making endless pots of tea, talking to the unhappy Coopers, the cheating over Maldwyn's boat temporarily forgotten.

Tomorrow things would be different. The fear had already been lifted from Yr Tro. The beach was still dark but the low rays of the sunrise were creeping slowly across the sea, scattering the beach with shadows. It touched the rocks and the bushes, bringing colour and freshness, revealing the beautiful, peaceful scene. It was no longer a frightening place in which killers roamed and secrets hung heavy on the air.

"I tell you what won't be different," Gordon said, when she tried to explain how she felt. "Grandad and Jake will still be enemies. Tonight is only a temporary cease-fire!" He turned and looked at her, the sun a halo around her lovely face, her hair lifting slightly with the gentle on-shore breeze, "Something else won't have changed," he said softly. "I love you, Bettrys. I love Cheryl too. Can we make plans to marry, adopt her and make us all legal?" He smiled as she hesitated before replying in that fascinating way of hers. "Just think, Cheryl will have

Mam and Granddad plus Jake and Carys as grandparents. We couldn't deprive the Coopers of a grandchild, even if Bryn chose to ignore her. Perhaps that might make old Maldwyn forget his anger against Jake.'

"That I doubt," she laughed. "I haven't been on Yr Tro very long, but I know them well enough to realise we'll still be listening to them arguing years from now!"

"Then you will?"

"Gordon, my darling. I will. Living here with you and with Cheryl would be perfect bliss."